MORE PRAISE FOR

CHOMP

"Hilarious. . . . Hiaasen extends his brand of Florida eco-adventures with this loopy foray into reality TV." —*Publishers Weekly*

"*Chomp* is a story for readers to sink their teeth into."
—*The Horn Book Magazine*

"An old-fashioned adventure story satisfyingly concluding with just deserts all around." —*The Bulletin*

"A finely tuned mix of satire and madcap adventure." —*Booklist*

"Laugh-out-loud funny. Old fans and new will be snapping up *Chomp*!" —*Bookends*

"Hiaasen may have outdone himself with this exceptional novel. . . . His best book for young people yet." —*Shelf Awareness*

"Hiaasen never loses control of his story, no matter how zany it becomes, and the novel retains its heart even as readers will be laughing their heads off." —*Book Reporter*

"Reminiscent of Edward Abbey and Christopher Moore, to name a few." —*Anole Annals*

"A brilliant mix of comedy and suspense. . . . The book's greatest strength lies in its seamless shifts from hilarious humor to nail-biting action." —*NorthJersey.com*

Carl Hiaasen

CHOMP

EMBER

Text copyright © 2012 by Carl Hiaasen
Cover art copyright © 2012 by Alfred A. Knopf

All rights reserved. Published in the United States by Ember, an imprint of
Random House Children's Books, a division of Random House, Inc., New York.
Originally published in hardcover in the United States by Alfred A. Knopf,
an imprint of Random House Children's Books, New York, in 2012.

Ember and the E colophon are registered trademarks of Random House, Inc.

Visit us on the Web! randomhouse.com/kids

HiaasenforKids.com

Educators and librarians, for a variety of teaching tools, visit us at
RHTeachersLibrarians.com

The Library of Congress has cataloged the hardcover edition of this work as follows:
Hiaasen, Carl.
Chomp / Carl Hiaasen.
p. cm.
"A Borzoi Book"
Summary: When the difficult star of the reality television show "Expedition Survival"
disappears while filming an episode in the Florida Everglades using animals from the
wildlife refuge run by Wahoo Crane's family, Wahoo and classmate Tuna Gordon set
out to find him while avoiding Tuna's gun-happy father.
ISBN 978-0-375-86842-9 (trade) — ISBN 978-0-375-96842-6 (lib. bdg.) —
ISBN 978-0-375-89895-2 (ebook)
[1. Reality television programs—Fiction. 2. Television—Production and direction—
Fiction. 3. Missing persons—Fiction. 4. Wildlife refuges—Fiction. 5. Everglades (Fla.)—
Fiction. 6. Florida—Fiction.] I. Title.
PZ7.H493Cho 2012 [Fic]—dc23 2011024920

ISBN 978-0-375-86827-6 (pbk.)

RL: 5.0

Printed in the United States of America

10 9 8 7 6 5 4 3 2 1

First Ember Edition 2013

Random House Children's Books supports the First Amendment
and celebrates the right to read.

This book is for Quinn, Webb, Jack and, of course, Claire, who suggested the toothy title.

For his insight and many true wild stories, I am grateful to Joe Wasilewski, a renowned wildlife biologist and world-class animal wrangler. Nobody is better at reasoning with a grouchy rattlesnake or a hungry crocodile.

CHOMP

ONE

Mickey Cray had been out of work ever since a dead iguana fell from a palm tree and hit him on the head.

The iguana, which had died during a hard freeze, was stiff as a board and weighed seven and a half pounds. Mickey's son had measured the lifeless lizard on a fishing scale, then packed it on ice with the turtle veggies, in the cooler behind the garage.

This was after the ambulance had hauled Mickey off to the hospital, where the doctors said he had a serious concussion and ordered him to take it easy.

And to everyone's surprise, Mickey did take it easy. That's because the injury left him with double vision and terrible headaches. He lost his appetite and dropped nineteen pounds and lay around on the couch all day, watching nature programs on television.

"I'll never be the same," he told his son.

"Knock it off, Pop," said Wahoo, Mickey's boy.

Mickey had named him after Wahoo McDaniel, a professional wrestler who'd once played linebacker for the Dolphins. Mickey's son often wished he'd been called Mickey Jr. or Joe or even Rupert—anything but Wahoo, which was also a species of saltwater fish.

It was a name that was hard to live up to. People naturally

expected somebody called Wahoo to act loud and crazy, but that wasn't Wahoo's style. Apparently nothing could be done about the name until he was all grown up, at which point he intended to go to the Cutler Ridge courthouse and tell a judge he wanted to be called something normal.

"Pop, you're gonna be okay," Wahoo would tell his father every morning. "Just hang in there."

Looking up with hound-dog eyes from the couch, Mickey Cray would say, "Whatever happens, I'm glad we ate that bleeping lizard."

On the day his dad had come home from the hospital, Wahoo had defrosted the dead iguana and made a peppercorn stew, which his mom had wisely refused to touch. Mickey had insisted that eating the critter that had dented his skull would be a spiritual remedy. "Big medicine," he'd predicted.

But the iguana had tasted awful, and Mickey Cray's headaches only got worse. Wahoo's mother was so concerned that she wanted Mickey to see a brain specialist in Miami, but Mickey refused to go.

Meanwhile, people kept calling up with new jobs, and Wahoo was forced to send them to other wranglers. His father was in no condition to work.

After school, Wahoo would feed the animals and clean out the pens and cages. The backyard was literally a zoo—gators, snakes, parrots, mynah birds, rats, mice, monkeys, raccoons, tortoises and even a bald eagle, which Mickey had raised from a fledgling after its mother was killed.

"Treat 'em like royalty," Mickey would instruct Wahoo, because the animals were quite valuable. Without them, Mickey would be unemployed.

It disturbed Wahoo to see his father so ill because Mickey was the toughest guy he'd ever known.

One morning, with summer approaching, Wahoo's mother took him aside and told him that the family's savings account was almost drained. "I'm going to China," she said.

Wahoo nodded, like it was no big deal.

"For two months," she said.

"That's a long time," said Wahoo.

"Sorry, big guy, but we really need the money."

Wahoo's mother taught Mandarin Chinese, an extremely difficult language. Big American companies that had offices in China would hire Mrs. Cray to tutor their top executives, but usually these companies flew their employees to South Florida for Mrs. Cray's lessons.

"This time they want me to go to Shanghai," she explained to her son. "They have, like, fifty people over there who learned Mandarin from some cheap audiotape. The other day, one of the big shots was trying to say 'Nice shoes!' and he accidentally told a government minister that his face looked like a butt wart. Not good."

"Did you tell Pop you're going?"

"That's next."

Wahoo slipped outside to clean Alice's pond. Alice the alligator was one of Mickey Cray's stars. She was twelve feet long and as tame as a guppy, but she looked truly ferocious. Over the years Alice had appeared often in front of a camera. Her credits included nine feature films, two National Geographic documentaries, a three-part Disney special about the Everglades and a TV commercial for a fancy French skin lotion.

She lay sunning on the mudbank while Wahoo skimmed the dead leaves and sticks from the water. Her eyes were closed, but Wahoo knew she was listening.

"Hungry, girl?" he asked.

The gator's mouth opened wide, the inside as white as spun cotton. Some of her teeth were snaggled and chipped. The tips were green from pond algae.

"You forgot to floss," Wahoo said.

Alice hissed. He went to get her some food. When she heard the squeaking of the wheelbarrow, she cracked her eyelids and turned her huge armored head.

Wahoo tossed a whole plucked chicken into the alligator's gaping jaws. The sound of her crunching on the thawed bird obscured the voices coming from the house—Wahoo's mother and father "discussing" the China trip.

Wahoo fed Alice two more dead chickens, locked the gate to the pond and took a walk. When he returned, his father was upright on the sofa and his mother was in the kitchen fixing bologna sandwiches for lunch.

"You believe this?" Mickey said to Wahoo. "She's bugging out on us!"

"Pop, we're broke."

Mickey's shoulders slumped. "Not *that* broke."

"You want the animals to starve?" Wahoo asked.

They ate their sandwiches barely speaking a word. When they were done, Mrs. Cray stood up and said: "I'm going to miss you guys. I wish I didn't have to go."

Then she went into the bedroom and shut the door.

Mickey seemed dazed. "I used to like iguanas."

"We'll be okay."

"My head hurts."

"Take your medicine," said Wahoo.

"I threw it away."

"What?"

"Those yellow pills, they made me constipated."

Wahoo shook his head. "Unbelievable."

"Seriously. I haven't had a satisfactory bowel movement since Easter."

"Thanks for sharing," said Wahoo. He started loading the dishwasher, trying to keep his mind off the fact that his mom was about to fly away to the far side of the world.

Mickey got up and apologized to his son.

"I'm just being selfish. I don't want her to go."

"Me neither."

The following Sunday, they all rose before dawn. Wahoo lugged his mother's suitcases to the waiting taxi. She had tears in her eyes when she kissed him goodbye.

"Take care of your dad," she whispered.

Then, to Mickey, she said: "I want you to get better. That's an order, mister."

Watching the cab speed off, Wahoo's father looked forlorn. "It's like she's leaving us twice," he remarked.

"What are you talking about, Pop?"

"I'm seein' double, remember? There she goes—and there she goes again."

Wahoo was in no mood for that. "You want eggs for breakfast?"

Afterward he went out in the backyard to deal with a troublesome howler monkey named Jocko, who'd picked the lock on his cage and was now leaping around, pestering the parrots and macaws. Wahoo had to be careful because Jocko was mean. He used a tangerine to lure the surly primate back to his cage, but Jocko still managed to sink a dirty fang into one of Wahoo's hands.

"I told you to wear the canvas gloves," scolded Mickey when Wahoo was standing at the sink, cleaning the wound.

"*You* don't wear gloves," Wahoo pointed out.

"Yeah, but I don't get chomped like you do."

That was hogwash. Mickey got chomped all the time; it was an occupational hazard. His hands were so scarred that they looked fake, like rubber Halloween props.

The phone rang and Wahoo picked it up. His father weaved back to the couch and flipped through the TV stations until he found the Rain Forest Channel.

"Who was it that called?" he asked when Wahoo came out of the kitchen.

"Another job, Pop."

"You send 'em to Stiggy?"

Jimmy Stigmore was an animal wrangler who had a ranch up in west Davie. Mickey Cray wasn't crazy about Stiggy.

"No, I didn't," Wahoo said.

His father frowned. "Then who'd you send 'em to? Not Dander!"

Donny Dander had lost his wildlife-importing license after he got caught smuggling thirty-eight rare tree frogs from South America. The frogs had been cleverly hidden in his underwear, but the adventure ended in embarrassment at the Miami airport when a customs officer noticed that Donny's pants were cheeping.

Wahoo said, "I didn't send 'em to Dander, either. I didn't send 'em anywhere."

"Okay. Now you lost me," said Mickey Cray.

"I said we'd take the job. I said we could start next week."

"Are you crazy, boy? Look at me, I can't see straight, I can't hardly walk, my skull's 'bout to split open like a rotten pumpkin—"

"Pop!"

"What?"

"I said *we*," Wahoo reminded him. "You and I together."

"But what about school?"

"Friday's the last day. Then I'm done for the summer."

"Already?" Wahoo's dad didn't keep up with Wahoo's academic schedule as closely as his mother did. "So who called about the job?"

Wahoo told him the name of the TV show.

"Not him!" Mickey Cray snorted. "I've heard stories about that jerk."

"Well, how does a thousand bucks sound?" Wahoo asked.

"Pretty darned sweet."

"That's one thousand a *day*." Wahoo let that sink in. "If you want, I'll call 'em back and give him Stiggy's number."

"Don't be a knucklehead." Wahoo's father rose off the sofa and gave him a hug. "You did good, son. We'll make this work."

"Absolutely," said Wahoo, trying to sound confident.

TWO

Hundreds of iguanas had died and tumbled from the treetops during the big freeze in southern Florida. As far as Wahoo knew, his dad was the only person who'd been seriously hurt by one of the falling reptiles.

Mickey Cray had been standing with a cup of hot cocoa beneath a coconut palm in the backyard when the dead lizard had knocked him stiff. Later, after he was brought home from the hospital, Mickey had ordered Wahoo to search the property, capture any iguanas that had survived the frigid weather and relocate them to an abandoned orchid farm half a mile away.

Wahoo hadn't searched very hard. It wasn't the fault of the iguanas that they'd frozen to death. They weren't meant to be living so far north, but Miami pet dealers had been importing baby specimens from the tropics for decades. The customers who bought them had no idea they would grow six feet long, eat all the flowers in the garden and then leap into the swimming pool to poop. When that rude reality set in, the unhappy owners would drive their pet lizards to the nearest park and set them free. Before long, South Florida was crawling with hordes of big wild iguanas that were producing hordes of little wild iguanas.

The cold snap had put an end to that, at least temporarily.

On the first morning of summer vacation, Wahoo found his father in the backyard scanning the trees.

"See any, Pop?"

"All clear," Mickey Cray reported.

Although months had passed since the accident, he was still paranoid about getting clobbered with another falling lizard.

"You must be feeling better," Wahoo remarked. He was pleased to see his dad up and moving around so early.

"My headache's gone!" Mickey announced.

Wahoo said, "No way."

"All those pills the doctors made me swallow, they didn't do a darn thing. Then all of a sudden I wake up and, boom, it's like a miracle." Mickey shrugged. "Some things just can't be explained, son."

But Wahoo had a theory that his father had been cured by five simple words: *one thousand dollars a day.*

Mickey said, "Go fetch some lettuce for Gary and Gail."

Gary and Gail were two ancient Galápagos tortoises that Wahoo's dad had purchased from a zoo in Sarasota many years earlier, when he was new to the wildlife business. These days there wasn't much demand from the TV nature shows for Gary and Gail, because tortoises were not exactly dynamic performers. Mickey Cray kept them around mainly for sentimental reasons. Each of the animals was more than a century old, and he didn't trust any of the other wranglers to treat them properly. The night before the big freeze, Mickey had gone out back and carefully cloaked Gail and Gary with heavy quilts so they wouldn't die. Wahoo had watched from his bedroom window.

"I don't suppose he's interested in these two," Mickey muttered while the tortoises munched loudly on their lettuce.

"No, they said he wants Alice," said Wahoo, "and a major python."

They were talking about their famous new client, Derek Badger. He was the star of *Expedition Survival!*, one of the most popular shows on cable. Every week, Derek would parachute into some gnarly wilderness teeming with fierce animals, venomous snakes and disease-carrying insects. Armed with only a Swiss army knife and a straw, he would hike, climb, crawl, paddle or swim back to civilization—or until he was "rescued." Along the way, he'd eat bugs, rodents, worms, even the fungus on tree bark—the grosser it looked, the happier Derek Badger was to stuff it into his cheeks.

Wahoo and his dad had watched *Expedition Survival!* often enough to know that most of the wildlife scenes were faked. They were also aware that at no time was Derek's life in actual danger, since he was always accompanied by a camera crew packing food, candy, sunblock, water, first-aid supplies and, most likely, a large gun.

"Derek's never done a show in the Everglades," Wahoo said to his father.

"They say he's a humongous pain in the butt, this guy."

"Just be nice, Pop. It's a lot of money."

Mickey promised to behave. "So, when do we get to meet the man himself?"

"His assistant is supposed to stop by later."

"What kind of python do they want—Burmese? African rock?"

Wahoo said, "Honestly, I don't think it matters."

They set to work building a pen for a young bobcat that was being delivered from a ranch up in Highlands County. The cat had been struck by a Jeep and suffered a broken leg that wouldn't mend, so it could never be released back into the wild. Mickey Cray had agreed to raise the animal, and he hoped to make it tame enough for TV work.

Bobcats were strong, meaning the pen had to be sturdy. Wahoo knew that a person with double vision shouldn't be using a nail gun, so he put his dad in charge of measuring and cutting the chicken wire. By noon Mickey's headache came roaring back, and he was in misery. Wahoo steered him to the house and made him lie on the couch and fed him four aspirins.

Minutes later, somebody started knocking on the front door. Mickey raised up and said, "That's probably the guy with the bobcat."

Wahoo looked out the window and saw a woman with a shining stack of red hair. She wore tan shorts and jeweled sandals, and she was carrying a leather briefcase.

"No cat," he said to his father.

"Well, open the darn door."

"But what if she's from the bank?" Wahoo whispered. The Crays were months behind on their mortgage payments.

Mickey peeked out the window. "She is definitely *not* from the bank."

Wahoo invited the woman inside. She introduced herself as Raven Stark.

"I'm Derek Badger's production assistant," she said. "I brought your contract."

"Excellent," said Mickey.

Wahoo noticed that Raven Stark had a strong accent. He tried not to stare at her hairdo, which looked like a sculpture made of red chrome.

She asked, "May I take a look around?"

"Nope," said Wahoo's father.

Raven Stark seemed surprised.

"First you've got to sign a release form," Mickey said. "I don't want to get sued if you fall into the gator pond and get bit."

She laughed. "I've been doing this a long time, Mr. Cray."

"You sign the release, my son will be happy to give you the grand tour."

A few years earlier, Mickey Cray had invited Wahoo's elementary school class to come see his wild animals. A boy named Tingley had ignored Wahoo's warning and reached into one of the cages to tug the tail of a grumpy raccoon, which had spun around and clawed the kid's arm so badly that it looked like a road map of Hialeah. Mickey paid for

Tingley's doctor bills, though not before telling his parents that their boy was dumb as a box of rocks. Ever since then, Mickey's insurance company insisted that everyone who came on the property had to fill out a legal form saying it wasn't Mickey's fault if they got hurt.

While Raven Stark signed the release, Mickey signed the contract from *Expedition Survival!* Wahoo noticed that he scrawled his name crookedly below the line where it was supposed to go, which meant his eyesight was still jumbled.

"How long is the shoot going to take?" Mickey asked.

Raven Stark said, "Until we get it right."

Wahoo's dad looked pleased. "So it's one thousand a day, plus location fees and the animal rentals."

"Correct." She took an envelope from her purse and handed it to him. "Here's eight hundred dollars as a deposit."

Mickey counted the cash and then turned to Wahoo. "Son, go show this fine lady whatever she wants to see."

Because it was going to be an Everglades show, Raven Stark was keenly interested in Alice the alligator. Wahoo led her to the pond and unlocked the gate.

Raven whistled. "That's a monster, eh?"

"Twelve feet," said Wahoo.

"How much?"

"One hundred and fifty dollars a foot, so that's . . ."

"Eighteen hundred even," Raven said. "No problem."

Wahoo couldn't wait to tell his father.

"Do you have another one that's smaller?" asked Raven.

"Yes, ma'am."

"Something Derek could wrestle?"

"Wrestle?"

"Maybe a four-footer," Raven said. "Five feet, max."

"I'll have to check with Pop." Wahoo foresaw trouble. His father didn't like anybody messing with the animals.

"Where are your pythons?" Raven asked.

Wahoo led her to the heavy glass tanks where the constrictors were kept. South Florida had become infested with huge exotic snakes that, like the iguanas, had been imported for the pet trade. Hurricane Andrew had blown apart several large reptile farms and scattered baby pythons and boa constrictors all over the place.

"Derek wants a beast," Raven stated.

Wahoo showed her a fourteen-footer that had been captured while devouring an opossum in a Dumpster behind the Dadeland Mall. The man who'd found the snake was supposed to turn it over to state game officers, but instead he'd sold it to Mickey Cray for three hundred bucks.

Raven agreed it was an impressive specimen. "But can he be handled safely?"

"It's a she," Wahoo said, "and she's a biter."

"Oh."

"Pop can work with her. She'll be okay."

"I hope so," said Raven Stark. "How much?"

"Seven hundred for the day." Wahoo tried to sound steady and businesslike. He wasn't used to handling the negotiations. The standard rental rate for pythons was fifty dollars a foot.

"Okay, fine. What did you say your name was?"

He told her.

"Is that 'Wahoo,' like the fish?"

Everybody made that assumption. "My dad named me after a wrestler," the boy explained.

"How interesting."

"Not really," said Wahoo.

"Can I ask what happened?" She pointed at the white bump on Wahoo's right hand, where a thumb should have been.

"Yes, ma'am. Alice got it."

"You're serious, aren't you?"

Quickly Wahoo said, "It wasn't her fault, it was mine."

One day he'd been showing off for a girl who had come over after school to see the animals. Wahoo had brought her down to the gator pond for a feeding, but he stepped way too close to Alice, who jumped up and snapped the thawed chicken out of his grasp, taking his thumb along with it. The girl's name was Paulette, and she'd fainted on the spot.

Changing the subject, Wahoo asked, "Where is Mr. Badger?"

"Paris," Raven said.

Wahoo had never heard of any dangerous jungles or swamps in Paris, so he assumed the famous survivalist was taking a vacation.

Mickey Cray came outside and joined them at the snake

tanks. Wahoo told him that Ms. Stark was interested in using Beulah, the big Burmese.

"Good choice," said Mickey. He appeared to be feeling better.

"You've seen the program, of course," Raven said.

"Sure," said Wahoo. "It's on Thursday nights."

"And rerun every Sunday morning," she said. "So you already know that we're all about verisimilitude."

Wahoo didn't even pretend to understand what the word meant. His father just looked at him and shrugged.

"Making it real," Raven explained. "On *Expedition Survival!*, we're all about making it real. Derek considers that his sacred mission, a bond of trust with our viewers."

Wahoo glanced at the massive snakes, coiled in their tanks. They were real enough; they just weren't wild and free.

The production assistant turned to Wahoo's father. "Any questions?"

Mickey smiled. "We put our animals on TV all the time. That's what we do."

Raven Stark bent down and tapped a scarlet fingernail on the glass panel that separated her from Beulah the python.

"Well, Mr. Cray," she said, "I promise you've never done a show like Derek's."

THREE

Derek Badger's real name was Lee Bluepenny, and he had no training in biology, botany, geology or forestry. His background was purely show business.

As a young man he'd traveled the world with a popular Irish folk-dancing group until he broke a toe while rehearsing for a street parade in Montreal. As he waited in the hospital emergency room, he happened to meet a talent agent who had gotten ill from eating tainted oysters. The queasy talent agent thought Lee Bluepenny looked tough and handsome, and asked if he'd ever considered a career in television.

As soon as Lee Bluepenny's dance injury healed, the agent arranged for him to fly to California and audition for a new reality show. The producers of *Expedition Survival!* loved Lee Bluepenny's new Australian accent, which he had shamelessly copied from the late Steve Irwin, the legendary crocodile hunter. The producers also liked that Lee Bluepenny could swallow a live salamander without throwing up. What they didn't particularly like was his name. Lee Bluepenny was okay for a jazz piano player or maybe an art dealer, they said, but it wasn't rugged-sounding enough for someone who had to claw and gnaw his way out of the wilds every week.

After trying out a few different names—Erik Panther,

Gus Wolverine, Chad Condor—the producers settled on Derek Badger, which was fine with Lee Bluepenny. He was so thrilled to be on television that he would have let them call him Danny the Dodo Bird.

Expedition Survival! got off to a rocky start. The first episode was staged in a jungle in the Philippine Islands, where the man now called Derek Badger was supposed to be lost and starving. Disaster struck on the second day, when Derek was bitten severely by a striped shrew rat that he was attempting to gobble for dinner. The rodent had appeared to be dead, but it was only napping. Derek's punctured lips swelled up so badly from the bite that he looked like he was sucking on a football. A medical helicopter rushed him to Manila for rabies shots.

Eventually the rough spots in the show were smoothed out, and *Expedition Survival!* turned into a smash hit. It wasn't long before Derek Badger was an international celebrity, and he quickly learned to act like one.

"How's France?" Raven Stark asked when she called.

"Heaven," he said. "The cheese here is fantastic."

"I'm sure," said Raven Stark, with a note of concern. Survivalists were supposed to be lean and fit, and one of her main responsibilities was to keep Derek from getting too flabby. It wasn't easy—the man loved to eat, and cheese was high on his list.

"Did you find me a proper alligator?" he inquired.

"Yes, a beauty." She could hear him chewing and smacking his lips.

"How big?"

"Twelve feet," said Raven Stark.

"Brilliant!"

"And they've got a slightly smaller one you can tussle with."

There was a pause on the other end that made Raven Stark uneasy.

Derek said, "But I don't want to wrestle the small one. I want to wrestle the monster."

It was exactly the response she had feared. "Too dangerous," she said.

"Excuse me?"

"We can chat about this later, Derek."

"Indeed we will. What about a python? I told you I wanted a python."

"The gentleman has offered us a very large Burmese, though it's not tame."

"Even better!" chortled Derek.

Raven Stark sighed to herself. She was accustomed to working around Derek's enormous ego, but there were times when she felt like reminding him that he was basically a tap dancer, not a grizzled woodsman.

"Anything else that's super-scary?" he asked.

"I noticed they had a large snapping turtle," she said.

"How large?"

"Large enough to take off a hand."

"Excellent," Derek said. "Set up an underwater scene— I'm swimming along through the Everglades, minding my own business, when the hungry snapper charges out from under a log and drags me to the bottom of the lagoon."

"Right. Except turtles don't eat people."

"How do you know?" Derek demanded.

"Call me when you land in Miami," said Raven Stark.

Wahoo had an older sister named Julie who was finishing law school at the University of Florida in Gainesville. His father was secretly proud of her, but he wouldn't let on.

"Just what the world needs—another darn lawyer," he'd grumble.

"I love you, too, Dad," Julie would say, and pinch his cheek.

Wahoo thought his sister was pretty cool, although he sometimes felt intimidated because she was so smart and funny and sociable. Wahoo was shy, and not as self-confident. Julie had always been a straight-A student while Wahoo wasn't: his best-ever report card was two A's, four B's and a C (in algebra, naturally).

"Just do your best," his mom would say. "That's good enough for us."

Mickey Cray never really took an interest in the children's schoolwork because he was too busy with the animals.

"Put the old man on the phone," Julie said when she called.

"He's out working with the pythons," Wahoo reported.

"It's about the *Expedition* contract. I see problems."

Wahoo always faxed the TV contracts to his sister for her to see, even though his father normally signed them without reading a word.

"What's wrong, Jule?"

"Like, on page seven, it says the show 'shall have unrestricted use of the designated wildlife specimens for the duration of the production period.' That means they can do pretty much whatever they please with the animals—and they don't need to ask Pop's permission."

"This is bad," Wahoo said. He remembered what Raven Stark had said about Derek Badger wanting to wrestle one of the gators.

"Did the old man take any money yet?" Julie asked.

Wahoo told his sister about the eight-hundred-dollar deposit. She said Mickey could still get out of the deal if he returned the cash.

"Too late. He already spent it," said Wahoo.

"On what—monkey chow?"

"The mortgage."

"Ouch," said Wahoo's sister.

"We're sort of broke, Jule. Ever since he got hurt, it's been tough."

"So that's why Mom went to China. Now I get it."

Wahoo didn't want his sister to worry, so he tried to sound upbeat. "Pop's been doing way better since we took this job."

"Who is this Derek Badger character, anyway?"

"You've never seen the show?"

Julie chuckled. "I don't even own a TV, little bro. All I do up here is crack the books."

"Derek Badger is a survivalist guy," Wahoo said. He explained the adventure format of the program.

His sister said, "Give me a break."

"He's huge, Jule."

"Tell Dad what I said about the contract."

"Do I have to?" Wahoo said.

He was only half kidding. He knew it would be his problem soon enough.

Mickey Cray was barefoot in the backyard with Beulah the python. He was admiring the markings on her skin—rich, chocolate-colored saddles on a sleek silvery background. Fourteen feet of raw muscle, and a brain the size of a marble.

Ever since he was a boy, Mickey had kept snakes for pets—green tree snakes, king snakes, rat snakes, water snakes, ring-necked snakes, garter snakes, even a few poisonous rattlers and moccasins. Mickey had caught them all. He still found them fascinating and mysterious.

Now the Everglades was overrun with foreign pythons that were eating the deer, birds, rabbits, even alligators—it was really a rough scene. The pythons weren't supposed to be there; Southeast Asia was their natural home. So the U.S. government and the state of Florida had declared war on them.

Wahoo's father understood why: the snakes were totally disrupting the balance of nature. A single adult Burmese could lay more than fifty eggs at a time. They were among the largest predators in the world, growing to a length of twenty feet, and at that size had no natural enemies. Even panthers avoided them.

Because of his knowledge and experience, Mickey Cray had been asked to go into the swamps and capture as many of the intruder reptiles as he could. The state was paying decent money, but Mickey said no. He knew that every python he caught would be euthanized, and he couldn't bring himself to take part in that. He liked snakes too much. That was the problem.

He sat down on the ground near Beulah and she glided slowly in his direction. Her brick-sized head was elevated, the silky tongue flicking slowly.

Mickey grinned. "When's the last time you got fed?"

Beulah responded by clamping down on Mickey's left foot and throwing a meaty coil around both his legs.

"Easy, princess," he said.

The python wrapped upward with another coil, and then another. Mickey quickly locked both arms in front of his chest to protect his lungs from being crushed, but he was out of shape and Beulah was extremely powerful.

"Wahoo!" he hollered. "Yo!"

"What?" called a voice from the house.

"Get your butt out here!"

The snake was chewing on Mickey's foot as if it were a

rabbit. He knew better than to struggle, for that would only cause Beulah to tighten her grip.

Wahoo came running. When he saw what the python was doing to his father, he yelled, "Don't move!"

"Oh, that's a good one," Mickey gasped. "I was thinking of dancing a jig."

"What the heck happened?"

"You forgot to feed her is what happened."

"No way! She ate last week, I swear, Pop."

"What did you give her—a cup of yogurt? Look at the poor girl, she's starving!"

Wahoo suspected his dad might be right—adult pythons often went weeks between meals. Maybe he *had* forgotten to feed her.

"Get the bleeping bourbon," Mickey said, "and make it fast." He was already gulping for air.

Wahoo ran back to the house and grabbed a bottle of liquor that his dad kept around for such emergencies. Pythons are equipped with rows of long, curved teeth that cannot be easily pried from their prey. The fastest way to make them let go is to pour something hot or obnoxious into their mouths.

Snakes don't have taste buds on their tongues like people do, so it wasn't the flavor of bourbon that Beulah hated. It was the sting. Wahoo got on his knees and sorted through the muscular coils until he located the toothy end of the creature, which had already swallowed half of his father's foot.

"You didn't even wear your boots?" Wahoo said.

Mickey grunted. "Get on with it already."

Wahoo uncapped the liquor bottle and dribbled the brown liquid directly down Beulah's throat. Within seconds the python began to twitch. Then she hissed loudly, unhooked her chompers and spit. Mickey purposely remained limp while Wahoo began unwinding the massive reptile.

Beulah didn't put up a struggle; she'd lost all interest in making a meal of Wahoo's father. The alcohol in the bourbon was highly irritating, and she kept opening and closing her mouth in distaste.

It took a few minutes for Mickey to catch his breath and for the circulation to return to his legs. He was able to hop along beside Wahoo as they lugged the big snake back to her tank. Then they went inside to take care of Mickey's foot, which looked like a purple pincushion.

"Promise you fed her? Tell the truth, son."

Wahoo felt awful. "I must have forgot."

"Springtime is when they get active and really start chowing down. I've only told you about a hundred times." With a groan, Mickey sprawled on the couch.

"Dad, I'm really sorry."

"Soon as we're done here, you go fetch her a couple of big fat chickens from the freezer. And nuke 'em good in the microwave, okay? Pythons don't like Popsicles."

"Yes, sir."

Wahoo emptied a tube of antiseptic ointment on his

father's foot, and with a butter knife he spread the goop over all the puncture holes. There were too many to count. Pythons weren't poisonous, but a bite could cause a nasty infection.

"I'm sorry," Wahoo said again. "I really messed up."

"Enough already. Everybody makes mistakes," his dad told him. "Heck, I shouldn't have been playin' with a snake that size, like she was a fuzzy little poodle."

"Hold still, Pop."

Mickey stared up at the ceiling. "Look, I know this ain't exactly a normal life for a kid your age."

"Don't start again," Wahoo said.

"No, I mean it," Mickey went on. "What would I do without you and your mom? I'm lucky she stuck around all these years."

"Yes, you are. Where's the gauze?"

Wahoo waited until his dad's wounds were bandaged before telling him what Julie had said about the *Expedition Survival!* contract.

"I knew the guy was trouble," Mickey muttered.

"So what do we do now?"

"Our job, son. We do our job." Mickey levered himself up, swinging his puffy, snake-bitten foot up on the coffee table. "I don't care what their stupid paperwork says—I'm the only one in charge of my animals. Mr. Dork Badger can go fly a kite."

"It's *Derek* Badger."

"Ha! You think it matters to these critters what his stupid name is?"

"No, Pop."

"Know what Beulah would say? 'All you stupid humans taste the same!' "

Wahoo found himself wondering if that was really true.

FOUR

When his mother called from China, Wahoo was brushing his teeth.

He heard his dad say, "Susan, your boys are miserable! Please fly home!"

Wahoo spit out the toothpaste froth and ran to the living room. Mickey cupped a hand over the phone and whispered: "It's eight in the morning in Shanghai—she's finishing breakfast."

"Can I talk with her?"

"Egg noodles again—she's gonna overdose on carbs."

"Please?" Wahoo said.

Mickey handed over the phone.

"So much drama," Wahoo's mom said to him. "For heaven's sake, doesn't your father ever give it a rest? You think I want to be here?"

"We took a big TV job. Actually he's doing better."

"But what about the headaches?"

"Gone, he says."

"Keep a close watch on him," Wahoo's mother advised.

She asked about school. Wahoo said he thought he did okay on his finals.

"Even Spanish?"

"That was a killer," he admitted.

"As long as you tried your best."

"Miss you, Mom."

"I miss you, too, big guy. This really sucks."

Wahoo swallowed hard to keep his voice from cracking. He didn't want her to know how bummed he felt because she was so far away. "I found your hotel on Google Earth," he said. "Looks pretty sweet from the satellite."

"Tell me about the TV thing," she said.

"It's real good money."

"But is it a good job?"

"Yeah, awesome," Wahoo said, thinking: *When you're broke, any job is a good job*.

Mickey Cray piped up: "Hey, my turn. Give it here."

Wahoo told his mother goodbye and went outside with a five-gallon bucket of cat food for the raccoons. He was the only kid in school whose father was a professional animal wrangler, and life in the Cray household definitely wasn't routine. Still, despite his missing thumb, Wahoo was able to do most normal things. He'd taught himself to write, shoot baskets and throw a baseball with his left hand. He could even turn a clean three-sixty on his wakeboard, when his dad had time to take him out on the boat.

One normal thing that the Crays couldn't do together was go on summer vacations. Mickey didn't trust anybody else to take care of the animals. One time, when Wahoo's aunt Rose had passed away, the whole family flew up to West Virginia for the funeral. Mickey had asked Donny Dander to look after the critters, which turned out to be an expensive mistake. The Crays were gone only three days, but during that short time two rare parrots escaped, a lemur caught the flu and Alice bit the tail off of a crocodile.

"Where's the darned aspirin?" Mickey hollered from the house.

"On the kitchen counter next to the coffee machine," Wahoo called back.

The raccoons were always excited to see him because Wahoo's arrival meant it was mealtime. When he entered the enclosure, they clustered around him, chittering noisily and tugging with their hand-like paws at his pockets. He poured the cat chow equally into four separate dishes, one for each corner, so that the hungry animals would split up. Whenever they stayed in one group, vicious fighting would erupt over the food. So loud was the screeching and snarling that one time a neighbor had phoned the police because she feared a gruesome murder was taking place behind the Cray house.

Wahoo slipped out of the raccoon pen, padlocked the gate and began washing his hands with a garden hose.

"Don't forget the soap, mate," said a voice behind him.

Wahoo spun around and there stood Derek Badger. At his side was Raven Stark.

"Take me to your alligator," Derek commanded.

"I'd better go get my dad."

"Hurry, then. Chop-chop."

Raven Stark spoke up. "Derek's totally exhausted. He traveled all night from Paris."

"A wretched flight," said Derek. "Didn't sleep a wink."

Wahoo had no trouble believing it. The man's eyelids were puffy, his pale cheeks were blotched and his hair—more orange than blond—was matted and oily. He wore black loafers with no socks, wrinkled white linen trousers and an untucked safari-style shirt that failed to hide his roundish belly. To Wahoo, Derek Badger looked more like a groggy tourist than a sturdy survivalist.

"I'm on a tight schedule," he said, glancing at his wristwatch.

Wahoo ran to the house and returned with his father. Raven Stark handled the introductions. Mickey managed a smile as he shook Derek's hand.

"We're lookin' forward to working with you," Mickey said, which wasn't exactly true but it sounded good.

Wahoo appreciated his father's effort to be respectful. Staging a nature show for a network star like Derek was a big deal. If everything went smoothly, it might lead to more TV jobs.

"Let's go see Alice, shall we?" said Raven Stark.

The gator was snoozing on the bank of the pond. Derek took one look at the huge reptile and said, "She's perfect." Then he turned to Raven Stark. "When can we move her?"

"Move her?" Mickey asked.

Raven Stark said, "We're going to be shooting on location out by the Tamiami Trail."

Wahoo thought: *Here we go.*

"She weighs six hundred and twenty pounds," his father said.

Derek chuckled. "No worries, mate. We'll hire a crane and a truck."

Mickey Cray stepped close to Derek. "Alice doesn't travel," he said. "You want Alice? Shoot the scene here."

Years earlier, Wahoo's father had constructed a small but convincing Everglades set at one end of the property. There was a lush pool ten feet deep, complete with pickerelweed and water lilies, for staging underwater scenes.

Derek didn't want to hear about it. "Save your pretty little lake for an air-freshener commercial."

Mickey said, "If it's good enough for Disney, it's plenty good enough for you, *mate*."

Wahoo worried that his father would say or do something so insulting that he'd lose the *Expedition Survival!* job even before it got started.

Raven Stark edged between the men. "What about the smaller gators?"

"They fit in the back of my pickup," said Wahoo's father. "They travel fine."

Derek looked down at Alice, who was still asleep. "She's the only one I want," he declared.

Then he turned and stalked off.

In a stiff tone, Raven Stark said, "Mr. Cray, you signed a contract."

"Which I intend to use as toilet paper—"

Wahoo cut in with a bluff: "Our lawyer looked at the contract. She said it won't stick."

Julie wasn't really a lawyer yet, but it wouldn't be long.

"Good luck finding another tame gator like Alice," Mickey said.

Raven Stark bristled. "We paid you a deposit, remember? Eight hundred dollars."

"Good luck finding *that*, too."

Wahoo volunteered to show the fake Everglades set to Derek so he could see for himself how authentic it looked. Raven walked to the car to get him, but she returned alone.

"He's on the phone," she reported soberly, "with our producers in California."

Mickey mumbled something sarcastic under his breath and headed back to the house.

"Look, we can still make this work," Wahoo said to Raven.

"Not if your father insists on being difficult."

"I'll deal with Pop, okay?"

"You're only a kid, no offense."

Wahoo tried to remain polite. "I'm *his* kid. He listens to me."

"And you guys need the money, right?" Raven looked around at the pens and cages. "It's got to be expensive, keeping all these animals. This would be a nice payday for your family, no?"

Wahoo felt his throat tighten. "Tell Mr. Badger we're on."

Raven was smiling. "How old are you, Wahoo?"

"Old enough to get it done," he said.

Back at the house, he found his father lying on the couch with an ice pack over his forehead.

Wahoo sat down beside him. "Pop, this show is really important."

"So's Alice." Mickey reached for the TV remote. "Hey, look what I TiVo'd the other night."

He touched a button and an episode of *Expedition Survival!* came on the screen—Derek Badger, roaming a rainy jungle in Costa Rica. A teaser at the beginning showed the star sleeping in a hammock made of vines while a fat hairy spider crawled up his bare arm.

Wahoo's father shook a scarred finger at the TV. "Five bucks says he kills that thing and fries it up for dinner!"

"I'm not taking that bet."

"You know there's a cameraman standing two feet away with a can of Raid, ready to blast that poor, pitiful tarantula."

"It's showbiz," said Wahoo.

"The guy's such a tool!"

"I know, Pop, but we need the work."

They watched the program for a little while longer. Sure enough, Derek Badger pretended to awaken just before the creeping spider reached his neck. Then he knocked it away and stomped it with a boot. He didn't fry the flattened victim, though; he grilled it over a small fire, all the time smacking his wormy lips and yammering about how he'd narrowly escaped a horrible, painful death.

However, Wahoo and his father knew something that most faithful viewers of *Expedition Survival!* didn't know—that tarantulas almost never bite people. When they do, the sting is no worse than a bumblebee's.

Grumbling in disgust, Mickey Cray switched off the TV and tossed the remote onto the coffee table. "The other shows we've done, even the lame ones, were all about the wildlife," he said, "but this is just about *him*."

Wahoo didn't like the idea of working for Derek Badger any more than his father did. "Pop, we've got bills to pay," he said. "Alice needs to eat, right?"

"Okay, but Alice doesn't travel. And that's final."

"Fine, Alice doesn't travel," said Wahoo. "But you've gotta admit, it would've been fun watching those bozos try to haul her out of the pond."

Mickey Cray laughed. "Oh yeah."

FIVE

Although she would never say it aloud, Raven Stark believed she was grossly underpaid. Her job title was "senior production assistant," but in reality she was also a babysitter, nurse, chauffeur, bartender, courier, valet, personal groomer and amateur psychologist.

Derek Badger was a handful.

"We're late," she said, knocking once more on the door of his hotel suite.

There was still no response, so she used the plastic key card. Derek wasn't inside the room; he was standing on the balcony, overlooking a golf course.

Raven said, "For heaven's sake, put on some clothes."

The star of *Expedition Survival!* was clad only in tartan boxer shorts and a pair of black knee-high socks. It wasn't a pretty sight.

"I refuse to work with that ignorant redneck," he said, meaning Mickey Cray.

"People are staring, Derek. Let's go inside."

"Are you telling me that's the only humongous alligator available in South Florida, which is the humongous alligator capital of the world?"

Raven was quite familiar with Derek's tantrums. "This particular specimen happens to be perfect for what we need."

"Perfect how?" he whined.

"Time to put on your pants. Let's go."

The script for Derek's Everglades adventure called for him to swim beside a huge gator, which required renting one that would tolerate Derek's nonsense and resist the urge to bite off his fool head. Mickey Cray's son had assured Raven that Alice had never purposely hurt anybody (he'd again blamed himself for the thumb removal), and that the reptile was accustomed to the noisy presence of camera crews.

"But we can't stage our biggest scene in some nitwit's backyard," Derek complained in the car, traveling to the Crays' house.

Raven assured him that the family's Everglades set didn't look like a backyard. "It looks like a real-life swamp. You'll be impressed."

Derek sniffed. "No, *they'll* be impressed when they see me jump that monster gator."

"Not happening. The insurance company says no way."

"They said the same thing about the cobra dance, but I did it anyway."

Thanks for reminding me, thought Raven.

They had been shooting an *Expedition Survival!* in Cambodia when Derek decided to play snake charmer with a spitting cobra that had been rented from a local handler named Mr. Na. When Mr. Na saw what Derek was doing, he leaped between Derek and the dangerous reptile just as it released a jet of deadly poison. A few drops landed in Mr. Na's hair, and as a precaution he rushed off to take a shower. Upon returning to the set of *Expedition Survival!*, Mr. Na was dismayed to learn that Derek had chopped up his pet snake with a rusty machete and eaten it for supper in the program's final scene.

"The Crays won't let you lay a finger on Alice," Raven said.

Derek chuckled to himself. "We shall see about that. What sort of people would name a dumb old alligator Alice?"

"The sort of people who treat it like one of the family."

"Hillbillies," Derek said. "Did you bring extra cash?"

The crew of the television program arrived early to set up. With amazement the cameramen and lighting technicians watched Mickey Cray lead Alice from her enclosure to the swamp-like Everglades set at the other end of the property. Swishing her thick armored tail for balance, the huge gator trailed Mickey like a puppy. He was carrying a plump thawed chicken under each arm, so Alice would have followed him anywhere.

Wahoo was busy tending the crippled bobcat, trying to coax it to eat. The poor thing was limping in circles around the new pen, still frazzled by the long truck ride from Highlands County. Every now and then the cat would scrabble up and down an old telephone pole that Mickey had planted for that very purpose. Still, it took Wahoo almost an hour to get the animal calm enough to nibble from a dish.

He arrived on the Everglades set just as Derek Badger was emerging from the air-conditioned motor coach that served as a dressing room. The vehicle was jet-black and as big as a Greyhound bus. Derek wore crisply pressed khaki shorts, a matching safari shirt and hiking boots splattered with wet oatmeal to look like mud.

"What a poser," Mickey said.

"Chill out, Pop."

"Don't we have some fire ants?"

"That's enough."

A rumpled assistant in orange sneakers and a corduroy vest began spraying something on Derek Badger's arms and legs. Wahoo assumed it was insect repellent until the man in the vest told Derek to shut his eyes and then misted his face.

"What *is* that stuff?" Wahoo asked Raven Stark.

"Spray-on tan," she said matter-of-factly.

Wahoo thought that even a showbiz survivalist should have a real tan, but evidently nothing about Derek Badger was real. The star went back to the motor coach to await his bronze glow while the TV crew snacked on donuts and bagels. Wahoo helped his father trim a patch of saw grass to clear space for one of the three cameras that would be filming the water scenes.

"How's Alice?" Wahoo asked.

"Pigged out and happy," said his dad.

The well-fed gator was resting at the bottom of the brackish lagoon. Every now and then a pair of bubbles would float to the surface, betraying the location of the animal's nose.

"Where's the gun?" Raven asked Mickey Cray.

"Oh, relax." He lifted his T-shirt to reveal the butt of a pistol that he was carrying on his waist. The contract with *Expedition Survival!* required Mickey to keep a firearm with him, in case something went wrong and one of the critters attacked.

"It's a .45," Mickey said. "Feel better?"

Raven went to retrieve Derek while Wahoo fetched the snapping turtle that would be featured in the first segment. Even though the turtle was bulky, Wahoo carried it at arm's length from his body. The snapper had a long, flexible neck and was lightning quick on the strike.

"Doesn't this one have a name?" Derek asked snidely. "How about Timmy the Terrible Turtle?"

Wahoo ignored him. He set the craggy reptile down beside the pool and backed out of the scene. The director, a shaggy-bearded guy, yelled, "We're rolling!"

Immediately Derek knelt down and positioned his glossy face beside the turtle's, although he wasn't nearly as close as the camera made it appear. Breathlessly he began reciting the lines he had memorized from his script:

"These snapping turtles are one of the most ferocious predators in the Everglades! They're camouflaged to look exactly like a mossy rock, and their sharp, powerful jaws unlock to reveal a juicy, worm-like tongue, which they deviously wiggle as bait—"

Derek abruptly halted and said, "Cut!" He motioned impatiently to Mickey Cray. "We definitely need to see Timmy's tongue."

"His name's not Timmy," said Wahoo's father, "and I can't make him open his yap if he doesn't want to."

"Then what are we paying you for?"

"Mainly to keep you out of the emergency room."

"Excuse me?"

Wahoo quickly stepped forward. "Mr. Badger, the turtle only wiggles his tongue underwater, when he's hungry."

"That's just great." Derek looked over at Raven. "I had a bad feeling about this whole operation—didn't I tell you?"

Wahoo's dad said, "You wanna see the inside of his mouth?" He broke a thin branch off a pine tree, stripped away the sprigs and handed it to the TV star. "Try this."

Raven grew concerned. "Derek, you be careful."

"Yes, Mum!" He laughed and got down on his knees again, this time a bit closer to the turtle. As soon as the cameras started rolling, he used the sharp end of the branch to poke at the pointy snout of the reptile, which shut its eyes and drew itself into its shell.

"C'mon, Terrible Timmy," Derek cooed, "say aaahhhh."

Wahoo knew he had to do something fast. Quietly he moved behind the cameraman nearest to Derek and made a pushing motion with both hands, a signal to back off. Either Derek didn't see him, or pretended not to.

The bite was a hissing blur. Everyone flinched at the crack of the branch being chomped in half, a few short inches from Derek's wide eyes. He gasped in surprise and tumbled sideways into the lagoon. The turtle wasn't far behind, paddling furiously toward the cool, quiet bottom, where Alice the alligator had been—until that moment—peacefully snoozing.

The director hollered, "Cut! Cut!"

Mickey Cray was applauding. "Hey, that's good stuff."

Two crew members hurried forward to drag Derek, cursing, from the water. The beak of the snapping turtle had peeled a sliver of flesh from the tip of his artificially tanned nose, now punctuated with a bright red dot of blood.

Raven Stark angrily cornered Wahoo and his father. "You two think this is funny? Derek could have been maimed!"

Mickey shrugged. "That's why they're called snappers, not yawners."

"You're the one who gave him that stick!"

"Well, it's better than using a finger," said Mickey. "Right, son?"

Wahoo nodded ruefully, displaying the fleshy bump where his right thumb once had been. Behind him Derek was bellowing at the director, ordering him to erase all the video footage of the turtle encounter.

"If I see one minute of that on YouTube, everybody on this crew is fired!" Derek warned as he toweled off. "And I mean *everybody*!"

Next they tried the python, Beulah.

Wahoo and his father uncoiled the beautiful, multi-hued constrictor and laid her out at full length. The script called for Derek to creep up and seize Beulah behind her head, instigating a fake life-or-death struggle. Mickey Cray didn't mention that Beulah had tried to eat his foot a few days earlier; the swelling had gone down and his limp was barely noticeable.

Over Derek's objections, Mickey insisted on conducting a rehearsal so he could demonstrate the safest way to handle the big snake.

Derek barely paid attention. "Piece o' cake, mate," he kept saying.

"Sometimes she bites," Wahoo reminded him.

"Ha! Never show you're afraid, because animals can sense it," said Derek. "Do you even know what true primal fear smells like?"

"Not really. Asparagus?"

Derek's eyes narrowed as he tried to figure out if he'd just been insulted.

As it turned out, Beulah showed no interest in biting anyone during the run-through. She was sleepy and sluggish, her belly still full from the microwaved chickens that Wahoo had fed her after she'd tried to make a meal of his father.

"Okay, this one's for real!" said the director. "Action!"

Soon Derek was crawling through Mickey Cray's manicured palmetto scrub, whispering dramatically into a bug-sized microphone clipped to his shirt collar:

"As if the Everglades weren't dangerous enough, in recent years this tropical river of grass has been invaded by lethal

predators from another continent—Burmese pythons! Imported by wildlife brokers for the exotic pet trade, hundreds and hundreds of baby pythons got scattered throughout the Glades when Hurricane Andrew destroyed breeding farms west of Miami. Now all those cute little buggers have grown into fierce levithanians, some of them twenty feet long!"

"Cut!" the director called.

"What's wrong?" snapped Derek. "That bit was totally brilliant."

"The word is 'leviathan,' not 'levithanian.' "

They attempted the scene nine more times, but Derek couldn't get the pronunciation right. Finally the director gave up. "Forget it, okay? Just say 'monster' instead."

Derek nailed it on the first take:

"Now all those cute little snakes have grown into voracious monsters, some of them twenty feet long! They can swallow a whole deer, a panther and, yes, even a human being.

"Today I'm crawling through the most remote, untouched and dangerous stretch of the Everglades, following the trail of an enormous wild python—and look! There she is!"

With a cameraman on his heels, Derek wriggled forward and pounced with a triumphant cry upon Beulah. He locked both hands two feet below her head, which is just about the worst place to grab a snake. Wahoo was surprised that Beulah didn't twist around and sink her chompers into Derek's fat face.

"I've got her! I've caught the beast!" he crowed.

The python wasn't particularly concerned. She hooked

her tail around one of Derek's ankles but didn't even tighten up. Grunting and huffing, he rolled back and forth on the ground, shaking Beulah by the neck, trying to provoke her to fight back.

It was like wrestling a fourteen-foot noodle. All Beulah wanted to do was curl up and take a nap.

Wahoo glanced at his father and didn't like what he saw. Mickey Cray was clenching and unclenching his fists.

Derek panted into the microphone:

"*Whatever happens, I can't let this jungle killer wrap her massive coils around my chest! She would literally crush the life out of me!*"

Mickey turned to his son. "That's what *I'm* fixin' to do," he whispered. "Literally."

"No, Pop, wait—"

It was too late. Wahoo's dad hurled himself furiously at Derek Badger, but the double vision caused him to miss.

Mickey got up, dusted off and tried again. This time he scored a direct hit, clinching both arms around Derek's pudgy midsection. He dragged him away from the dizzy python and began to squeeze with all his might.

"Cut! Cut!" cried the director. "Are you nuts? Somebody stop this lunatic!"

The crew members seemed entertained by the scuffle. No one except Wahoo made a move to rescue Derek. By the time Wahoo was able to unfasten his dad, the famous survivalist's face had turned the color of cranberries. He was down on all fours, coughing and whimpering with Raven Stark at his side, brushing the leaves and twigs from his hair.

"Now you've done it," Wahoo said.

His father looked somber. "Let's move Beulah back to her tank."

Mickey took the front half while Wahoo hoisted the tail section.

"That's the worst excuse for a python I ever saw!" It was Derek, lurching to his feet. "You call that a snake? Ha! I call it an overstuffed earthworm."

Beulah opened her shovel-sized mouth and burped, displaying rows of hook-shaped teeth. Derek cringed and hopped backward.

"Take a hike," advised Mickey Cray.

"What?"

"You heard me, Dork Man."

Raven stood speechless. Wahoo noticed one of the cameramen chuckling.

Derek stiffened. "Listen, mate, we've got a contract."

"Are you kidding?" said Mickey.

Wahoo and his dad began hauling the hefty python toward the snake tanks.

"Hey! What about the gator?" Derek Badger shouted after them.

"Over my dead body," Mickey said.

"Three grand for a scene with Alice! Cash!"

"Pop, you hear that?" Wahoo whispered.

"Hear what?"

"Thirty-five hundred!" Derek called out.

"Pop, come on."

"Keep walking."

"Four grand!" cried Derek. "Four thousand dollars!"

Mickey Cray turned around, smiling. "*That* I heard."

SIX

Wahoo sat at the kitchen table, tapping the keypad of a calculator. His father was stretched out on the sofa. Outside, the rain poured down and the yard was turning to mud. The taping of *Expedition Survival!* had been suspended until the weather cleared.

"How much do we owe the bank?" Wahoo asked.

Mickey Cray grunted. "I don't recall."

"I bet Mom knows."

"Down to the penny." Mickey sat up. "Hey, let's call her."

"We can't, Pop. She said once a week, remember?" Wahoo would have loved to hear his mother's voice, but she'd warned about phoning too often. "It costs, like, ten bucks a minute," he reminded his dad. "Plus, it's the middle of the night in Shanghai."

"Put that stupid calculator away," Mickey said sourly. "Let me deal with the bleeping bank."

Wahoo's mom, who hated to hear cussing, made his father put a dollar in the cookie jar every time he said a bad word. Consequently, Mickey had trained himself to use "bleep" or "bleeping" instead. He'd gotten the idea from watching reality police shows, which replaced the criminals' profanity with electronic toots.

Wahoo said, "I'm not trying to be nosy, Pop."

He had a friend at school whose parents had lost their house to the bank because they couldn't make the mortgage payments. Now the whole family was crammed into a small apartment in Naranja. Wahoo knew his mother was determined not to let that happen to them—that's why she'd taken the job in China.

Still, he worried.

"Relax, would ya? We'll be okay," Mickey said.

Clutching the TV remote, he lay back down. He flipped through the channels until he found a show called *When Animals Go Bonkers*. The first segment featured a crazed Canada goose attacking a garbage truck. Mickey didn't even crack a smile; his thoughts were a million miles away.

Wahoo was troubled to see his father acting so listless and distracted. He grabbed a weather jacket and walked outside.

Rain always made the animals sleepy, so the backyard was peaceful. The TV crew had stowed its equipment and gone to lunch. Only the hum of Derek Badger's humongous motor coach could be heard over the patter of raindrops. As Wahoo passed by the vehicle, he looked through a side window and saw Derek standing with Raven Stark in front of a mirror. With a tissue she was dabbing makeup on his nose, undoubtedly trying to conceal the button-sized turtle bite. Wahoo smiled to himself and kept walking.

Alice the alligator was floating serenely in the faux Everglades pond. It was three times as large as a regular backyard swimming pool and twice as deep. Mickey Cray and two friends had dug out the hole and poured the gunite themselves. Wahoo, who was only five at the time, had taken a turn with the shovel, too.

"Hey, girl," he said to Alice. He waved to her with his thumb-less hand, a private joke.

Every year, the new kids at school would stare at Wahoo's knobby scar and ask what had happened. Initially they wouldn't believe the story, then they'd want to hear all the gory details. His classmates were always amazed when he told them he hadn't felt any pain at first.

In truth, Wahoo hadn't even realized anything was wrong until Paulette, the girl he'd been trying to impress, shrieked and keeled over. Only then had Wahoo looked down at his hand and seen the empty, bloody socket where a perfectly good thumb had been attached.

He'd wrapped the nub with his sweatshirt and dashed for the house, leaving Alice munching happily on the chicken and unseen appetizer. By the time the ambulance had arrived, Wahoo was in a world of hurt.

He never saw Paulette again. Her parents moved her to a private school where the boys came from normal homes and kept hamsters or goldfish as pets, not giant flesh-eating reptiles. Wahoo understood completely.

Yet he wouldn't have traded his childhood for anybody else's.

He said goodbye to Alice and went to check on the injured young bobcat, which was still acting skittish. His dad trudged past, hatless in the downpour, and pointed toward the gator pond. Wahoo sat down and tried speaking softly to the wild cat, which eyed him with uncertainty.

When the rain finally let up, someone in the motor coach began blasting the ridiculously loud air horn; it sounded like a Mississippi tugboat. Then the door of the big bus banged open, and a familiar voice yelled: "Get a move on, mates! *La siesta* is over!"

Wahoo rose and said, "Showtime."

The bobcat, showing good sense, scooted up the telephone pole.

While Raven Stark was applying makeup to his wounded nose, Derek Badger asked, "Are snapping turtles edible?"

"Not that particular turtle, no."

"But what a fabulous campfire scene—cooking it up over a bed of hot coals. I could use the snapper's shell as a soup kettle!"

"Mr. Cray would never agree," Raven said. "Now hold still."

Derek frowned. "So what am I supposed to eat to survive? For the show, I mean."

"The script calls for bullfrogs and crawdads."

"What else? I want something truly disgusting."

"Centipedes," said Raven. "Florida has some seriously vile centipedes."

"But we already did centipedes—down in South Africa, remember?"

Raven consulted her Everglades research notes. "Wild mushrooms, lichens, cabbage palms—"

Derek groaned. "Boooor-ing. What about an opossum?"

"They're too cute. We'll get angry letters."

"Opossums aren't cute. They're ugly as the devil!"

"Not everyone thinks so." Raven Stark had recently visited FAO Schwarz, a very famous toy store in New York City, where she'd noticed a whole shelf of hand puppets that were made to look like smiling, pink-nosed opossums. They were fairly adorable.

"How about maggots?" she asked Derek. "We can dig up plenty of maggots."

"But they're rather small, aren't they? How many would I have to eat?"

"All depends." Sometimes Derek needed a dozen tries to get the campfire dinner scene just right. "I should think no more than a pound or so," Raven speculated.

"A slam dunk," he said gaily.

"You do know we're talking about fly larvae, right?"

He leaned closer to the mirror and started brushing his hair. "Speaking of food, who's doing our catering? Please tell me it's Candy and Anabelle."

Although loyal viewers of *Expedition Survival!* never would have guessed, Derek Badger dined like a king during his televised survival missions. No matter how remote the jungle setting, his contract required sumptuous five-star menus: steak, lamb, lobster, sockeye salmon, homemade pasta, pheasant or venison, accompanied by fresh garden vegetables and of course an array of rich, artery-clogging desserts.

Naturally, these feasts were consumed off camera, so as not to spoil the illusion of hardship.

"Candy and Anabelle are on a job in Argentina," Raven Stark said, knowing her boss would be miffed. "We're using Leticia Oxford's outfit."

"Not again! That fool nearly poisoned me," Derek cried. "Remember that dreadful Brie?"

There had been an incident, two years earlier, involving a wheel of spoiled cheese. In Leticia Oxford's defense, the temperature that day in the Guyanese rain forest had reached 107 degrees, and the supply of ice had been limited.

"It's Bear Grylls, isn't it?" Derek whined, referring to one of his rival TV survivalists. "I'll bet that's who Candy and Anabelle are catering. Tell the truth, Raven. Are they cooking for that little twerp?"

"The rain's stopped."

Derek cocked his head to listen. "Well, so it has."

"Alice awaits," Raven said.

"Yes, in all her glory." He put down the hairbrush and inspected his turtle-nipped nose once more in the mirror. Then he mashed the horn on the steering wheel, flung open the door of the motor coach and hollered, "Get a move on, mates. *La siesta* is over!"

* * *

The first time Mickey Cray got chomped, he was only four years old.

His mom (Wahoo's future grandmother) was sweeping the patio when she let out a yell. Mickey ran outside and found her waving a broom at a small garter snake, which he promptly snatched up by the tail. The frightened reptile twisted around and sank its sharp little nippers into Mickey's tender wrist.

He stood there, staring in wonderment. It was just about the coolest thing he'd ever seen.

From that day on, Mickey Cray was fascinated with creatures small and large, furry and scaly. He spent every minute of his spare time in the woods and wetlands, chasing after snakes, chameleons, turtles, toads, eels, even baby gators. If it slithered, scampered or hopped, Mickey would grab for it.

As a result, he frequently got bitten. That wasn't his favorite part of the outdoor experience, but the pain was nothing, really, compared to the fun he was having. Rare was the evening when he rode his bicycle home with no fresh puncture wounds or bloody spots on his jeans. His parents knew better than to ask about the squirming pillowcase he'd be carrying, as long as he remembered to lock whatever creature it held in the utility room.

Mickey's family had hoped his passion for wildlife was just a youthful phase, but he never outgrew it. His mother and father were amazed when he met a bright and seemingly normal young woman who didn't mind his motley collection of animals, and they were even more amazed when she agreed to marry him.

But that was Susan—she was amazing, period.

Mickey missed her like crazy, and she was 8,297 miles away. Wahoo had gone on the Internet and computed the distance, which had turned out to be depressing for both of them.

Not only did Mickey have a heavy heart, he was fighting another skull-splitting headache.

"The Curse of the Iguana," he muttered to himself, slouched in the rain.

The falling droplets dimpled the brackish pool. Two fat bubbles appeared, and Alice rose slowly. Only her plank-sized snout and knuckled brow broke the surface.

"You're lookin' good," Wahoo's father said to the gator. "Heck, you *always* look good."

In his world, Alice was a much bigger star than Derek Badger. Mickey had found her when he was a teenager and she was practically a hatchling, so she was as close to being tame as any ravenous, pea-brained dinosaur could be. Female alligators rarely grew so huge in the wild, but Mickey fed his favored specimen generously, and often.

"We'll be out of your hair tomorrow," he said to Alice, who hovered motionless and unblinking. "This TV guy, he's a royal bonehead. Just roll with it, okay?"

Wahoo's father sometimes held one-sided conversations with the animals, but he wasn't a whack job; he never imagined that they could actually talk back. They all came to know his voice, though. Of that he was certain.

Finally the rain stopped and Mickey straightened up, dripping like a dog. Alice sank slowly toward the depths of the pool.

An air horn blew, and then a man hollered something about a *siesta*. The words were hard to make out, but the Australian accent was unmistakable.

"Mr. Dork Badger," Wahoo's father said to himself.

Then, to his favorite reptile, now at the bottom of the pond: "Don't worry, princess. He tries anything funny, I'll personally bite his head off."

SEVEN

The underwater camera, bolted to an aluminum rod, was operated by remote control. Another camera was stationed at ground level by the side of the pool, while a third was mounted with a microphone on a high boom extending above the set.

Derek Badger waded in up to his ankles; he wore a spotless safari shirt and creased khaki hiking shorts. Strapped to one leg was a black-handled diver's knife.

"Don't worry—it's just a prop," said Raven Stark. She was fanning Derek's face while the TV lights were being arranged.

"Looks like a real knife to me," Mickey Cray said. He was down on one knee, chewing a wad of bubble gum. Wahoo could see the bulge from the .45 pistol tucked under his dad's shirt.

Alice was still ten feet deep, invisible.

Derek peered into the pond. "Well?" he said.

"Go for it," the director told him. "We're rolling."

" 'Kay, mate."

Derek slipped up to his neck into the water, careful not to muss his hair. "No mistakes!" he shouted at the crew, and went breathlessly into the script:

"Soon the sun will be setting over the Everglades, and I find

myself in a perilous predicament. I must now swim across this deep, murky pond to reach dry ground, where I can camp for the night and hopefully start a fire.

"Getting across this water is absolutely crucial to my survival, but here's the problem—in the bush I've discovered fresh signs of an extremely large alligator, and I mean HUGE, lurking close by! Unfortunately, I don't know where this massive beast is hiding right now, but it surely can't be far. . . ."

Wahoo glanced over at Mickey, who didn't look enthralled.

Derek was treading water, facing the camera mounted on the shore:

"The American alligator is one of the most primitive brutes on the planet. In millions of years this toothy species hasn't changed hardly at all, and there's a good reason for that. You see, gators are perfect predators—powerful, silent and unbelievably fast!

"If that monster were to attack me right now, the only chance I'd have of escaping alive would be to fight back ferociously, desperately, and gouge it in the eyes. . . ."

Wahoo watched his father's expression darken.

Meanwhile, the guy with the remote control for the underwater camera was urgently pointing at the screen of his video monitor, trying to get the director's attention. Apparently Alice was on the move.

Mickey Cray stood up. Wahoo's eyes flicked toward the cattails, where he'd concealed a long bamboo pole. The pole could be used to poke the alligator if she decided to attack.

Derek slowly began swimming across the pool, calling back to his imaginary viewers:

"Well, wish me luck. Here I go!"

Wahoo and his father sidled closer to the video monitor and peeked over the cameraman's shoulder. The screen showed a view from the submerged camera—Derek's pale arms stroking and his legs kicking, leaving a wake of foam and bubbles.

And there was Alice, suspended beneath him, gazing up at the odd, obnoxious creature that had invaded her space.

"This is insane," Wahoo whispered.

"Naw, she won't touch him," said his father. "Not on a full belly."

But there was an edge of tension in Mickey's voice.

"What if you're wrong, Pop?"

"Don't think like that. Who knows Alice better than I do?"

Sure enough, Derek Badger made it safely across the pond and slogged up into the shallows. The last line of the scene was supposed to be: *Whew! That was a mighty close call!*

But what he said was: "Hey, where was that stupid bloody gator?"

Mickey looked pleased. Wahoo felt a wave of relief—Alice had been a good sport.

The director assured Derek that the scene had turned out fantastic. "Your tippy toes were just millimeters from her jaws! Incredible stuff!"

Derek trudged around the bank of the pond and rejoined the crew. "I want to do another take," he said sullenly.

"But why? Come see the replay—it's perfect." The director looked at Raven for backup. She pleaded under her breath with Derek, but he wouldn't budge.

With a sigh of surrender, the director said, "Okay, then. Let's try another one."

Wahoo's father stepped forward. "Naw, we're done. You got what you need."

Derek, who was smoothing his hair, gave no sign of hearing a word. Raven said, "Just one more take, Mr. Cray. That'll do it."

"Only if he gets rid of that bleeping knife."

"But I told you, it's just a toy—"

Wahoo's dad reached over and snatched the dive knife from the sheath on Derek's leg. He pressed the point of the blade to the tip of his forefinger, and a crimson bubble appeared. Raven cleared her throat. Derek shrugged, turning away.

Mickey wiggled the knife and arched his eyebrows. "That's some toy." He closed one hand firmly around the handle, as if testing the grip.

The mischievous glint in his dad's eyes made Wahoo uneasy. "Give me that thing, Pop. I'll put it somewhere safe."

"Don't worry. I got just the place."

Mickey wiped the blade on the collar of Derek's safari shirt, the blood droplet leaving a small brownish smear.

Then he tossed the knife high in the air and watched it spiral down into the middle of the pond, where it disappeared with a *sploosh*.

Derek was now paying attention. "Are you totally, completely out of your mind?"

Mickey clicked his teeth. "You got fifteen minutes, brother. One more shot."

The TV crew began scrambling. Somebody brought Derek a clean shirt, and Raven retouched the makeup on his nose. The director checked the angles on all three cameras while his assistants adjusted the lighting.

A swelling appeared in the glassy pool—Alice, rising to take a breath. This time the full breadth of her back broke the surface, the black scales glistening like barnacles. She was as wide as a railroad track.

Derek said, "Ha! Nice of you to finally make an appearance."

Everyone on the crew stopped to gaze at the enormous creature that floated only a few feet away. Wahoo could tell they were impressed. He could also see they were jittery about being so close to such an animal.

"Don't you move!" Derek barked at the reptile. He wheeled on Mickey: "Make sure she stays right there till I'm back in the water."

Wahoo's dad just shook his head.

The director yelled, "Action!" and Derek jumped into the pond. He was about as graceful as a potbellied pig.

Alice immediately sank out of sight.

"No! No!" Derek squawked. "Where'd she go now?" He was dog-paddling in circles.

Wahoo was glad that the dive knife was sunk out of Derek's reach—there was no telling what he might do to provoke the gator. Watching the underwater monitor, Wahoo saw her hunkered once again at the bottom of the pool.

"Start your lines!" the director called.

Derek refused. "Not till that silly bloody lizard pops up again."

Raven leaned close to Wahoo and inquired how long Alice could hold her breath.

"Hours," he replied.

"Are you serious?"

"Her personal record is three," Mickey interjected. "Three hours and fifteen minutes. It was during one of the hurricanes."

"Oh, brilliant." Raven glanced crossly at her wristwatch. "We don't have three hours to kill."

The director said, "Yeah, let's bag it."

"No, keep rolling!" It was Derek, now tangled in the lily pads. "Keep rolling!"

Wahoo's father murmured, "What a jackass," and headed for the house.

"Where are you going?" Raven asked.

"To get some aspirin."

"Bring the whole bottle," she said.

Ten minutes passed, then fifteen more. Derek continued to flounder around the fake Everglades lagoon while Alice remained out of sight.

The man operating the remote control for the underwater camera said the battery was running low. "Want me to put in a new one?"

"Don't waste your time," the director said. "This is hopeless. We'll just use the first take."

Wahoo looked toward the house and wondered if his dad was all right. He would have gone to check on him, but he didn't want to leave as long as Alice was alone in the water with Derek. . . .

Five, ten, fifteen more minutes dragged by. Finally the director said to Raven, "That's enough. Get him out."

Derek angrily waved them off. "No way! I'll stay here all night if I have to—"

"Hey!" It was the guy in charge of the underwater camera. "Look at this."

They gathered closely around the video monitor—the director, the cameraman, Raven and Wahoo. Slowly but surely, Alice was rising from the bottom of the pool. Her great fluted tail fanned the water gently, stirring a haze of greenish mud.

On the way up, the alligator paused with her blunt nose only inches from the camera's lens. Even with her mouth shut, the lethal downward teeth were on full display, a crooked picket fence along her upper jaw.

"Wow," said the director. "Check out those pearlies."

"She definitely needs an orthodontist," joked the cameraman.

From the pool, Derek shouted, "What're you looking at?"

Suddenly the picture went black. The underwater camera's battery was dead.

"Where'd she go?" Raven asked anxiously.

The director stroked his scraggly beard. "This is not ideal."

Wahoo stepped to the edge of the pond and called to Derek. "She's coming up!"

"Well, it's about bloody time," he said.

"Don't move!"

"Ha! Are we still rolling, mates?"

During their 150 million years of existence, alligators have survived global upheavals that wiped out thousands of other species—volcanic eruptions, raging floods, sizzling droughts, melting glaciers and crashing meteorites. After all the other great dinosaurs vanished from earth, the hardy gator remained.

The most serious threat to emerge was man, who in the twentieth century began killing the reptiles for their hides, which were used to make expensive purses, belts and shoes. By the 1960s, alligators had been slaughtered to the brink of extinction throughout the southeastern United States, their main habitat. Eventually the government stepped in and halted gator hunting until the species bounced back, which didn't take long.

Nothing in nature is tougher.

Contrary to media hype, wild alligators are born with the instinct to avoid people and will usually stay away if given a choice. However, gators that become accustomed to a human presence soon lose all fear, which creates serious problems for both species.

It was impossible for Wahoo to know what was going on in Alice's prehistoric brainpan as she rose to the surface of the pool. But compared with all the epic disasters that her ancestors had endured, a flabby fake Australian probably wouldn't have been viewed as a serious threat. On the other hand, she had never before encountered a human so fool-hardy.

Whether Alice failed to see Derek Badger because he was in the lily pads, or whether he purposely positioned himself to intercept her, the result was the same. Somehow he wound up straddling her back, like a tipsy cowboy on a bronco.

"Wooo-hooo!" he hollered idiotically.

All Raven Stark could say was: "Oh Lord."

Wahoo was astounded that Alice was holding still. Apparently she was trying to figure out what exactly was on top of her, and if there was any room left in her tummy for dessert. Young egrets and herons sometimes mistook alligators for logs and perched on them, only to be gobbled in a blur.

"Get off!" Wahoo yelled.

Derek hooted back.

The director sternly motioned for Wahoo to be quiet. He didn't want any voices other than Derek's on the audio loop of the scene.

Time slowed to a crawl. Wahoo knew that Alice wouldn't tolerate such nonsense for long. He was alarmed to see Derek lie down lengthwise along the gator's spine and try to wrap his arms around her, locking his fingers into the rubbery ridges of her hide. It was a pose that lasted for approximately one second.

Members of the Crocodilia order of reptiles don't buck like horses do when shedding an unwanted rider. Instead, they thrash and spin. Derek managed to hang on for three full revolutions before being launched airborne. Alice was still twirling violently when he splashed down for a landing. Wahoo feared he would be killed.

Both ends of an alligator possess lethal power—the jaws can crush a person like a grape, while a swift blow from the heavy tail can smash every important bone in the human body. Derek happened to reenter the pond at the biting end of Alice, and through pure misfortune his khaki shorts became snagged on two of her eighty teeth. This connection caused him to begin rotating in unison with the spinning reptile, creating a frothy turmoil on the water.

Raven Stark screamed for help, but none of the crew knew what to do. Jumping in the pool to help Derek seemed like a sure way to get mangled or drowned. Wahoo snatched the bamboo pole from the cattails and thrust it outward in

.ek might be able to grab on, but Derek was too
.onfused.

.oo gave up and tossed the pole aside. Jabbing it at
.uce would have accomplished nothing but to agitate her
even more—the unhappy gator wanted only to be rid of her
pesky human leech.

"Shoot that thing!" Raven shrieked, and Wahoo realized
she was addressing his father, who'd reappeared at the scene.

"Shoot it! Shoot it!" she begged.

Mickey Cray removed the .45 from his belt and handed it
to his son. Then he calmly kicked off his shoes and dove into
the water, where he grabbed a fistful of oily, orange-tinted
hair as Derek Badger bubbled past.

The director ordered the cameramen to keep the video
rolling. Wahoo's heart was pounding in his eardrums. He
was so riveted on the chaos in the pool that he didn't see
Raven approach him from the side and lunge for the gun.
She plucked it from his hand and aimed the barrel at the
portion of the turbulence that looked more reptile than
human.

"No, don't!" Wahoo cried, yet she pulled the trigger
anyway.

Click. Click. Click.

Raven gaped in disbelief at the pistol. It was empty, of
course. Wahoo's father hadn't loaded a single bullet.

"This is madness," said Raven, trembling.

She looked back at the pond. Alice had vanished again,
but there stood Mickey in the shallows, Derek spluttering

in his grasp. Derek's knees were skinned, his mouth was bleeding and his khakis had been torn off, but otherwise the famous survivalist seemed to have survived the crazy gator ride without serious injury. Wahoo was amazed.

His dad waded from the pool and deposited Derek in a dripping heap on the ground. "Here's your so-called star," he said to the director. "Now pack your gear and get off my property."

Then he grabbed the gun away from Raven and walked back toward the house. Wahoo hurried to catch up. He didn't say a word. Nothing upset his father more than the mistreatment of an animal.

When they reached the porch, Mickey said, "I guess we're not gettin' the rest of the money."

"That's okay, Pop." Wahoo's heart was still racing. It had been a close call—too close.

"That moron's lucky all he lost was his pants."

"We're lucky, too," said Wahoo.

Mickey peeled off his wet clothes and hung them over a chair. "Bring me the phone," he said. "And I don't care what bleeping time it is in China."

EIGHT

The crew carried Derek Badger to his motor coach, dried him off, bundled him in a fuzzy *Expedition Survival!* bathrobe and put him in bed.

Raven Stark stayed to fuss over him. "I thought we'd lost you this time," she said.

"Where's my green tea?" he asked irritably.

The director popped in. He said the trucks were being loaded to go.

Derek displayed the raw scrapes on his knees and a scabby lip. "This is all your fault."

The director thought: *I'm not the clown who climbed on the alligator's back.*

Raven said, "The most important thing is that nobody got seriously hurt."

"No, the most important thing is my show," Derek snapped.

He was trying to sound tough, but it was just an act. The tussle with the reptile had frightened him. He'd truly thought he was going to drown, or be devoured. Over the years there had been other mishaps while staging wildlife encounters, yet nothing as harrowing as his encounter with the swamp beast called Alice.

"By the way," Derek said to the director, "consider your-self fired."

"I brought something to show you."

"A letter of resignation, perhaps?"

The director held up a disk. "The pond scene," he said.

"Destroy it immediately!"

"Not so fast," the director said.

Derek glowered. "Are you threatening to blackmail me?" He looked over at Raven and snapped, "You're my witness. Obviously he wants a payoff."

"Just chill out," the director said. He inserted the disk into a DVD player that was mounted under a high-def TV.

Derek motioned for Raven to fluff his pillows. He said, "Let him have his fun and be on his way."

Raven sat on the edge of the bed to watch the scene. She was prepared to be depressed. Her boss, the executive producer of *Expedition Survival!*, would be furious to learn that the Everglades episode was being scrapped. It cost big money whenever something like this happened, because the director and crew still had to be paid.

On one memorable occasion, Derek had leaped from a baobab tree in Madagascar and sprained both ankles. The script hadn't called for him to jump; a baby gecko had scur-ried up his shorts and frightened him.

On another set, in Mexico, Derek had clumsily tripped over a tortoise and sprawled into a yucca plant. His face had swollen up like a puffer fish. For two weeks afterward, he had worn a veil and refused to go out in public.

While shooting a program in Australia—a very expensive trip—Derek had ignored the local wrangler's warnings and tried to tackle a wallaby, which he'd hoped to fry up as one of his televised campfire dinners. The result: five broken ribs, a torn Achilles tendon, sixteen stitches in his scalp and five days in the hospital.

In each instance, filming had to be canceled and the expenses settled. Raven knew that if *Expedition Survival!* hadn't been such a smash hit, Derek would have been booted off the show a long time ago.

"Let's get this over with," she said to the director.

He pressed the Play button on the DVD console. Thirty-three seconds later, he turned it off.

Raven took a heavy breath. Derek sat bolt upright and goggle-eyed.

"Well?" the director said.

"That . . . was . . . bloody . . . *brilliant!*" Derek punched the air jubilantly with both fists. "I almost died, didn't I? That vicious monster almost killed me!"

Witnessing the scene all over again, even on a video disk, had left Raven a bit shaken.

The director said, "Do you still want me to destroy it?"

Derek roared. "Destroy it? Are you crazy, mate? This stuff is killer. This is genius. Am I right, Raven? Is this not the *bomb?*"

"The bomb it is," said Raven quietly.

"That crazy redneck—did you see what he did?"

"A total madman," the director agreed.

Derek lowered his voice. "Can you edit him out of the scene?"

"No problem. Snip, snip."

"Excellent!"

Raven said, "But he saved your life, Derek."

"And he shall be compensated handsomely."

With a hopeful smile, the director asked, "Does this mean I'm not fired?"

"Fired? Ha!" Derek bounded from the bed and threw an arm around the man's neck. "You, my friend, just got yourself a big fat raise."

As Wahoo and his father had predicted, Susan Cray knew exactly how much the family owed the bank for overdue mortgage payments: "Seven thousand nine hundred and twelve dollars and four cents."

"Don't forget, I just sent 'em eight hundred bucks," Mickey said.

"Yes, honey, I already subtracted that."

"Oh."

"We're also two months behind on your truck," she said.

"You sure about that?"

"May I speak to Wahoo?"

"He's right here." Mickey handed the phone to his son.

"Sorry we woke you, Mom."

"How's the job going?"

"Not so great."

"What happened?"

"Long story," Wahoo said. Too long for an expensive overseas phone call. "How's China?"

"I'm homesick, big guy. Is your dad feeling okay? Tell the truth."

"Some days are better than others."

Susan Cray sighed. "He's as stubborn as a darn mule. You keep an eye on him."

"I'm trying," Wahoo said.

Somebody knocked on the door and Mickey went to open it.

"Let me talk to him again," said Wahoo's mother.

"He'll call you back, Mom—when it's daytime over there, I promise."

Derek Badger and Raven Stark were standing in the living room. Wahoo said goodbye to his mother and set down the phone. Then he told his father to put away the fire extinguisher.

"I'm serious, Pop."

"But they're supposed to be gone!"

Raven said, "We need to chat, Mr. Cray. Please?"

"I don't 'chat.' " He pulled the trigger on the fire extinguisher, blasting a cloud of white vapor toward the ceiling. "Now get out!"

"Knock it off," said Wahoo.

Derek puffed his chest. "Mate, there's no need to be cranky. We come in peace."

It was hard to take the man seriously because he was dressed in a purple bathrobe and matching slippers. Mickey placed the fire extinguisher on the kitchen counter. Wahoo suggested that everybody sit down, which they did.

Raven said, "Derek's got something he wants to say."

"Imagine that." Mickey was rubbing his temples.

Derek leaned forward. "That wrestling scene with the alligator—"

"Alice is her name."

"Yes, Alice. The scene turned out fabulously, Mr. Cray. Perhaps the most extraordinary thirty-three seconds of footage in the history of *Expedition Survival!*"

"But you almost got drowned."

"Exactly! And the best part is it was *real.*"

"You're seriously gonna use that in your show?" Mickey asked, and right away Wahoo knew what his father was thinking.

"Of course we intend to use it," Raven said.

"It'll be all over YouTube the same night," Derek added. "Trust me—we're talking worldwide viral. Millions of hits!"

Mickey's eyes narrowed. "That means you're gonna pay us the rest of the money, right?"

Derek chuckled. "Not only are we going to pay you all of it, we're hiring you to lead us into the Everglades to put the finishing touches on this masterpiece. What do you think of that?"

Wahoo felt slightly queasy.

"What do you need *me* for?" his father said to Derek. "You're gonna fake the rest of it, same as you always do."

Derek didn't seem even slightly insulted. He twirled the sash on his robe and said, "You're the most fearless man I've ever met, Mr. Cray. With you guiding us on location, we won't need to 'fake' anything."

"In our line of work," Raven cut in, "it's known as 're-creating' events for the camera."

Wahoo spoke up. "He can't go. He's got another job lined up that starts tomorrow."

Mickey threw him a puzzled look. "What job?"

"You know, Pop. That scorpion scene for the Rain Forest Channel." Wahoo was hoping his dad would get the hint and play along. A swamp trip with Derek Badger promised nothing but trouble.

Mickey scratched his head. "I don't remember booking a scorpion gig."

"And even if you did," Derek said with a wink, "will it pay you two thousand dollars a day for *four* days?"

Wahoo was stunned. With that kind of money, they could cover what they owed on the house *and* the truck. His mother wouldn't have to give a nickel of her China paycheck to the bank.

"Hold on—what about the boy?" Wahoo's father said to Derek. "He's my right hand."

"Then make it twenty-five hundred—plus we'll give him screen credit as 'First Assistant Wrangler.' "

Mickey stroked his chin. "Let me think on this."

Derek looked aggravated. "Are you serious? This is the opportunity of a lifetime."

Wahoo didn't know whether he should be flattered or suspicious that Derek had agreed to put him on the payroll. Five hundred dollars a day was more money than he'd ever made on any job. He was also secretly excited at the idea of seeing his own name among the crew credits that would roll on the screen at the end of the broadcast.

Yet while part of him wanted his dad to accept Derek's offer, another part of him feared something bad would happen. The real Everglades was a very different place from the homemade marsh in the Crays' backyard.

Feeling torn, he excused himself from the meeting and jogged down to see about Alice. She was still pouting; only her black nostrils showed on the surface of the pool. Wahoo sat down on a plastic milk crate and watched a baby leopard frog hop across the lily pads.

Soon a piece of pale, ragged cloth floated to the top of the water. Wahoo used the bamboo pole to retrieve it: Derek's torn khaki shorts. Two large, hollow alligator incisors remained stuck in the fabric.

"You'll grow new ones," Wahoo said to Alice. The

average gator went through three thousand teeth in a life-time of chomping.

"Yeah, she'll be pretty as ever." It was his father, who'd come up behind him. "And she knows it, too."

"What did you tell 'em, Pop?"

"You mean the Dorkster?" Mickey Cray smiled. "He showed me the video. They put it on a disk."

"Come on. Did you take the job or not?"

"They're gonna cut me out of the gator scene. Make it look like an 'escape' instead of a rescue. One minute that knucklehead will be spinning like a propeller underwater, and next minute he'll be lyin' on the shore—as if he got free from Alice all by himself!" Mickey seemed more amused than upset. "You said it yourself: showbiz!"

"You told them yes, didn't you?"

"Son, we seriously need the dough."

Wahoo couldn't argue with that. He said, "After what happened today, maybe Derek learned his lesson."

"Sure. And maybe the raccoons will start their own la-crosse team." Wahoo's dad kicked the TV star's shredded shorts into the cattails. "Now go fetch a chicken from the freezer. Let's walk sweet old Alice back to her pen."

"*Two* chickens, Pop. She earned it."

NINE

That evening, they drove down to Florida City and stocked up at the Walmart: sodas, Gatorades, bug spray, sunblock, coffee, bacon, powdered eggs, granola bars, Pringles, frozen hot dogs, black beans, matches and first-aid supplies, including a bottle of five hundred aspirins for Mickey.

When they got to the register, Wahoo slipped ahead of his father and paid for the supplies with cash.

Mickey eyed him warily. "Where'd you get that money?"

"Robbed a bank," Wahoo said. Actually his mother had left three hundred dollars inside an envelope in his sock drawer, for emergencies.

Mickey said, "Don't be such a wise bleep."

"Okay, I didn't rob a bank. I won the lottery."

"I'm warning you."

"Here, grab a couple of these bags," Wahoo said. He'd promised his mom he wouldn't tell his dad about the cash in the drawer.

They were loading the provisions into the back of the pickup truck when Wahoo heard someone call, "Wait up!"

He turned around and saw Tuna Gordon, a girl from school. She had curly ginger hair and was small for her age, but she wasn't shy. Wahoo didn't know her well, although she had caught his attention in biology class because she knew the Latin names of all the local snakes and lizards.

"I need a ride," Tuna said. She wore a camo weather jacket, blue jeans and bright green flip-flops. Her canvas tote bag looked as if it weighed more than she did.

"This a friend of yours?" Mickey asked Wahoo.

"She's in my biology class."

"Algebra, too," said Tuna.

Wahoo's father was looking at the tote bag. "Which way are you headin', hon?"

"Anywhere," she said. "Wherever you guys are going."

When she stepped closer, they saw she had a black eye.

"Who did that to you?" Mickey asked.

"I fell down the stairs."

"Baloney."

"Then never mind," Tuna said, and turned to walk away.

"Hold on." Wahoo motioned her to come back. He didn't know what to say or how to act. *Who in the world would hit a girl?* he wondered.

His father asked Tuna where she lived. She pointed toward a dented old Winnebago at the far end of the parking lot.

"Okay, but where do you keep it?" Mickey asked.

"Right there."

"You live at the Walmart?"

"They let motor homes stay for free," Tuna explained. "We got electric and water, everything we need. It's not so awful."

Mickey's father shook his head. "If you like campin' in a parking lot."

Wahoo knew Tuna was telling the truth. In fifth grade he'd met a boy who had spent a whole summer with his family towing a Gulf Stream trailer from one Walmart store to another, all the way from Myrtle Beach, South Carolina, to Portland, Oregon.

"What really happened to your eye?" Wahoo asked.

"I told you. I fell down."

Mickey said, "That's bull. Somebody slugged her."

Tuna's cheeks turned red. Wahoo was shocked that his father would say it aloud and embarrassed for Tuna that it was probably true.

Mickey bent down and whispered, "Was it your old man?"

Tuna pulled away. "So what if it was?"

"Has he been drinkin' tonight?"

Her eyes welled up. "Every damn night," she said quietly.

"Where's your mom?" Wahoo asked.

Tuna covered up a sniffle. "Up north with my grandma."

Mickey Cray was staring darkly across the parking lot at the Winnebago, and Wahoo knew he was considering paying Mr. Gordon a visit. Such a confrontation could only end badly, with police cars and ambulances. Wahoo's father had absolutely no use for creeps who beat on small animals, especially kids.

"You're coming with us," Wahoo said to Tuna, "on a *real* camping trip."

Her eyes brightened. "Seriously?"

"We're heading out to the Everglades for a few days."

"Sweet."

Mickey said, "I'll be right back," and started striding toward the camper where Tuna's father was drinking.

Wahoo ran up and cut in front of him. "No, don't."

"He's got a gun," Tuna said, "by the way."

Mickey frowned. "Then somebody better take it away from him."

"Stay out of it, Pop. She's safe now." Wahoo unclenched his father's right hand and pressed a twenty-dollar bill into it.

"What the bleep is *this* for?"

"Now that we've got company, we'll need more food for the trip," Wahoo said. He looked over at Tuna. "You like Coke or Mountain Dew?"

"Anything's good," she said.

Wahoo gave his father another five bucks. "Mountain Dew it is."

Mickey shoved the cash in his pocket and muttered, "You two wait in the pickup." Then he trudged back toward the Walmart. Wahoo kept an eye on him, to make sure he didn't make a detour to Mr. Gordon's RV.

Once they were seated in the truck, Tuna said, "Look, I don't want to mess up your vacation."

"It's not a vacation. It's a job," said Wahoo.

"What kinda job?"

When he told her, she didn't believe him.

Swaddled in his fluffy purple robe, Derek Badger watched the replay of the alligator scene over and over.

"Crikey, this is golden," he murmured.

Raven Stark sat beside the director at a small dining counter in Derek's motor coach. A map of the Everglades was spread in front of them.

"Have you arranged for a chopper yet?" Derek called from his bed.

"It's on my list," Raven said patiently.

Derek loved using helicopters to shoot high aerial scenes of himself traipsing through the bush, making it appear as if he were all alone. The key was to find a place where there were no obvious signs of human habitation. Fortunately, the Everglades covered a vast region, and much of it was remote.

"Where's the new script?" Derek demanded.

"The writers are still working on it," the director said.

"I want fresh pages by tomorrow morning. Understood?"

The pages were being rewritten to put the gator "attack" at the very end of the show. Because the scene was so brief, it would be shown several times in slow motion and dragged out to fill the last ten minutes of the program.

For the earlier part of the show, the director would need other videotaped segments—Derek hacking his way through the saw grass, building a campsite and, of course, cooking some poor luckless creature for supper.

"What about using your face-to-face with the snapping turtle?" the director asked. "It's really not so bad—"

"I told you to erase that!" Derek exploded.

"All right. Consider it done," the director said, although he had no intention of destroying the turtle tape. The nose-nipping scene would be digitally added to a secret DVD of Derek's spectacular blunders that would be played on a giant flat screen when the crew of *Expedition Survival!* held its annual end-of-the-season party, which Derek never attended because he considered himself too important. The DVD was always the high point of the evening—even Raven had found herself weeping with laughter.

She wasn't laughing now, scanning the map of the Everglades.

At first the Miccosukee tribe had agreed to let *Expedition Survival!* base its operations at one of its settlements along the Tamiami Trail. Unfortunately, Raven had just been informed by a tribal lawyer that Mr. Badger and his crew were no longer welcome.

"Because of the incident involving the Navajos," the attorney had explained stiffly. "We found out about it on the Internet."

Raven had grimaced at the memory.

Derek had been doing a cave-camping scene in New Mexico when he'd brainlessly decided to use an ancient Navajo prayer pipe to scratch an itch on his back. The sacred relic had snapped into three pieces, greatly upsetting the tribal leaders. Derek had been ordered to depart the reservation and never return.

Now, on the eve of the Everglades taping, Raven was scrambling to find a new place to use as a headquarters.

The director tapped a place on the map. "What about here, down in Flamingo?"

Raven frowned. "That's in the national park."

"So what? Call 'em."

"I think we're on some sort of blacklist."

"You're joking," the director said. "Because of what happened at Yellowstone? Geez, that was three, four years ago."

"Not my fault!" Derek protested from the folds of his robe. "I didn't know it was a bloody eagle nest."

That wasn't true. Everyone on the set had warned him it was an eagle nest. Before climbing the old cottonwood, he'd strapped on his Helmet Cam, thereby making sure that the whole idiotic crime had been recorded. A park ranger who'd arrived during the fiasco retrieved the eagle egg as soon as Derek descended from the tree, depriving the survivalist of a tasty breakfast omelet and possibly a prison term.

For disturbing a federally protected species, Derek had been slapped with a ten-thousand-dollar fine that was hastily paid by the producers of *Expedition Survival!* Miraculously, the story had never leaked out to the media.

Everglades National Park was a long way from Yellowstone, so it seemed possible to Derek's director that the authorities in Florida were unaware of the nest-robbing incident.

"Fine," Raven said. "I'll call the park superintendent and give it a shot."

Her lack of enthusiasm annoyed Derek. "Be sure and tell them we're the number one rated survival show on TV!"

"Right."

"Broadcast twice weekly across all eight continents!"

"*Eight* continents?" whispered the director.

Raven put a finger to her lips. "Let it go."

Derek beckoned them both to his bedside. "This is pure gold," he said, touching the Replay button again and setting the alligator scene in motion. "It's a once-in-a-lifetime, near-death experience."

Neither Raven nor the director could disagree. If it weren't for Mickey Cray, Derek probably wouldn't have survived the struggle with Alice.

"The rest of the show," he said dreamily, "must all build up to this incredible, heart-stopping moment. We'll spare no expense!"

Raven waited for Derek to finish savoring the replay so that she would have his full attention. She said, "Mr. Cray would like to know which animals to bring along when we go on location."

"Tell him not to bring any."

"But—"

"No tame animals, darling. This time we're going totally raw and wild."

Raven glanced apprehensively at the director, who said to Derek, "Why not have a few ringers handy, just for backup? They've got a gimpy bobcat that I'm sure we could use in a scene or two—"

"No more faking it, mate. From now on, we're putting the 'real' back in 'reality.' "

Raven didn't like the sound of that.

Derek basked on the bed like a walrus, jowly and content. "Surely our talented Mr. Cray can track down some beasties for me to tangle with in the deep, dark Everglades," he said. "I'm totally psyched about this show, aren't you?"

The director was the opposite of psyched. Surviving the alligator scare obviously had inflated Derek's already-bloated ego and filled his head with foolish notions.

"But what if we don't come across any wild animals?" the director asked. "Then we've basically got fifty minutes of you schlepping through the muck."

From somewhere inside his robe Derek produced a sprinkle-covered donut and crammed it in his cheeks. "No worries. Cray and his lad will come through—God knows we're paying 'em enough."

Raven went outside to think. The director caught up with her by the primate pen, a safe distance from the motor coach. There was no way Derek could hear them over the shrill din of monkey chatter.

"I'm not loving this scenario," the director confided.

"Me neither," Raven said grimly. "That's his third donut since lunch. Pretty soon he'll be too fat to fit in his khakis."

"No, it's the show I'm worried about. We've never done one with strictly wild animals."

Raven decided to be positive. "This is just a phase. Derek will come to his senses, you'll see."

"If he doesn't, then everything depends on that crazy redneck—and he's not exactly a charter member of the Derek fan club."

"Think positive," Raven said.

At that moment, a disgusting glop of something flew out of the monkey pen and splatted in her hair.

"You have *got* to be kidding," she said.

The director ran for cover as the monkeys threw more, yowling uproariously.

TEN

Mickey Cray was surprised to learn that Derek Badger didn't want any of his captive critters on location. Mickey had never wrangled for a nature show that used only wild animals, nor had he ever encountered a person less qualified than Derek to handle untamed specimens.

"How 'bout if I bring a water moccasin? I got a three-footer so calm that a baby could play with it," he said. "Or maybe a couple of the raccoons—they're always fun to have around the set."

Raven Stark said no thanks. "Derek wants to do this totally wild and raw."

"Slow and dumb doesn't mix with wild and raw."

"Thanks for your input, Mr. Cray."

"Seriously. The man almost got killed by the world's laziest alligator."

Raven said, "See you bright and early."

The next morning, Mickey got the kids up first. While he went out back to check on the animals, they ate a quick breakfast and loaded the truck. Wahoo told Tuna that she should call her father to let him know she was all right.

"I already did," she said. "He hadn't even noticed I was gone."

"Didn't he ask where you were?"

"Nope. He was too busy yelling." She tossed her tote bag into the back of the pickup. Her black eye looked worse than it had the night before.

Wahoo said, "Your dad could go to jail for what he did."

"What if I told you I hit him back? Let's just say he won't be riding any motorcycles for a while."

They spritzed each other with bug repellent and walked down to the pond because Tuna wanted to have a look at Alice.

"Wow. That's a major *Alligator mississippiensis.*"

"A queen," Wahoo agreed.

"To think, she almost ate the great Derek Badger."

"She wasn't trying to eat him. He climbed on her back and she spazzed out."

Tuna grinned. "Whatever. It's still epic."

Expedition Survival! was one of her all-time favorite TV shows, and she was excited about the opportunity to see Derek Badger in action. Wahoo didn't want to burst her bubble by revealing that the man was a menace to all other life-forms. She'd figure that out for herself.

"Do you think I'll get to meet him?" she asked. "Would he autograph my jacket?"

Before Wahoo could compose a diplomatic answer, a racket arose from a nearby enclosure—the raccoons, demanding food.

"*Procyon lotor,*" Tuna said.

Wahoo wanted to know how she'd learned the scientific names for so many animals. She explained that the study was called taxonomy, which classified all living things into categories based on traits and common ancestors. The first part of the scientific name identified the genus, and the last part was the species.

"Every organism, from a fungus to a whale, has its own special place on the taxonomy chart. You should Google a guy named Linnaeus," said Tuna. "Speaking of names—not Latin names—we both ended up as fish. How'd *that* happen?"

"I wasn't named after the fish. I was named after a wrestler."

"Yeah, but the wrestler was probably named after the fish," Tuna said. "I was named for my aunt, who worked at a sushi bar. Any which way you look at it, we're both named for something with scales, gills and fins. Personally, I'd prefer to be called something else."

"Me too."

"I see you as a Lance."

"No way," said Wahoo. "If you call me Lance, I swear, I'll start calling you . . . *Lucille*."

Tuna seemed delighted. "Cool. I could roll with Lucille."

Wahoo's father walked up and said it was almost time to go. Donny Dander was at his side, awaiting instructions on what to feed the Crays' array of animals, and how often.

"If I come home and find any of 'em sick—and I mean one little monkey with a runny nose—you're in deep trouble," Mickey warned. "I will haunt you like a bleeping ghost."

"Take it easy, bro," Donny said. After what had happened

the last time—when the parrots escaped, a lemur got sick and Alice mauled the crocodile—he knew better than to make Mickey mad.

"I'll treat 'em like they're my own," Donny promised.

Mickey massaged his forehead. "Yeah, that's what I'm afraid of."

Leading the convoy to the Everglades were two equipment trucks hauling all the lights, scaffolds, wiring, batteries, sound boards and video cameras. Next was a rented minivan transporting Raven Stark and the crew, followed by the huge luxury motor coach carrying only Derek himself. Last in line was Mickey's pickup truck.

They were on the road barely ten minutes when Wahoo saw his father wash down four aspirins with a slug of coffee.

"How are you feeling, Pop?"

"Like a million bucks."

"Can you see okay?"

"One of everything. Quit worryin'."

But Mickey's hands were locked in a death grip on the steering wheel, and he was squinting like a stamp collector through the windshield.

"What's wrong?" Tuna asked.

Wahoo told her about his father's iguana injury. Tuna, who was sitting between them, said, "I've got some medicine that works pretty good."

"I'm fine," Mickey insisted.

"Then how come your eyes are watering?"

"Mind your own business." He dragged a sleeve across his face to dry his cheeks.

Tuna said, "I'll be right back."

Before Wahoo could stop her, she slid open the back window of the cab compartment and squirmed out onto the open bed of the truck, among the groceries and camping gear. His father watched worriedly in the rearview mirror as she rummaged calmly through her tote bag.

Wahoo told his father to slow down. Tuna was so small that he feared she'd be bounced skyward if the pickup hit a bump.

Frowning, Mickey laid off the accelerator. "It was a big mistake, inviting that girl to come along."

"What else could we do?" Wahoo said. "Send her back to her dad so he could punch her around some more? Plus, he's got a gun!"

"Call the cops is what we should've done."

"And where would she go if her old man was in jail? Stay all alone in that crappy motor home? In a Walmart parking lot?"

Mickey said, "Settle down. What's done is done."

Tuna slithered back through the window and repositioned herself between Wahoo and his father.

"You oughta be an acrobat," Mickey said. "Join a circus or somethin'."

Tuna uncapped a small brown bottle and tapped out two pink tablets. "Say aaahhh," she instructed him.

"Are you nuts?"

She jabbed him sharply in the gut. When he opened his mouth to moan, she flicked the pills into his throat. He had no option but to swallow.

"Akkk-akkk!" he said.

"It's a killer on migraines," Tuna informed Wahoo.

Sure enough, within minutes Mickey's eyes quit watering and his hands relaxed on the wheel. When Wahoo asked if he was feeling better, he denied it.

"Tell the truth, Pop."

"Okay, maybe a little better. But so what?"

"Aren't you even going to thank her?"

"Hey, I'm sorta busy right now. Driving?"

Wahoo turned to Tuna and said, "He's too stubborn to say so, but thank you for the medicine."

She smiled. "You're welcome, Lance."

Ahead of them, Derek Badger's enormous black motor coach jounced and swayed on the road to the Everglades.

The man's name was Sickler, and a year earlier he'd been run out of Tennessee for selling fake rubies at a fake mine outside of Gatlinburg. Now he had a souvenir shop on the Tamiami Trail, a two-lane road that crosses southern Florida between Miami and Naples.

There Sickler peddled counterfeit Seminole artifacts and charged tourists twenty dollars a head for a one-hour airboat tour—five bucks more when they asked for a box lunch. He promised a full refund if they didn't spot at least one alligator during the boat ride, which they always did. That's because Sickler had purchased an eight-footer from a taxidermist in Homestead and nailed it to a cypress log half a mile from the dock. He named the stuffed gator "Old Sleepy," and the tourists never caught on.

For the sum of one thousand dollars, Sickler had agreed to let the crew of *Expedition Survival!* use his store and dock as a center of operations. He'd never seen the show because his television had been malfunctioning for years; the only channel that came in clearly was the Pastry Network, which was the main reason that Sickler weighed two hundred and ninety-one pounds.

"We'll need all three of your airboats," Raven Stark told him.

Sickler said that was fine. "But it'll cost you another grand."

"Five hundred," said Raven. "End of discussion." She handed him the cash.

Derek Badger sauntered up and introduced himself. "Would you like me to autograph the wall of your shop?"

"I'll whip your hide if you do," said Sickler. "I just re-painted the place."

"Easy, mate. Don't you know who I am?" Derek looked at Raven. "Is he for real?"

"Let's go look at the new script," she suggested.

Derek remained focused on the portly Sickler. "What

can we expect to encounter out there?" he asked, jerking his marshmallow chin toward the shimmering wetlands.

Sickler, who ventured into the wilderness as seldom as possible, sensed that Mr. Badger and his TV crew were seeking an element of danger.

"Poison snakes," he replied ominously. "And gators, for sure."

"What kinds of snakes?"

"Water moccasins, diamondbacks. We're Snake Central."

Derek's face glowed. "That's fantastic!"

"And now we got them killer pythons from Asia. They grow thirty feet long and eat the tourists right off the boardwalk." This was utter nonsense, but Sickler laid it on thick.

"Panthers?" Derek inquired hopefully.

"You bet." Sickler thinking: *In your dreams, pal.*

Maybe a hundred panthers were left in the entire state. Every so often a federal game officer would stop by the shop to ask if the airboat drivers had seen any sign of the big cats, which was sort of pointless. Powered by large automobile engines, the airboats were equipped with deck-mounted aviation propellers that worked as giant fans, pushing the flat-bottomed crafts at high speed. They were so loud that panthers heard them coming from miles away and ran for cover.

Raven raised a hand. "How about bears?"

"Absolutely, ma'am," said Sickler, who hadn't seen a

bear since a field trip to the Atlanta zoo with his third-grade class, forty years earlier.

But Derek was sold. "We've come to the right spot! Now, where's Cray?"

"Right here."

The wrangler was leaning against a soda machine in a corner of the souvenir shop, where he'd been listening to Sickler's baloney.

"Can you deal with a bear?" Derek asked Mickey. "What about panthers?"

Mickey gave Sickler such a cold, cutting stare that the crooked proprietor sheepishly excused himself and waddled off to the stockroom.

To Derek, Mickey said, "Whatever's out there, I can handle."

The TV star raised a cheery thumb. "That's all I need to hear, mate." Through a window he caught sight of the catering truck, and he hurried out the door on a quest for boysenberry pancakes.

Raven, who'd lain awake all night worrying about the show, asked Mickey if she could have a word with him.

"Aw, don't worry," he told her. "We're not gonna run into any bears or panthers."

"Promise me you'll stay close to Derek," she said. "We *cannot* have a repeat of what happened with your alligator. Is that clear?"

"Lady, do I look like a bleeping babysitter?"

"He nearly died."

"Yeah, because he's a fool," Mickey said. "There's no known cure for that."

"Then do whatever's necessary to keep him from getting harmed."

Mickey chuckled. "You got a call from your bosses in California. Am I right?"

Raven blinked, but her tone remained firm. "We need Derek in one piece. He's the whole franchise."

"The franchise, huh?" Mickey whistled sarcastically. "Then I guess we'd better make sure a cottonmouth doesn't crawl into his sleeping bag and bite him on the butt."

Now it was Raven's turn to chuckle. "Oh, Derek won't be camping with the rest of us, Mr. Cray. He'll be staying at the Empresario."

"Isn't that a hotel?"

"One of Miami's finest," Raven said.

Mickey was puzzled. "How's he gonna get from the middle of the Everglades to the middle of the city every night?"

Raven touched a red fingernail to her ear. "Hear that?"

"What?"

"Listen."

Mickey heard it now. "I should've guessed," he muttered. It was the sound of a helicopter.

ELEVEN

Wahoo had been riding in airboats since he was two years old, but this was the biggest one he'd ever seen. It was designed to carry a driver and fifteen stout tourists.

Wahoo's father said, "It's nuthin' but an old tin barge."

"Hop in, mates!" Derek Badger chirped.

The other passengers included Raven, the director, two cameramen (without their cameras) and Tuna.

"And who would you be?" Raven asked.

"Oh, I'm the taxonomist," Tuna replied as she took her seat.

Wahoo said, "It's okay, Ms. Stark. She's with us."

Raven looked doubtful. "A *taxonomist?*"

Tuna nodded cheerfully.

"What happened to your eye, young lady?"

"I fell down the stairs. What happened to your hair?"

Raven's face purpled. "I don't know what you mean."

Derek rose and demanded to speak with Mr. Sickler.

"He ain't comin'," said the airboat driver, a beefy, dull-eyed man called Link.

"And why not?" Derek couldn't understand why anyone would pass up the opportunity to take a nature ride with a world-renowned survivalist.

"Because he too big," Link said.

Derek misunderstood. "You hear that?" he sneered to the others. "Mr. Sickler is too 'big' to be bothered with the likes of us."

"Nossir, he too big for the boat," Link explained. "He climb in now, we sink like a rock."

Everybody laughed except Derek. Before starting the engine, Link handed out earmuffs to dampen the roar. Raven had difficulty fitting hers over her stupendous cliff of red hair, Tuna and Wahoo watching with amusement.

The airboat skimmed along a watery trail through the saw grass for only a couple minutes before Link cut the power and glided the craft to a stop.

"Bull gator," he announced triumphantly, as if expecting a cash tip.

The specimen was an eight-footer that appeared to be sunning on a log. Its mouth was yawning wide.

Mickey Cray busted out laughing. Obviously Sickler hadn't informed the driver that this wasn't an ordinary group of suckers.

"What so funny?" Link demanded.

"That poor thing's stuffed," Mickey said, yanking off his earmuffs.

"No, it ain't!"

Derek Badger stared curiously at the motionless reptile. It was a closely guarded secret that *Expedition Survival!* occasionally used taxidermied animals when the live ones were not cooperating. Still, he couldn't tell if the alligator was real or not.

Raven elbowed the director, who spoke up. "We're not here for the tour," he said to Link. "We're scouting locations for a TV production."

The driver pondered that information, then said, "That-un's Old Sleepy. He be round here 'morrow, you wanna get some video for your show."

Mickey moved to the bow. "That gator's way beyond sleepy."

"Let it go, Pop," Wahoo implored.

"But they're lyin' to everybody! It's a scam."

"Tourists don't know any better," said Wahoo.

His father's shoulders stiffened. "I wasn't talkin' about the tourists, son. I was talkin' about nature—it's an insult to nature, putting a stuffed specimen in the middle of the swamp."

Tuna whispered, "He's got a point."

Wahoo grunted. "Don't encourage him."

"Mister, sit down," Link snapped at Mickey from the stern of the airboat.

"Yes, Mr. Cray, *please*," said Derek. "Who cares if the alligator's fake?"

"But he ain't!" It was Link, looking both confused and indignant.

For a moment Wahoo wondered if the man actually believed that Old Sleepy was alive, napping in the exact same place and in the exact same pose, week after week, month after month, never moving a muscle.

Mickey was squinting and rubbing his brow again. "Show

some pride, brother," he said to Link. "Tell Sickler to put that stupid thing in the gift shop, where it belongs."

Link scowled hatefully. Derek spun around and muttered something to Raven that Wahoo couldn't hear.

"Outta my boat!" Link commanded.

Mickey looked at Wahoo and shrugged. "See what we're dealing with?"

"Sit down, Pop."

"Not a bad idea," said Tuna.

Derek huffed. "We're wasting valuable time. Let's go."

Wahoo's father pointed wryly at Old Sleepy. "You want to practice your wrestlin' skills, Mr. Beaver? That's one gator you can probably handle."

"Very funny," said Derek through clenched jaws.

Link was also not amused. He charged to the bow of the airboat, seized Mickey Cray by the seat of his pants and heaved him like a sack of cement into the water.

The director crammed a knuckle into his mouth to stifle a laugh. Wahoo's father, who was an excellent swimmer, began paddling on his back in a circle, like a lazy otter.

"Paradise," he said.

Derek snapped two fingers at Raven, who told the driver to start the engine.

Link grinned, showing more gums than teeth. "We be gone."

"But what about Mr. Cray?" Tuna cried.

Considering Link's temper, Wahoo decided his father was probably safer in the water than he was on the boat.

"Don't worry about Pop," he said, repositioning his ear-muffs. "He'll find his way."

The crew of *Expedition Survival!* was using Sickler's Jungle Outpost and Juice Bar because Raven Stark's request to base the program in Everglades National Park had been rejected. A secretary for the park superintendent had informed Raven that, because of the earlier egg-robbing incident at Yellowstone, Derek Badger had been blackballed from the entire federal park system.

"For how long?" Raven had asked.

"Eternity," the secretary had replied politely.

Sickler's place turned out to be a convenient one for scouting video locations using airboats. The director of *Expedition Survival!* selected for the first camp a tree island, far out of sight of the highway. The island was surrounded by a natural moat that was shallow enough to wade, but then the crew encountered a fierce tangle of thorny vines and clawing shrubs. It required tough work with sharp blades to hack a path into the cool canopy of the interior.

Sickler's boat drivers spent the remainder of the afternoon shuttling back and forth between the dock and the campsite, hauling the TV crew's tents, provisions and gear. Wahoo and Tuna found some shade on the porch of the souvenir shop and waited there for Mickey to return. They made small talk and avoided the topic of fathers.

Tuna captured a brilliant green anole lizard and helped

Wahoo memorize its scientific name, *Anolis carolinensis,* which was a mouthful.

Then, out of nowhere, she asked, "You got a girlfriend, Lance?"

"Please quit calling me that."

"So that's a yes?"

"No, Lucille, I do *not* have a girlfriend."

"How come?"

" 'Cause I'm too busy."

"Oh please. Boys are never too busy for girls," Tuna said.

Wahoo was desperate to change the subject. He had told her the truth—he'd never had a real girlfriend. Most of his time, outside of school and sports, was spent tending his father's animals. It was a high-maintenance, two-man operation.

"I had a boyfriend once," Tuna volunteered. "His name was Chad and he could do a hundred push-ups. Unfortunately, he had the personality of a cabbage, so I dumped him."

"Dumped him where?"

"Ha-ha," she said. "Aren't you ever gonna tell me what happened to your thumb?"

Wahoo was thrilled to be talking about something else, even a foolish injury. "Alice ate it," he said. "My fault, totally."

"Can I see?"

Without waiting for permission, Tuna reached over and

took his right hand. She touched two fingers to the bony scar in such a gentle and curious manner that Wahoo didn't mind at all. The delicate lizard, which she'd placed like a green brooch on the collar of her camo coat, jumped to the deck of the porch and disappeared between the planks.

"If we lose this job," Wahoo said, "the bank's going to take our house." He was startled to realize he was holding her hand, and she was squeezing back. "Yesterday they left a message on my cell phone. Actually, it's *our* cell phone. Me and Pop share."

Tuna puffed her cheeks in sympathy. "I know all about banks. That's how we ended up living at the Walmart. But here's the difference, Lance: nobody's drinking up your mortgage money the way my old man did. At least your dad's out there trying."

"You saw what happened on the airboat today—it's only a matter of time before he gets us fired from the show."

"No, he won't," Tuna said, "because we won't let that happen."

"You don't know him like I do."

"And you don't know *me*." She smiled and let go of his hand. "Now look sharp. You've got company."

Raven Stark marched up the steps of the porch and asked to speak with Wahoo privately. Tuna departed with an impish wave, leaving Wahoo stranded.

"Listen to me, young man," Raven began sternly. "Your father's pushing his luck. . . ."

The remainder of her lecture was drowned by the rising whine of a helicopter revving. Raven glanced irritably over her shoulder. Turning back to Wahoo, she shook a finger and mouthed the words, "One more chance, buster!" Then she bustled off toward the vacant lot where the chopper carrying Derek Badger was preparing to depart.

Wahoo heard someone call his name and he jogged down to the water. The director and a few remaining crew members were waiting in Link's airboat to be ferried to the campsite for the night. Tuna had saved a place for Wahoo in the bow. He picked up his backpack and stepped aboard.

"What about your dad?" she said.

One look at Link and Wahoo knew there was no point in asking him to wait; the guy didn't want Mickey on his boat again. Link unhitched the dock rope and climbed up in the driver's perch, slapping a hairy left hand on the steering stick. He turned the ignition, and with his right foot he pumped the gas pedal, revving the engine.

Instantly the large propeller began to turn. The airboat eased along briefly before gathering speed and shooting forward through the grassy, cinnamon-tipped sedge. Link took the first bend fast, producing a steep sideways slide that never failed to delight the tourists. For balance Tuna locked arms with Wahoo, who would have enjoyed the moment had he not been distracted by an object that appeared dead ahead in their path, no more than a hundred yards away.

"Stop!" Wahoo yelled as they flew closer, but Link couldn't hear him over the engine. It seemed impossible that from his elevated seat the driver didn't see what Wahoo—and now the others—plainly did:

A bare-chested man stretched out upon a black, knobby object, which he was paddling like a surfboard across the water.

"Look out!" Tuna hollered.

By now, the other passengers were waving and shouting, too. Yet the airboat wasn't veering away or even slowing down. Link sat erect and stone-faced as the wind made his grungy hair dance.

Psycho! Wahoo thought. Shaking free of Tuna, he yanked off his backpack, raised it above his head with both hands and hurled it at the control deck.

Somehow he got lucky. The flying satchel knocked Link's boot off the gas pedal, sending the boat into a sputtering stall. It skimmed to a halt only a few feet from Mickey Cray, who calmly grabbed on and hauled himself aboard.

"Howdy, pilgrims," he said.

The other riders sat speechless. Their disbelieving eyes went back and forth from the dripping, shirtless man to the bizarre craft upon which he'd been traveling—a stuffed alligator bolted to a log.

"Anybody got a towel?" Mickey inquired.

Wahoo said, "Sit down, Pop."

Link was glaring at both of them. "Yeah. Sit your butt down."

Passing overhead, Raven Stark peered out the window of a rented Bell 407 helicopter and tried to make sense of the strange scene below. Sitting in front of her was Derek Badger, who was preoccupied by other matters.

"Call the hotel," he told Raven through her headphones. "Tell them to move me to a room with a Jacuzzi. Chop-chop!"

TWELVE

Susan Cray said her husband had the ideal occupation because he got along so much better with animals than he did with people. Sometimes that included his own family.

"Let me get this straight," Wahoo said curtly to his father. "You went into the water—"

"That dumb goon threw me."

"—with the cell phone in your pocket! Seriously?"

"He was way outta line—tellin' me I don't know a dead gator from a live gator!"

Wahoo tossed another branch on the fire. "Fantastic, Pop. Now we're in the middle of nowhere without a phone."

Mickey seemed unconcerned. "We can always borrow your girlfriend's."

"Not to call China we can't," said Wahoo. "And she's not my girlfriend."

The Crays had pitched their own small camp away from the TV crew because Mickey didn't want to be around Derek Badger. Deep in the hardwoods, they were shielded from a breeze that would have otherwise kept away the mosquitoes. Now they were losing blood by the pint to the ravenous swarms.

Wahoo had set up a separate pup tent for Tuna, who

poked out her head and said, "I hear you two characters talking about me."

Mickey didn't miss a beat. "Does your cell have one of those international chips? Don't worry, I got a credit card."

Barely, thought Wahoo.

Tuna pointed up at the clouds. "No signal way out here, Mr. C. Maybe when we're back at the dock."

"Sorry, son," Mickey said to Wahoo, pretending Wahoo was more bummed than he was. Twice they'd tried to reach Susan Cray from the house before leaving on the Everglades trip, but all they'd gotten on the other end was static.

Tuna announced she was taking a walk. Wahoo's father told him to go with her.

"What for?"

" 'Cause you're a gentleman." Mickey looked serious. "Don't make me ask twice."

Wahoo brought a flashlight, mainly to make sure they didn't step on any water moccasins or pygmy rattlers. A curtain of low ragged clouds blocked out the stars and the moon. The night air was warm and heavy; Wahoo wondered if a thundershower was coming. Above the western horizon they saw white pulses of heat lightning.

Centuries of water flow had shaped the island like a teardrop, the tallest trees clustered at the fat end. Tuna rattled off their Latin names as she walked: *Myrica cerifera* (wax myrtle), *Annona glabra* (pond apple) and *Magnolia virginiana* (swamp bay).

Wahoo asked if she had a photographic memory.

She said, "No, dear, I just study."

Before long they heard voices, and through the trees they saw the campsite of the *Expedition Survival!* crew. No fire was burning, but the clearing was well lit by cheesy bamboo tiki torches.

A young woman from the catering company was cooking T-bone steaks on a big stainless-steel stove of the type used at fancy river camps in places like Alaska. The director, cameramen and sound technicians sat in a half circle of folding chairs, drinking beer, slapping at bugs and laughing boisterously.

"Turn off the flashlight," Tuna whispered to Wahoo. "Let's get closer."

"No way. We're not gonna spy."

"It's not spying, Lance, it's *observing*."

They crouched in a thicket of coco plums and inched forward. The crew members were taking turns telling stories. Wahoo couldn't make out every word, but he got the gist. Even the catering lady was giggling.

"Who are they talking about?" Tuna asked Wahoo.

"Take a wild guess."

"Not Mr. Badger?"

"I'm pretty sure."

They stopped moving so they could hear better. The

next story, which was recounted uproariously by the show's director, involved a close-up scene in which Derek accidentally snorted a live earthworm up his nose.

"They make him sound like a horse's ass," Tuna whispered cheerlessly.

"You know how people talk when the boss isn't there."

Tuna hadn't been around Derek long enough to know the truth. She was a genuine fan, one of millions, so it would take a while for her to accept that the real-life Derek was a different person from the one she saw on TV. Earlier, Wahoo had noticed her disappointment when she'd learned Derek was staying at a luxury hotel, not roughing it in the swamp as he pretended to do on the show.

She tugged Wahoo's sleeve. "Somebody's coming!"

"Be still."

One of the cameramen had left his chair and was cautiously making his way into the unlit wooded area where Wahoo and Tuna were hiding. He was only a few steps away when he stopped beside a bay tree and began to unzip his pants.

Oh no, thought Wahoo. *Not here.*

In the shadows he couldn't see Tuna's expression, but he could sense her alarm. He touched her arm so she would stay calm—if the two of them were caught snooping, Raven would immediately fire Mickey, just as she'd threatened to do.

Tuna gently pushed Wahoo's hand away. Next she did something completely unexpected: she grabbed one of the coco plum bushes and began to shake it.

The cameraman who was about to relieve himself froze at the rustling noise in the darkness. Tuna wasn't finished. She let out a low, rising growl that an untrained ear could easily have taken for an unhappy bear or an ill-tempered bobcat, or even a mama panther.

With a yelp, the cameraman wheeled and took off running for the campsite, crashing out of the tree line at full speed.

"Something big's out there!" he hollered to the other crew members. "I heard it!"

A wave of laughter followed, for the frightened fellow had neglected in retreat to pull up his zipper.

Tuna said, "That was seriously rude. He almost peed on our heads!"

Wahoo was on edge. "Let's get outta here."

"Wait a minute—he dropped something."

"Come on, *Lucille*! Before one of the others needs a potty break."

"I said hold on."

She darted up to the bay tree and snatched an object off the ground. Wahoo, who was already slipping away, heard twigs cracking as she hurried to catch up. Only when they were safely out of sight, deep in the trees, did he turn on the flashlight to see what the cameraman had left behind.

"What is this?" Tuna asked, riffling the pages. "Some sort of book?"

Wahoo took it from her and held the cover sheet up in

the narrow beam of light. He said, "It's not a book. It's a script."

The title, printed on the first page, was **Expedition Survival! Episode 103—Florida Everglades.**

Tuna gave Wahoo an inquiring glance. "Guess we oughta give it back, huh?"

"For sure," he said. "First thing tomorrow."

She chuckled. "But tonight you're gonna read it, aren't you? Don't lie to me, Lance."

"I'm absolutely gonna read it," he said.

What better way to prepare for another Derek Badger fiasco?

NOON—ANGLE FROM HELICOPTER—high above the Everglades.

A dark speck is moving ant-like through the endless, shimmering marsh. Gradually the aerial camera ZOOMS CLOSER AND CLOSER on our lone figure, sloshing and slashing through the dense grass.

It's DEREK BADGER. He is plainly exhausted from his hike, dripping sweat. His cargo pants are filthy and torn, and his shirt is unbuttoned to the waist.

CUT TO CLOSE-UP with a Steadicam, moving side by side with DB.

DEREK: *I've been fighting my way through this swamp for four, possibly five hours straight—I've lost track of the time. The heat is*

*virtually unbearable, and the mosquitoes are so thick that I have to
stop every few minutes to cough them out of my lungs!*

*You can see why they call this place a river of grass. But it's not the
same soft green grass that's growing in your backyard. Check this
out—*

Derek bends down and breaks off a piece of saw grass, which he
holds up for the camera.

CUT TO CLOSE-UP of Derek's forefinger as he slides the edge
of the grass blade across his skin, drawing blood.

DEREK: *See? Like a barber's razor! They don't call it saw grass for
nothing.*

He licks the droplet from his finger and continues his lonely
trek. . . .

DEREK: *Time is running out. It's absolutely essential that I locate
a safe place to build a small fire and dry out these soggy clothes,
hopefully before the sun goes down. That's when the predators come
out—alligators, panthers, bears and pythons big enough to devour a
full-grown man!*

*As always, I've brought no food or water on this expedition.
Everything I eat and drink—and, believe me, I'm bloody famished—
will come from the natural bounty of this savage but magnificent
wilderness.*

CUT TO MEDIUM SHOT: Derek digs into a pocket and pulls
out a Swiss army knife and a plastic straw.

DEREK: *See? This is all I brought—my trusty Swiss knife and a clean straw. Two simple—but essential—tools of survival.*

DB marches on.

CUT TO STEADICAM SHOT from Derek's point of view, the saw grass flattening ahead of him as he trudges forward.

DEREK'S VOICE (surprised and hushed): *Whoa! What was that?*

CUT BACK TO MEDIUM SHOT OF DEREK, as still as a statue. He's peering with great intensity into the brown, shin-deep water.

DEREK (whispering): *I just felt something slither between my ankles! It was either an eel or a snake, hopefully not a poisonous one. The Everglades is literally crawling with deadly cottonmouth moccasins. One bite, even from a baby, and I could be a dead man.*

Ah! There it goes again!

Derek drops to his knees with a splash. He stabs both arms into the murky water, probing and groping until . . .

DEREK: *Gotcha!!!*

He pops to his feet, holding up a very confused, very angry
_____.

DEREK: *Crikey, what a feisty little bugger.*

CUT TO CLOSE-UP OF THE _____, writhing and snapping.

DEREK: *I'm afraid it's not your lucky day, mate.*

Dangling the _____, he turns to look into the camera.

DEREK (triumphantly): *Dinner!*

CUT TO MEDIUM SHOT OF DEREK, turning a shoulder to the camera as he twists the neck of the _____, killing it instantly. He coils its limp body and places it in a pocket of his cargo pants. Then he resumes his journey.

DEREK (somberly): *I get no pleasure from taking the life of any wild creature, but if I don't eat, I won't have the strength to keep going. When you're in a desperate survival situation, you must do whatever it takes to stay alive.*

Hovering above, the helicopter-mounted CAMERA pulls back its focus until once again Derek is a speck on the savanna, which unfolds in all directions as far as the eye can see. He is completely alone....

Wahoo slapped the script closed. "I can't show this to Pop. He'll go ballistic."

Tuna looked bothered. "What kind of animal is the blankety-blank supposed to be?"

"Whatever's handy. A snake, a frog, a turtle—you've seen the show. Derek always fries up *something.*"

They were hunkered by the dwindling campfire and using the flashlight for reading. Mickey Cray snored in his tent.

"I watch his show every week," said Tuna, "and I never knew the whole thing was written out beforehand. I thought all that stuff just, you know, happened."

Wahoo had to remind himself that most people had no idea how nature programs were produced. Lots of time and money were spent making every animal encounter appear spontaneous and real, even though the scenes were carefully planned in advance.

"Derek's probably piggin' out on a big juicy steak at the hotel tonight," Tuna said morosely.

"And a humongous slice of Key lime pie."

"Then why does the script say he's gotta go kill a blankety-blank for food?"

"Because," Wahoo said, "that's one of the things he's famous for."

Tuna planted her chin in her hands. "All those times on TV when he swallowed some little mouse or salamander, I thought he was really starving. Am I stupid or what?"

"You're not stupid. They don't exactly advertise what goes on behind the scenes."

Wahoo stood up to stretch. He was still stuffed from their modest camp dinner of hot dogs, black beans and rolls. For dessert Mickey had handed out Chips Ahoy cookies.

Tuna said, "Your old man's not gonna go along with this scam, is he? Trap some poor old snake or toad just so Derek can cook it up on the show?"

"Not Pop. No way."

"Good!"

"It's late. I'm going to bed," Wahoo said.

"I might stay up and read some more."

"Are you sure you want to?"

Tuna nodded. Her brown eyes were bright and intent in the amber glow of the fire.

He handed her the flashlight and the script. "Remember, it's just show business."

"Not to me," she said.

When Derek Badger became agitated, he sometimes misplaced his fake Australian accent.

"You call this a lobster?" he snarled at the attendant who delivered his dinner to the hotel room. "I've eaten bloody *shrimp* that were bigger!"

The man mumbled an apology, covered the tray with a silver lid and rolled the cart out the door.

"And next time bring me a real one from Maine," Derek barked after him.

The star of *Expedition Survival!* was marinating regally in the Jacuzzi, which had a grand window view of Biscayne Bay and the Miami skyline. All evening he'd been thinking about the Everglades show—specifically, how to make it the most thrilling, hair-raising episode in the history of reality TV.

Derek was highly motivated to do something spectacular. His contract with the Untamed Channel expired soon, and his agent was bargaining to get him a new three-year deal for a lot more money.

And he definitely needed it. During the off-season, he'd purchased a ninety-nine-foot yacht that was currently being refurbished at a boatyard in West Palm Beach. Among the additions were a billiard parlor, a mini–movie theater and a gymnasium that Derek probably would never use. It was an extremely expensive project, more expensive than he'd ever dreamed. Just painting a new name on the yacht's transom—he was calling it the *Sea Badger*—cost eighteen hundred bucks.

Those cheap weasels at the network had offered to renew Derek's contract with a 10 percent raise that he considered highly insulting, and well below what was necessary to maintain the proper lifestyle of an international television star (and now yachtsman). That's why the Everglades episode *had* to be his best ever, a blockbuster. Then, fearing that another outdoor show might try to hire him away, the suits at the Untamed Channel would have no choice but to accept Derek's extravagant demands.

The scene with Alice the alligator had turned out marvelously terrifying—by now Derek had replayed the clip at least twenty times—and he felt inspired to make the rest of the program equally memorable. Lolling in the Jacuzzi tub, watching the jets of water make his belly quiver like a bowl of vanilla pudding, he envisioned many future talk-show appearances for himself, captivating Jay Leno or Anderson Cooper with breathtaking tales from the Florida swamp.

Most people who were nearly drowned by a twelve-foot gator would feel grateful to be alive and not eager to repeat the foolhardy behavior that had gotten them into that situation. No such contemplations entered the mind of Derek

Badger as he sipped French wine and admired through soapy toes the twinkling lights of downtown Miami. His reckless brush with death actually made him feel invincible.

Ironhearted.

Indestructible.

"Here's to Alice," he said, raising his glass in a private toast.

The decision not to use any more of Mickey Cray's animals was risky, but risk was exactly what Derek desired. He knew that wild critters were more aggressive and unpredictable than captive ones. The disappointing python scene was a prime example—Cray's lazy snake was about as fierce as a garden hose.

To capture maximum drama on video, Derek wanted the real deal, wild and raw. The caution and common sense that would govern the actions of a clear-thinking person were in his case overpowered by a blinding hunger for more fame and wealth.

He was very much looking forward to being poked, stung, scratched, clawed, chewed and chomped by authentic denizens of the Everglades.

And he would get his wish.

THIRTEEN

Wahoo was accustomed to his father's snoring, which sounded like a dump truck stripping its gears. That's not what awakened him.

It was a dream about Tuna.

Her dad was furiously chasing her around the Walmart parking lot, and Wahoo was trying to tackle him so she could get away. In the dream, Tuna's father had no face—only a slab of pocked gray flesh where his mouth, nose and eyes should have been. Wahoo's imagination simply couldn't picture a man who would try to harm his daughter that way.

Wahoo crawled from his sleeping bag and emerged from the tent he shared with his father. A light rain had fallen overnight, and the sky remained overcast. The sun had been up for an hour, but the air beneath the tree canopy was cool and funky-smelling from the exotic vegetation. In the distance, a great blue heron croaked defiantly.

Mickey Cray arose with a series of wolverine snuffles. Anticipating a demand for hot coffee, Wahoo restarted the campfire. There was no breeze, and the mosquitoes were delighted to see him. Tuna came out of her tent, mumbled a sleepy "G'morning" and sat down cross-legged on the ground.

Wahoo's father noticed the script in her hands and asked, "What're you readin', hon?"

"Shakespeare," she answered, casually flipping over the script to hide the title page. "I'm playing Ophelia in a summer production of *Hamlet*."

Wahoo was impressed by her quick thinking and the classy-sounding fib.

"Shakespeare, huh?" said Mickey, with no shred of interest. He reached for the pot of coffee. "Hey, you wouldn't happen to have any more of those headache pills, would ya?"

Tuna said, "I'll trade you two of 'em for a cup of that java."

"Fair enough."

"Pour one for me, too," said Wahoo.

Mickey laughed. "Since when do you drink this stuff?"

"Take your pills, Pop."

Tuna suggested that they go get breakfast at the main camp, from which tantalizing smells wafted through the bay trees. Wahoo's father again insisted on cooking, a humble but tasty serving of bacon and powdered eggs. He said that dining with Derek Badger would ruin his appetite.

Soon they heard airboats, which meant that the crew of *Expedition Survival!* was preparing to load the gear and ride to the location of the opening scene. Tuna, Wahoo and Mickey hurried through the woods and joined up with the others, who were filling canteens with cold water from a fifty-gallon cooler and stuffing their pockets with granola bars. Raven Stark was there, though Derek had not yet arrived.

It took a while to pack the equipment and get everybody

seated. Tuna, Wahoo and his dad were assigned to ride with Link, who wasn't exactly overjoyed to see them.

"Not you," he growled from the driver's platform.

Tuna gave a friendly little wave. "Play nice," she said, and wedged herself safely between Wahoo and Mickey.

Link poked Wahoo's father in the back. "I keep my eye on you. We clear?"

Mickey ignored him. Wahoo looked up and said, "We are absolutely clear."

"Clear as a church bell," Tuna added.

The ride lasted longer than Wahoo had expected, the three airboats flattening pathways through a prairie of tall saw grass that hadn't been crossed in a long time— at least not by humans. After almost an hour, the lead boat carrying the show's director halted at the edge of a wide-open pond that was teeming with dragonflies and wading birds called purple gallinules. The other boats stopped in the same place, and all the passengers removed their earmuffs.

A walkie-talkie attached to Link's belt began to crackle with instructions. Wahoo recognized the director's voice.

"Four minutes," he announced. "Be ready."

In the first boat, a cameraman scrambled to position himself on the bow. At the front of the second boat stood Raven, wearing a flamingo-pink sun hat as wide as a sombrero. Derek Badger was nowhere to be seen.

"Where the heck is he?" whispered Tuna.

Mickey snickered. Wahoo pointed to an object in the

sky. It was a helicopter approaching rapidly from the east, the *thwock-a-thwock* of its rotors growing louder.

"He's gonna do the Jump!" Tuna exclaimed. "Sweet."

Parachuting into the wilderness was one of Derek's signature moves, although other TV survivalists occasionally used the same stunt. The difference was that Derek insisted on jumping from the aircraft while blindfolded. This was not only dumb but also pointless, as Wahoo's father remarked whenever they watched the program.

The chopper slowed down until it froze in a hover high above the fleet of airboats. A familiar-looking figure could be seen at the open door, his boots braced on the skid. Poised beside him was another man aiming a video camera.

"Five," said the voice coming over Link's handheld radio, "four, three, two, one . . . and *action!*"

The figure let go of the helicopter and dropped free, spreading his limbs like a spider. A moment later the chute opened, a green-striped starburst against the drab background of gray clouds. Mickey cupped his hands over his forehead to better follow the path of the glide.

"I told ya!" Tuna said excitedly. "Look at him fly!"

Wahoo anticipated a clumsy landing, but the parachute came in softly and right on target, fluttering to rest in the center of the pond.

"Cut!" the director shouted into his walkie-talkie. "That was brilliant! Now let's go get him."

All three airboats blasted off in unison; nobody had time to fit on their earmuffs. Link was the first to get there. He cut the engine and coasted on a line toward the billow of silk. Wahoo could see that Derek had successfully detached himself from the parachute and was treading water.

Link stepped past the other passengers and poised himself for the retrieve. Once he was within reach, he grabbed the straps of Derek's skydiving pack and hoisted him aboard. Everybody applauded except Wahoo and his father.

Because it wasn't really Derek. It was a professional stuntman whose safari shirt had been padded with foam and whose hair had been dyed orange-blond to match that of the TV star.

As soon as the stuntman peeled off his blindfold, Tuna stopped clapping and her face fell.

The director called out, "Nice job, Ricky!"

"Easy ride," said the stuntman.

He was at least ten years younger and thirty pounds lighter than Derek, and his tan looked real—not sprayed on.

"Did you know about this?" Tuna demanded of Wahoo. "Did you know the Jump was bogus?"

Wahoo said, "I swear I didn't." But he wasn't all that surprised.

"Okay, people, heads up!" The director raised both hands clasped together, as if aiming a gun.

The helicopter had looped back around and was slowly descending toward the airboats gathered in the pond. A large metal basket with a man inside was being lowered on a cable. The man was dressed the very same way as the parachutist, and his pudgy bare legs dangled through the canvas webbing of the basket.

"Pathetic," Tuna said.

As the chopper dropped lower, the gusts from its whirling blades churned the surface of the pond and made the lily pads flutter and shimmy. When the dangling basket was almost touching the water, the real Derek Badger stood up, tied on his blindfold and hopped out.

The helicopter shot straight up, dragging the basket out of the scene.

"Action!" barked the director, and the cameraman in the front of his boat resumed taping, zooming in on the now-swimming figure.

On cue, Derek began grunting dramatically with each stroke. Within seconds he'd managed to tangle himself in the cords of the waterlogged parachute.

"Help!" he gasped.

The director responded with an enthusiastic, upraised thumb.

"No, I'm bloody serious," Derek bleated. "Somebody help me before I drown!"

"Cut!" Raven Stark shouted. "Cut! Cut!"

"Okay," the director said impatiently. "Let's cut."

Mickey Cray looked quite amused when he turned to Wahoo and Tuna.

"His Phoniness has arrived," he said.

* * *

The director called a short break before the big scene in which Derek would trek alone across the saw grass plain. Having seen the script, Wahoo knew what was coming. His father didn't.

"Yo, Mr. Cray!" the director shouted. "Can we have a word?"

The other airboat drew closer, and Mickey stepped aboard. The meeting was brief. Mickey slipped into the waist-deep water and motioned for Wahoo to do the same.

As they waded through the lily pads, Wahoo said, "They need a snake, right?"

"In fifteen minutes. How'd you know?"

"What else did they tell you?"

"They want me to make it swim up to Dorko so he can grab it."

"Pop, there's something else."

"Lemme guess." Mickey's eyes moved back and forth across the pond, scanning for slithery movements. "He's gonna kill it."

"That's right."

"And cook it for supper."

"So they showed you the script?" Wahoo asked.

"Naw, they didn't have to." His father lunged forward and reached into the water. He came up empty-handed, saying, "That was just a little bugger."

Wahoo hadn't even seen it. His dad's eyesight was astounding; obviously the double vision had gone away.

"So, what are you gonna do?" Wahoo asked.

"Just wait and see."

"Hold on, Pop—not a cottonmouth!"

Mickey smiled mischievously. "*That* would be intense."

"No, that would be crazy. You'll wind up in jail."

Cottonmouths, also known as water moccasins, were foul-tempered and hard to handle. They were also highly poisonous.

"Don't even think about it," Wahoo warned his father.

"It's not like the man's definitely gonna die—I'm sure these folks are smart enough to keep a snakebite kit in the first-aid bag. But if not . . ."

"Okay, Pop, that's enough."

"Hey, I'm only kidding. You need to chill."

Wahoo spied a small ribbon snake scooting through the reeds and started sloshing in pursuit. His dad told him to let it be. By now they were fifty yards from the airboat. Wahoo could see Tuna standing in the stern, close to Link. They appeared to be talking, although Wahoo couldn't imagine what the conversation might be.

"Whoa!" Mickey signaled for him to stop. "There's a good one."

"I don't see anything."

"Be still, son. He went down." Mickey stared into the tea-colored water, ready to pounce.

"Is it a moccasin?" Wahoo was trying not to sound anxious.

"Aha!" his father exclaimed, and thrust both arms underwater. He brought up a banded water snake about three feet long.

Wahoo was relieved. Water snakes release a foul musk, but they aren't venomous. This one whipped back and forth, snapping wildly, before Mickey got a grip behind its neck and dunked it again, to wash off the stink.

"Four minutes to spare," he reported after checking his wristwatch.

"Not too shabby," Wahoo admitted. He'd never seen a better snake catcher than his father.

But now what? he wondered.

As they slogged back toward the boats, Mickey didn't seem upset about what was supposed to happen to the newly captured reptile.

"Hey, let's call him Fang," he said.

Wahoo shook his head. "Let's not."

"How come?"

"Because." Wahoo was annoyed. Why give the poor thing a name if it would be roasting on Derek's TV campfire by sunset?

The director's grin seemed to split his sweaty beard.

"Super!" he crowed when Mickey showed him the captured snake. "Derek, have a peek at tonight's delicious entrée!"

"Oh, surprise me," said Derek, who was busy getting his tan freshened and his facial makeup retouched.

As soon as Wahoo climbed back in Link's airboat, Tuna grabbed the fleshy part of his left arm and twisted.

"Ouch!"

"You said your old man wouldn't let 'em do this," she hissed. "You promised!"

"I didn't think he ever would."

"That's not good enough, Lance."

"Look, we really need this job," Wahoo said.

"Not. Good. Enough." She gave another sharp twist and let go.

Derek entered the water gingerly as the helicopter rumbled into position above.

Tuna leaned close to Mickey Cray and cupped a hand to his ear. "Where's the blankety-blank?"

"Huh?"

"The snake," she whispered.

"Oh. You mean Fang."

"That's real funny."

Wahoo's dad unbuttoned the last three buttons of his shirt so that Tuna could see where he was stowing the pretty rust-and-tan-colored reptile, which was now curled up peacefully.

"*Nerodia fasciata*," she said. "But that's not from Linnaeus. He called it *Coluber fasciatus*."

"I like Fang better."

"You would."

Wahoo slid closer. "So, what's the plan, Pop?" Hoping he had one.

"Heat," Mickey replied with a wink.

Tuna made a puzzled face. "What?"

Mickey jerked his chin toward the snake, which was resting against his bare belly. "Heat is good," he said.

Tuna shrugged. "Whatever."

But Wahoo understood what his father had in mind. *Maybe it'll work,* he thought, *and maybe it won't.*

The director ordered all the airboats to move behind a nearby tree island so that they wouldn't be visible to the camera up in the hovering chopper. For Derek's adventure to be believable, the Everglades had to appear empty and never-ending.

A dark speck is moving ant-like through the endless, shimmering marsh. Gradually the aerial camera ZOOMS CLOSER AND CLOSER on our lone figure, sloshing and slashing through the dense grass.

It's DEREK BADGER.

Taping that part of the scene proved easy, thanks to the steady hands of the helicopter pilot and cameraman. The director had supervised from behind the island, using a portable video monitor and a two-way radio.

To the pilot, he said, "Another masterpiece, Louie!"

"Thanks, buddy. We've got some weather moving in, so we're gonna head home and refuel."

"Be back here at six to pick up the boss and Ms. Stark."

"That's a roger."

The director holstered his radio and turned to the air-boat drivers. "Okay, let's hurry up and roll!"

Derek was in a grouchy mood when they got to the spot where he was waiting, truly a lone figure on the horizon. "What took you so bloody long?" he whined. "There's a whole flock of buzzards waiting for me to keel over."

The cameraman in the director's airboat eased carefully into the water. He was toting an expensive Steadicam that allowed him to wade beside Derek while shooting, with very little motion or bumpiness in the picture.

"Everybody ready?" the director hollered. "And . . . action!"

Derek said, "Wait! What's my line?"

Raven stood ready with a copy of the script. "Your line is: *I've been fighting my way through this swamp for four, possibly five hours straight—I've lost track of the time.*"

"Right," said Derek. "Let's do it."

"Take two. Action!"

"*I've been fighting my way through this swamp for hours and hours—I've lost all track of time. . . .*"

When he got to the part where he was supposed to feel something swim between his legs, Derek stopped. The director brusquely motioned for Mickey to get in the water.

"Where's your scaly little pal, Mr. Cray?"

"Right here. What's my cue?"

"The line is: *Ah! There it goes again!* That's when you release the snake near Derek."

"No problem."

"And be sure to keep your paws out of the shot!" Derek interjected.

Wahoo thought: *Uh-oh. Here we go.*

Yet somehow his father remained calm. "All due respect, Mr. Beaver, this ain't my first rodeo," he said mildly.

"It's Badger, not Beaver!"

Gently Mickey removed the newly named Fang from inside his shirt. Its reddish tongue flicked inquisitively as the snake coiled around Mickey's forearm.

Hearing a distant rumble of thunder, Wahoo and Tuna glanced up at the darkening sky.

The director looked, too. He clapped and said, "Okay, ready? Three, two, one and . . . action!"

Derek continued:

"I just felt something slither between my ankles! It was either an eel or a snake, hopefully not a poisonous one. The Everglades is literally crawling with deadly cottonmouth moccasins. One bite, even from a baby, and I could be a dead man.

"Ah-ha! There it goes again!"

Reptiles are cold-blooded, which means their energy and alertness vary greatly depending on the temperature. During periods of chilly weather, a snake's metabolism slows down, and it becomes sluggish and sleepy. The warmer the air, the more active and lively it becomes.

By letting the banded water snake rest for so long against his skin, a comfortable 98.6 degrees, Mickey Cray had made sure the creature would be wide awake and full of attitude by the time he released it back into the pond. He also knew it would not take kindly to being grabbed again.

"*Gotcha!*" Derek crowed, carelessly snatching the snake by its middle.

From that moment on, the script was in tatters.

As Mickey had anticipated, Fang went nuts. First it bit Derek on one arm, then it bit him on the other. It bit him on a knuckle. It bit him on a wrist. It even bit him on the chin.

"Crikey!" he whimpered over and over, but he wouldn't let go of it.

Tuna pressed against Wahoo's shoulder. "Wow" was all she said.

The director was so stunned by what he saw that he forgot to yell "Cut!" Sitting behind him in the airboat, Raven Stark hunched down and covered her eyes.

Meanwhile, the cameraman toting the Steadicam dutifully zoomed in on the bloodbath. Derek struggled in vain to gain control of the twisting, squirming, snapping reptile while at the same time he tried to recite his lines:

"*Looks like it's not—ouch!—your lucky day, mate.*"

His determination to kill and eat his supercharged captive was fading with each new puncture wound. Still, he labored to keep a brave face for his TV fans.

"*Dinner!*" Derek squeaked unconvincingly. Then: "Aaaggghhh!"

Nerodia fasciata had found one of his thumbs and begun to chew.

Derek flapped his wounded hand and toppled backward, producing a barrel-sized splash. By the time three guys from the crew had fished him out, he was spitting up pond water and the snake was long gone.

"Good Fang," Mickey said quietly.

Tuna looked at Wahoo, and Wahoo looked away, trying hard not to laugh.

FOURTEEN

Derek Badger was rushed back to the camp, where his bite marks—tiny but numerous—were slathered with antibiotic cream. He was so shaken by his battle with the feisty water snake that he declared he was finished for the day.

"Call the chopper," he said to Raven. "I'm going back to the hotel."

She informed him that the helicopter was grounded in Miami due to bad weather.

"That's ridiculous," Derek said just as a wave of thunder grumbled ominously in the western sky.

"They can't fly in lightning. It's too dangerous," said Raven.

"Dangerous? Ha! Have you forgotten who you're talking to?"

When Mickey Cray approached, Derek held out his arms to display the result of the reptile's attack.

Mickey said, "That's what happens when you go raw."

"But you're the wrangler! We're paying you big bucks to control these animals."

"Look, Mr. Beaver—"

"Stop calling me that!"

"There's no such thing as a snake whisperer," said Mickey.

"I have some fat, sleepy ones back home that wouldn't nip even if you tied them in a knot. But you wanted wild, and wild is what you got."

Derek jutted his chin to reveal yet another U-shaped series of dot-sized punctures, which glistened from the medicine cream. "This is all your fault, Cray!"

Mickey felt no urge to apologize. He turned his attention to Raven.

"So what's next? You want me to trap a raccoon? Or maybe a skunk?"

"We're taking a break," she said.

"Good plan. There's some heavy-duty weather moving in."

Derek muttered, "Thanks for the bulletin." Then, to Raven: "Try the chopper pilot one more time. Make it fast."

Mickey returned to his mini-camp, swallowed a couple of Tuna's headache pills and stretched out on his sleeping bag for a nap. To prepare for the oncoming downpour, Wahoo and Tuna were staking a blue plastic tarp over the fire pit so the wood stayed dry. Just as they finished the job, a double flash of lightning lit up the clouds. A blistering crack of thunder followed.

The airboats all took off toward Sickler's dock. Minutes later, the wind kicked up and the rain began to fall hard. Wahoo and Tuna scrambled into her tent and closed the flap, the squall drumming loudly on the canvas.

Outside, another heron squawked between thunderclaps, prompting Tuna to remark: "That would be *Ardea herodias*, commenting on the foul weather."

Wahoo was mystified by this odd talent of hers. He said, "How many Latin names have you memorized?"

"I don't know—a couple hundred maybe."

"But why?"

"Because I like to," she said. "Every single species on earth has been classified that way by science. I'll never learn them all, but I'm gonna try."

Wahoo couldn't get over it. "My brain hurts when I've got to memorize one little poem for English class. What's the secret?"

"I told you. I study a lot." Tuna paused to wait out another roll of thunder. "Before the bank took our house, I'd just go in my room, lock the door and start Googling like a fiend. Some nights I worked on insects. Other nights it might be fish or amphibians, whatever. I'd sit there and say their scientific names over and over again until they stuck in my head."

"Too much like homework. I couldn't do it," Wahoo said.

"Sure you could—if your old man was trashed out of his skull and acting like a maniac. Then you'd find a place of your own to hide," she said, "and something to keep your mind off all the craziness."

Wahoo felt his face turn hot and he thought he might be sick. He excused himself with a mumble and pawed his way out of the tent. Sucking raw shallow breaths, he began walking nowhere in particular, through the teeth of the storm.

The rain lashed his cheeks, and soon his clothes were soaked. Fingers of blue lightning split the sky, but he never flinched; he just kept tromping like a zombie. Tuna's story had made him feel angry and guilty at the same time—angry at her father for hurting her, and guilty because his own life was so good, so easy. Compared to hers, Wahoo's world was paradise, a day at the beach. Nobody ever got drunk and tore up the house. Nobody ever punched him in the eye.

"Get out of the rain, for heaven's sake!"

"What?" Wahoo looked up and realized he was standing in the main camp.

Raven Stark motioned for him to come under the big fabric awning where the catering service was headquartered. Most of the crew members had gathered there to wait out the storm, which had somehow failed to disturb a single red hair on Raven's head.

"What's the matter with you?" she asked Wahoo. "All we need is for you to get barbecued by a lightning bolt. Then your crazy father would sue us."

Wahoo was still in a sad daze. "Where's Mr. Badger?"

"Over there." Raven waved toward a white hexagonal tent that was being puckered by gusts of wind. The entrance had been zippered tight. "He'll come out after the thunder stops," she said. "Here, put this on before you catch cold."

She gave Wahoo a shiny blue weather jacket that had

the *Expedition Survival!* logo stenciled in gold lettering on the front. He peeled out of his dripping shirt and wrapped the jacket around his bare shoulders.

On a nearby table sat a telephone in a black case that looked waterproof.

"Do you get a signal way out here?" Wahoo asked.

Raven said, "It's a satellite phone, dear. I could get a signal on Mount Everest."

"Can I borrow it?"

She looked amused by the request. "Exactly who are you going to call?"

"Please?"

"Sit down, young man."

As she toweled off his hair, Wahoo groped through his pockets until he located the piece of paper with the number written on it. The paper was wet, so he opened it slowly to keep it from falling apart.

Raven removed the phone from the case and turned it on.

"I'll pay you back," Wahoo said.

"No worries. This is a company phone."

He handed her the number. "It's in China," he whispered. "Look, whatever it costs, you take the money out of my paycheck."

She smiled skeptically. "Who can you possibly know in China?"

"My mom. She's working there."

"Doing what?"

"She's a language teacher."

Fortunately, Raven seemed to believe him. She checked her watch and said, "Your mother's probably sleeping now. It's the middle of the night in that part of the world."

Wahoo nodded. "Yeah, I know. Please?"

The thunderstorm was sliding to the east, and the rain had softened to a drizzle.

As Raven dialed the number, she said, "Let me tell you a secret: I use this phone to call my mom back home every day, no matter where I am."

"Where does she live?" Wahoo asked. From Raven's accent, he figured it was someplace exotic, like South Africa or New Zealand.

"Fairhope, Alabama," said Raven.

"You sure don't sound like you're from Alabama."

She handed the satellite phone to him. "Ten minutes, okay?"

Susan Cray wasn't sleeping; she was sitting up in bed, staring at a bulky old-fashioned telephone. When it rang, she knew who was calling even before she answered.

Ever since Wahoo was little, he and his mom had shared an unusual mental connection that was almost telepathic. One day, in kindergarten, he'd fallen on the playground and received a nasty gash on his head. Susan Cray had arrived at the school before the ambulance did—before, in fact, Wahoo's teacher had phoned to tell her about the accident.

Susan had confided to her son that a strange and anxious sensation had swept over her at work, and that she'd known instantly that he needed her.

The same thing had happened on the afternoon that Alice the alligator accidentally ate Wahoo's thumb. Susan Cray had arrived at the house right behind the paramedics—and no one had called her about the mishap.

When she picked up the phone in Shanghai, the first thing she said was: "What happened?"

"Nothing, Mom. I just called to say hi."

"Well, that's very sweet," said Susan Cray, "but I don't believe you."

"I'm fine. Pop's fine. The job is going . . . okay."

"But what?"

"I didn't say 'but' anything," Wahoo noted.

"You don't have to. I can hear it in your voice."

"Okay, there's this girl—"

His mother groaned.

"Mom, come on."

"I'm listening."

"She sort of ran off with me and Pop."

"Sort of?"

"Her dad beat her up," Wahoo said.

Susan Cray was silent on the other end.

"Her mom's gone. She didn't have anywhere else to go." Wahoo was still waiting for a response. When he didn't get one, he said, "So we brought her along on the job. She's out here in the Glades with us."

Finally his mother spoke. "How old is your new friend?"

"She's in my same grade at school."

"Your father should have called the police."

"He wanted to," Wahoo said. "But if they locked up her old man, she'd be all alone. Mom, they live in the Walmart parking lot."

"Get out."

"I'm serious. In a crappy old RV."

Susan Cray said, "The police wouldn't let her stay there alone. They'd find someone to take care of her."

"You mean, like foster parents?"

"Or family. Doesn't she have any aunts or uncles?"

Wahoo said he hadn't asked.

"Well, find out."

"This wasn't the first time it happened. Her dad, he drinks all the time."

"That's awful."

"It's hard to listen to her tell about it." Wahoo heard his voice quaver and he thought, *What's the matter with me?*

His mother said, "She needs somebody to talk with. You have to be strong."

"I know. It's just . . ."

"Just what?"

"She's *little*, Mom. I don't understand how a person could do that to their own kid. He slugged her with his fist!"

On the other end, Wahoo's mother sighed. He could picture her expression.

"You can't make sense of it," she said, "so don't even try. There are some seriously messed-up people in this world."

Raven Stark reappeared at Wahoo's side and tapped her wristwatch. He held up a finger, seeking one more minute on the satellite phone.

Susan Cray was saying, "When this job is over, you and your dad should take your friend to the police station so she can report what happened."

"But the black eye might be gone by then."

"They'll still believe her. They'd *better* believe her."

"Miss you, Mom."

"I miss you, too, big guy. What's her name? Your new friend."

"It's not important."

"Are you kidding? Tell me."

Wahoo braced himself. "They call her Tuna."

Susan Cray laughed warmly. "Wahoo and Tuna! Maybe it's fate."

"I knew you'd think that was funny."

"Hey, you've got to admit. It's quite a fishy coincidence."

"I'd better go now," said Wahoo. "This lady needs her phone back."

"Not before you tell me how your father's doing?"

"Much better, Mom. Really."

"Does that mean he's behaving himself?"

"Well," Wahoo replied carefully, "we haven't been fired yet."

The weather got worse, not better. One band of thunder-showers was followed by another, and then another. Late in the afternoon, Derek Badger emerged from his private luxury tent and glared at the roiling sky.

"Still no chopper?" he said peevishly to Raven Stark.

"It doesn't look good," she allowed, which was an understatement. The radar app on the director's iPhone showed a series of flame-orange waves sweeping in from the west.

"The helicopter can't possibly take off or land in this mess."

"Then how am I supposed to get back to the hotel?" Derek protested.

Sometimes Raven was surprised by her own patience. "It doesn't look good," she said again. "We might be spending the night out here with the crew."

Predictably, Derek pitched a tantrum, cursing and hollering like a brat. He drop-kicked a plastic bottle of mosquito repellent into the woods. He dumped a tray of turkey sandwiches into the mud. He snapped off a dead oak branch and hurled it wildly, inconveniently slicing a hole in his own tent.

And of course he vowed to fire the helicopter pilot for insubordination.

The childish performance ended abruptly when a spear of lightning struck no more than a hundred yards from the camp. Derek turned gray and retreated into his leaky quarters, where he cowered until nightfall.

Dinner was served late, during a break in the storm—braised chicken, wild rice, buttermilk rolls and a garden salad. The wondrous aroma was too much for Derek, who crept out of his tent and joined the others beneath the caterer's canopy. The wicks of the tiki torches were too soggy to hold a flame, and no one had thought to stockpile dry wood, so the crew members built a fire using folding chairs that they tore apart with hammers.

After his third helping of chicken and rice, Derek croaked out a burp and asked, "What's for dessert?"

"Cheesecake," the chef replied, "with bing cherries."

Derek beamed. "Hallelujah! Bring it to baby."

Firmly, Raven said, "One small slice for you." She was scoping out his gut, a bulging orb that threatened to bust the buttons off his safari shirt.

"Oh, lighten up, Mother," he said. "After the terrible day I've had, I deserve to eat as much as I please."

His attack on the cheesecake was a gross spectacle. Raven could only stare in disgust. The director and the cameramen turned their backs on the scene; someone broke out a deck of cards, and a game of gin rummy was organized.

By the time Derek finished gorging, there wasn't a crumb on the platter. His snakebitten chin was shining from the creamy combination of cake goo and antibiotic ointment. He dabbed a paper napkin to his mouth and nodded at Raven.

"The scene we shot this afternoon," he said in a half whisper, "did you look at the footage?"

"Not yet."

"Here's a thought—what if we said it was a cottonmouth that fanged me?"

"Then we'd get boxes of angry letters from snake collectors and herpetologists who would notice that it *wasn't* a cottonmouth."

Derek smirked. "Come on, Raven, use your imagination. CGI?"

He was referring to computer-generated imaging, a technique often used in movies to create illusions and special effects. "Those little geeks in postproduction," he said, "they can turn it into a cottonmouth or rattler, or any kind of snake we want. Then we can shoot a scene where I'm injecting myself with the antidote and saving my own life!"

Raven sat back and folded her arms. "You said we were done faking it. You said you wanted to put the 'real' back into reality."

Derek was annoyed to be reminded of his recent conversion to integrity.

"Whatever," he muttered lumpishly.

The sky strobed, a jagged stutter of ice-blue light. A ripple of thunder rattled a tray of silverware.

Derek frowned. "Get someone to patch that hole in my tent. Chop-chop."

"Fine," said Raven.

"While we're on the subject, don't they make one of

those bloody things with air-conditioning? It must be ninety degrees in there—"

Just then, a piercing scream arose behind them. They spun around and saw one of the catering staff, a lanky middle-aged woman sporting a green hairnet, hopping frenetically. She was pointing at a long-tailed clump of fuzz that lay quivering on the cake platter.

Raven stood up and gasped. "What *is* that—a bird?"

Derek was standing, too. "Birds don't have big ears," he said.

"A rat!"

"No. Rats don't have wings." Approaching the platter, he leaned down to examine the furry, twitching intruder. When he turned back to Raven, he was grinning.

"Just as I suspected—a bat!"

She said, "Lord, that's a big one."

"Indeed." Derek's eyes twinkled in the golden flickering of the campfire.

"It must be sick or hurt," Raven said. "I'll go get Mr. Cray."

"Wait, I've got a better idea." Derek motioned to the director. "How long will it take you blokes to set up some lights?"

The director folded his cards. "Seriously?"

Raven looked down at the woozy bat, then back at Derek Badger.

"Oh no," she said.

"Oh yes!" He licked his upper lip. "Let's do this!"

FIFTEEN

Raven Stark had asked Wahoo to stay and eat with the crew, but he said no thanks. When he got back to camp, Tuna was sitting on a corner of the tarp, reading by flashlight.

"Nice outerwear," she said. "Does this mean you're officially part of the team?"

He took off the *Expedition Survival!* jacket and put on a dry T-shirt. From his father's tent came the familiar croaks and snuffles of snoring. Mickey had gone to bed early.

"I scared you off, huh?" Tuna said.

Wahoo shook his head. "The stuff about your dad, it's sort of . . ."

"Heavy."

"Definitely." Wahoo sat down beside her. "You ever thought about going to the cops?"

The question hung there in the empty night and then evaporated, like a wisp of smoke.

Tuna said, "Today the airboat driver asked about my black eye. He thought it was you who socked me."

"He actually said that?" Wahoo was mortified. "What did you tell him?"

"The truth, of course, and guess what? His old man used to do the same thing to him and his little sister."

So that's what Link and Tuna had been talking about on the boat. Once again, Wahoo wasn't sure what to say.

"Even on Christmas they got slapped around is what he told me," Tuna said.

"Did *they* call the police?"

"I didn't ask." Tuna closed the book and handed the flashlight to Wahoo. "Hey, I didn't mean to freak you out."

"No, it's all right. Anytime you want to talk."

"The rain's quit. Let's get some food."

They pulled up the tarp, which had kept the kindling dry. Wahoo started the fire and cooked hot dogs wrapped in bacon strips. It wasn't a fancy catered meal, but it tasted great. Dessert was Fruit Roll-Ups.

Afterward, Tuna began telling him about the wild orchids of the Everglades. "There's one called the ghost orchid. It's incredibly rare and beautiful!"

Wahoo wasn't paying close attention. He was thinking about what his mom said when he told her about Tuna.

"Earth to Lance. Am I boring you?"

"Sorry," Wahoo said. "I was just—"

"What?"

"You said your mother's up north."

"In Chicago," Tuna said.

Wahoo didn't want to seem pushy, but there were things he needed to know. "When's she coming home?"

Tuna shook her head. "I'm not sure. My grandma's real sick."

"Did you tell your mom what happened? What your dad did to you?"

"She's got enough to worry about."

"But—"

"Listen, he's slugged her before, too," Tuna said.

Again Wahoo was stunned. He couldn't picture his dad ever hurting his mother. Living with Mr. Gordon must have been terrifying.

"Mom wanted me to go up with her to take care of Grandma," Tuna said, "but I decided to stay here and finish out the school year. So she took Daddy aside and said, 'If you lay a hand on that girl while I'm gone . . . ' Anyhow, it didn't stop him."

"When did all this start?" Wahoo asked. "The hitting, I mean."

"Doesn't matter. Sometimes you wait for somebody to change, and you end up waiting too long. Soon as Mom gets back, we're outta there."

"But isn't there anyone else you could stay here with until then? Aunts or uncles?"

"I'm tired, Lance."

"Sorry. This is none of my business."

"Hey, we're good." Tuna smiled sadly. "If it was happening to you, I'd be asking the same questions." She said good night and ducked into her tent.

Wahoo had no hope for sleep. He moved closer to the fire and poked the embers with a stick. Aiming the flashlight up in the branches, he counted a half-dozen air plants topped with dark red flowers. They looked like crazy Halloween wigs. Something fluttered with hushed wings among the treetops—probably a barred owl or a hawk.

From the other pup tent came a faint moan. Wahoo peeked inside and saw his dad was having a nightmare. Gently Wahoo shook him awake.

"My head," Mickey murmured.

"You want Tuna's pills?"

"All I want is to feel normal again." He sat up, blinking.

Wahoo held up four fingers in the flashlight's beam. "How many do you see, Pop?"

"*Quatro.*"

"Very good."

"What if that bleeping iguana gave me a brain tumor?"

"That's not even funny." Wahoo had worried about the same thing after Googling his father's medical symptoms. "A concussion won't give you a brain tumor," he asserted, although he wasn't absolutely certain.

"You know what I dreamed?" Mickey said. "I dreamed some poacher got after Alice. It was ugly."

As Wahoo helped him out of the tent, he couldn't help but notice that the muscles in his father's arms and shoulders were still as taut as ship cables. Even after weeks of inactivity, the man was in fairly solid shape.

"Tell the truth, Pop. You ever had a dream that turned out to be true? I mean good or bad?"

"Never once."

"There you go. Alice is just fine."

Mickey cocked his head and sniffed at the sky. "Rain again?"

"Hey, I talked to Mom," said Wahoo.

"What! When?"

"While you were asleep. Ms. Stark let me call on her sat phone."

"You should've got me up," Mickey said crossly.

"She thinks we should take Tuna to the police so she can tell them what her dad did."

"Yeah, then what?"

"Exactly."

Mickey rubbed a knuckle across his stubbled chin. "What if the cops just take a report and send her back home? Or lock up her old man, like you said—then where the heck's she supposed to live?"

The wind picked up, cooler than before. Wahoo zipped on the *Expedition Survival!* jacket and said, "Let's think on this. We don't have to decide tonight."

"Well, boys, let me know when you do!" It was Tuna speaking, from inside her tent. "It's only my life you're talking about."

Wahoo had no time for another apology, because at that instant a tremulous cry pierced the darkness, followed by another and still another. . . .

The Florida mastiff bat is the largest in the southeastern United States, reaching a length of almost seven inches. Its short, glossy hair can be black or cinnamon, and a thin, mouse-like tail extends well beyond its winged membrane. The wings are long and slender.

Believed to have been carried by hurricane winds from Cuba to Florida years ago, the mastiff is quite rare and considered an endangered species. By day it sleeps, often in the shady crevices of palm fronds. It emerges not at dusk, as other bats do, but in the deep of night. A swift flier, the mastiff travels great distances in search of food. It feasts mainly on insects and has no natural appetite for the flesh or blood of humans.

The specimen that ended up in the *Expedition Survival!* catering tent was a young female whose internal sonar had malfunctioned as she'd swooped low in pursuit of a flying beetle. After bouncing at high speed off the canvas, the creature had landed in a muddle on Derek Badger's cheesecake platter.

Like other nocturnal animals, the mastiff is extremely sensitive to light. The one that crashed at the TV camp was therefore frightened by an artificial blast of whiteness much brighter than that of the sun. The bat couldn't see where this strange, blistering glare was coming from, nor could she see the cluster of humans that surrounded her.

With leaf-sized ears she absorbed strange vocal vibrations that only heightened her confusion:

"*Deep in the Everglades, the swamp is unforgiving and food is scarce. Survival depends on making the best of the situation, and that means eating whatever you can get your hands on.*

Tonight the heavy squalls and dangerous thunderstorms have made it impossible for me to leave camp to hunt for the juicy bullfrogs and crayfish that I was hoping to cook for supper.

"But by sheer luck—and, believe me, that's what you need out here—the violent weather has literally dropped on my platter a tasty morsel that will provide enough nutrition to get me through another brutal day in this tropical wilderness.

"Here, have a look. . . ."

Mastiffs, like most species of bats, are equipped to hang upside down. However, they are not accustomed to being snatched by their tails and dangled in midair.

And even when half blinded by light, they are able at close range to recognize the presence of predators, particularly if such a predator has a shiny chin, a big oval mouth and vivid, orange-tinted hair.

"There are probably only fifteen grams of meat on this fellow's bones. But when you're as hungry as I am, this little bugger looks as juicy as a T-bone steak!

"Unfortunately, the rain has soaked all the tinder, so I can't make a fire for cooking. That leaves me only one choice, I guess.

"Now, please don't try this yourself—wild bats can be vicious, and their teeth are needle sharp. Remember, I'm an experienced survivalist. I know how to handle these unpredictable rascals. . . ."

The mastiff bat that Derek Badger slowly lowered toward his gaping maw wasn't vicious. She simply didn't want to be eaten.

And so she reacted defensively and without hesitation.

She chomped down on the first chompable target that came within reach, which happened to be Derek's plump, purple-blotched tongue.

"*Aaaieeeeeegh! Aaaieeeeeegh! Aaaieeeeeeeeeeeeeeeeeeegh!*"

The shrieks were not part of the script that he'd hastily composed on a paper napkin following the bat's unexpected arrival. The shrieks were totally spontaneous.

"Don't move! Don't move!" Raven Stark cried, but Derek did move. He tipped backward into a wet patch of ferns, the flapping mammal still attached to his bloody face.

"Cut!" barked the director. "Somebody go get Cray!"

Wahoo's father stood over the fallen TV star, who lay rigid and goggle-eyed. The front of his safari shirt was dappled with wet crimson splotches, and the bat dangled from his mouth like a bizarre holiday ornament.

"Unbelievable," Mickey said.

"Do something!" Raven pleaded.

Mickey turned to his son. "I'll need my serious gloves."

While Wahoo ran back to the other camp, Tuna stepped closer to take a look. "What kind of bat is that?" she asked. "It's a freetail, I know, but what species?"

Wahoo's father shrugged. He directed the crew to re-aim their bright lights toward the spot where Derek Badger had fallen, illuminating the scene like a hospital operating room. As soon as Wahoo returned with the heavy gloves, Mickey fitted them on and told everybody to stand back.

"Is he still breathing?" Raven said. "Please tell me he's still breathing."

"They're *both* breathing." Mickey knelt beside Derek and pondered how to remove the frightened creature without also removing the tip of Derek's tongue.

Wahoo happened to know his father wasn't fond of handling bats. They were tricky to wrangle and, like other mammals, they sometimes carried diseases. However, this was an emergency, and nobody else at the campsite was qualified to deal with it.

Mickey leaned in to whisper in one of Derek's ears: "Blink twice if you can hear me."

Derek blinked two times. The director clapped in relief, and some of the other crew members cheered.

"Hush!" Mickey snapped over his shoulder. Then, to Derek: "Don't worry, we'll get your dumb butt out of this mess. The trick is to not make your furry little friend any madder than it already is. So you've gotta stay still, *mate*, no matter how much this hurts. Blink once if you understand."

Again Derek blinked. Mickey instructed Wahoo to strip the leaves off a fern, which left only the soft green stem. Wahoo handed it to his father, who said, "Perfect."

"What are you going to do?" Raven asked skeptically.

"Tickle it," said Wahoo's father.

"You can't be serious."

"I believe he is," said Tuna.

Wahoo observed that the crew was preparing to videotape the delicate procedure. Normally Derek would have protested indignantly, not wanting his TV audience to see their super-masculine hero disabled by a creature weighing two ounces. On this occasion, though, he remained mute.

Mickey got down on the ground so that he was level with the bat, which regarded him unpleasantly with moist black eyes. It didn't appear to Wahoo and Tuna that the bewildered animal was enjoying the flavor of Derek Badger.

Using the flexible stem of the fern, Wahoo's father went to work on the bat's belly, lightly prodding and stroking. Very soon the mastiff began to twitch and squeak.

"Zoom in for a close-up! Hurry!" the director ordered the cameraman.

Wahoo waved his arms and motioned for everyone to remain still. He feared that the agitated bat would let go of Derek and then glom on to his father.

In fact, the critter had only one item on its agenda: escape.

There are no scientific studies that address the question of whether or not bats can experience the sensation of being tickled, the way people do. But whatever Mickey was doing with the fern stem, it worked. With a shudder, the bat unhooked its fangs from Derek's swelling tongue.

"Now kill it! Kill it quick!" Raven cried.

"Don't be ridiculous," said Wahoo's father.

The animal made a spitting noise and repositioned itself on Derek's spray-tanned forehead, where it stretched its bony wings. Unlike most other bats, mastiffs can lift off from a flat surface, and that's what this one did. On the next gust of wind it took flight, zigzagging through the hot beams of the TV lights until it disappeared into the dark canopy of the hardwoods.

Wahoo and Tuna high-fived each other, while the director called out, "Bravo, Mr. Cray. Well done!"

Raven rushed anxiously to Derek's side, babbling something about rabies and distemper. Wahoo's father assured her that the bat wasn't sick. "She bit Mr. Beaver out of self-defense, pure and simple."

Derek showed no reaction to being called Beaver, another indication that he might have been in shock. Several crew members gathered around and carried him to his tent. Raven followed gravely, carrying a first-aid kit.

To Wahoo and Tuna, Mickey said, "Come on. Let's get some sleep."

A slashing rain chased them back to their camp. It poured all night long on the tree island, and no living thing stirred.

Except one.

SIXTEEN

The airboat awoke Wahoo. He figured it was coming to get Derek Badger and take him away for medical treatment.

Emerging from the tent, Wahoo saw Tuna reading a green book. It was a field guide to Florida mammals. She kept it in her canvas tote bag with several other books, journals and sketch pads. Tuna never let the bag out of her sight.

"Here's our prime suspect," she announced. "It's called a mastiff bat. *Eumops glaucinus floridanus*."

She showed the photograph in the field guide to Wahoo. "Yeah, that's the one," he agreed.

"I'm gonna learn the Latin names of all tropical bats, starting today."

"You seen my dad?"

"He went for a hunt." Tuna was eating a lame breakfast— trail mix and Mountain Dew. "I bet they're taking Derek to Miami for rabies shots," she said.

"Which way did Pop go?"

"Relax, Lance. He said his head feels fine."

Their campsite was a mud pit because of the overnight rain. Wahoo didn't bother trying to start the fire and cook some food. He settled for two snack bars and a lukewarm lime Gatorade.

"So, what happens now?" Tuna asked.

After seeing Derek's trance-like condition the night before, Wahoo assumed that the Everglades episode of *Expedition Survival!* would be canceled and that his father's wrangling job was over.

"I guess we pack up and go home," he said.

"Home, sweet home." Tuna chuckled bitterly. "I can't wait."

Wahoo noticed that the bruise beneath her eye had faded a bit, taking on a yellowish tinge. "Maybe you can stay with us for a while," he suggested.

She was flipping through the bat chapter of the book. "I'm sure I'll hear from Daddy, soon as he needs his laundry done. That's the usual program. He's the king of fake tears and phony apologies."

"You've run away before?"

Tuna looked up. "Sure. Twice."

"And you go back."

"Yeah, but it's not like forever. Mom's serious about leaving him."

Wahoo had an idea. "Soon as Pop and I get paid for this job, we'll get you a plane ticket to Chicago."

"No," said Tuna, "but thanks anyway." She turned away, trying not to choke up.

"School's out for the summer. There's no reason for you to stay here."

She tucked the field guide in her bag and popped to her

feet. "Look, I know you guys are tryin' to help, but I'll be okay. I can deal with my dad until Mom gets home."

"All right," said Wahoo, thinking: *But the man's got a gun.*

Tuna broke into a smile when she spotted three striped butterflies, flitting in a casual ballet through the hammock.

"Hey, Lance, check it out!" she said. "Zebra swallowtails. *Eurytides marcellus!*"

Wahoo wondered if the butterflies were traveling together or had met by coincidence. High overhead he saw a string of somber turkey buzzards, riding the thermals under a mat of gray-blue clouds. The sun had been up for some time, but the heavy sky gave no clue it was morning. Wahoo was tired of the lousy weather, tired of being wet.

His father stepped out of the scrub holding a pair of Everglades rat snakes. They were good ones—five-footers, dark orange with grayish stripes and butter-colored underbellies.

"Look who I found," he said cheerily.

"Biters?" asked Wahoo.

"Big-time."

Tuna agreed that the snakes were beautiful, but she kept a distance.

"All right, Lucille," said Wahoo, "tell us what Mr. Linnaeus would call 'em."

"Wait, I'm tryin' to remember." She closed her eyes in concentration. "The scientific name is *Elaphe* something-or-other. It'll come to me."

Wahoo grinned. "Way to go, Pop. I think you stumped her."

Mickey wasn't listening to the conversation. He heard something nearby—the heavy snapping of branches. "We got a visitor," he said.

Link, the hulking airboat driver, stalked into the clearing. He wore a grime-streaked undershirt, faded Wranglers and rotted hiking boots with no laces. He scanned the campsite, sneering slightly when his eyes settled on Mickey and the snakes.

"Where's he at?" Link demanded.

"Who?" said Wahoo.

"The TV man."

Tuna stepped forward. "You mean Mr. Badger?"

"Yeah. He be gone."

Wahoo's father muttered, "If only." He had an *Elaphe* entwined on each arm.

"Keep dem tings 'way f'me," Link warned.

"Aw, don't be a baby."

"TV man be gone from his tent dis mornin'."

Tuna said, "Maybe he went for a hike."

"Or mebbe he out here wid you."

Mickey laughed. "That's right, Sherlock. We kidnapped him in the middle of the night! I remember now."

"Pop, lay off," said Wahoo. Link was built like a refrigerator, and he didn't have a rollicking sense of humor.

"Dey tole me to come'n git him," the airboat driver went

164

on. "Take him back to Sickler's. Hospital sent a ambulance on account of he got bit by a otter."

"Actually, it was a bat," Tuna interjected.

Wahoo couldn't imagine why Derek Badger took off, or where he might have gone. The tree island wasn't very large, maybe fifteen acres. "We'll help you find him," he said to Link.

While Mickey bagged the rat snakes in a pillowcase, Tuna and Wahoo varnished themselves with bug spray. Link accepted a Gatorade, which he downed in four gulps. Then they all set out through the vines and the hardwoods in search of the missing reality TV star. Wahoo's father led the way.

Before long, they crossed paths with the director and the crew, accompanied by a distraught Raven Stark, her red hair laced with spiderwebs.

"We've looked everywhere," she lamented. "Derek's gone! Vanished!"

"Not possible," said Mickey.

The director pulled him aside and whispered, "What if a bear got him?"

"Florida bears don't eat people. Plus, there'd be blood and bones."

"Then he must be lost out here someplace. . . ."

Mickey said, "He's not lost. He's hiding."

They were gathered at the low, skinny tail of the island, where the trees thinned out.

"Hiding?" Raven exclaimed. "From what?" She turned and called Derek's name.

Wahoo and Tuna felt obliged to do the same. There was no response. Mickey advised the group to split up once more and work their way back toward the main camp.

"Here. Take a walkie-talkie," said the director.

That's when they heard the loud growl of the airboat engine, cranking up. Link at first appeared confused, then angry.

"DAT'S MINE!" he bellowed, and lowered his shoulders, crashing like a mad buffalo through the underbrush.

The director cursed, and Raven let out a despairing moan. Wahoo and Tuna could hardly believe what was happening.

Mickey Cray shook his head. "It just gets better and better."

The executive producer of *Expedition Survival!* was a man named Gerry Germaine, a crabby, bullet-headed fellow who drove a canary-yellow Ferrari and wore loafers that cost nine hundred dollars. The sprawling office from which he ruled his television empire was in Studio City, California, not far from downtown Los Angeles. In addition to *Expedition Survival!*, Gerry Germaine produced three other popular reality shows—*Rattlesnake Roundup*, *Shrimp Wars* and *Polar Madness*, which featured a quarrelsome family that lived on a melting iceberg.

Gerry Germaine seldom watched his own TV programs, but he paid close attention to the budgets. Derek Badger was a constant problem, and his latest salary demands had angered the bosses at the Untamed Channel, which broadcast all of Gerry Germaine's reality shows. Having recently purchased an expensive vacation home in Aspen, Colorado, Gerry Germaine wanted to remain on good terms with the Untamed Channel. Therefore it was his view that *Expedition Survival!* would do just fine without Derek Badger, whose frequent tantrums and mishaps were expensive.

"What do you mean by 'gone'?" Gerry Germaine asked Raven, who had contacted him on her satellite phone from the Everglades.

"Last night he was bitten by a bat."

"What else is new?"

"A seriously ticked-off bat. Derek was bleeding all over the place," Raven said. "And this morning, when we checked his tent, he was gone."

"Hmmm."

"It appears that he stole—let's say 'borrowed'—an airboat. We don't know why."

"Where did that klutz learn to drive an airboat?" wondered Gerry Germaine.

"Two years ago we taped that show in the Louisiana bayou. The one where Derek finds an old beat-up airboat and uses his Swiss army knife to fix the engine so he can escape—remember?"

"I remember the bills," Gerry Germaine said. "Twenty-four hundred bucks we paid some Cajun fisherman for 'vessel repairs.'"

Raven cleared her throat. "That's the one. Derek crashed it into a cypress stump."

"Naturally." In his mind, Gerry Germaine was sorting through the options. "What's your plan to find him?"

"Well, the local sheriff has a search team."

"Absolutely not. I don't want to see this all over the media."

"But he's hurt," Raven said. "He needs help."

"How badly hurt? You think he might . . . *die?*" Gerry Germaine had pondered such coldhearted fantasies before. It would be a humongous night for the show's TV ratings if Derek Badger failed to survive one of his survival expeditions. It would also open the way for him to be replaced with another actor who wasn't as pompous, demanding and clumsy. Plenty of guys would jump at the job, for half the pay.

Raven said, "It's possible the bat had rabies. Derek could be losing his mind."

Out of curiosity, Gerry Germaine Googled "rabies symptoms" on his laptop.

"We need to keep this ultra-hush-hush," he said, "especially if your boy's gone off the deep end. The show definitely doesn't need that kind of publicity."

He could easily imagine the scene: Derek blathering and

wild-eyed as deputies hauled him out of the marsh. There was no telling what kind of nutty nonsense the guy might spout with news cameras poking in his face. The Untamed Channel was a family network, run by fussy businesspeople who didn't like being embarrassed.

"No cops yet," Gerry Germaine said firmly.

Raven was silent on the other end.

"Get the crew together and do what you can to find him."

"And if we can't?" Raven asked.

"Then call me back."

"We'll need the helicopter, Gerry."

"Whoa, there, missy. Badger's contract says he gets a chopper ride back to his hotel every night. It doesn't say a word about chartering one of those fuel hogs if he happens to go bonkers and runs away. You know what it costs to keep a helicopter in the air?"

"Eight hundred dollars an hour," Raven said, "last time I checked."

"More like a thousand."

Raven was dumbfounded that Gerry Germaine was giving her grief about hiring the chopper to help with the search.

"Four hours," he told her, "not a minute more."

"But this is a man's life we're talking about!"

"Good luck," said Gerry Germaine.

He hung up the phone and continued reading on his

office laptop. Rabies, it seemed, was a most unpleasant disease.

By the time Sickler's other two airboats arrived at the tree island, Derek Badger had been gone for more than an hour and Link was seething. Another thirty minutes was spent debating how and where the search should be conducted. Eventually it was decided that Mickey Cray and Raven Stark would go with one driver, while Link and the show's director would ride with the other. Nobody anticipated that the first boat would break down and require towing by the second. The result was a waste of the entire morning that put everybody in a testy mood.

Four big cruiser airboats were called in from the Mic-cosukee reservation to haul the crew, its video equipment and the catering team back to Sickler's dock. Over a tense lunch of barbecued chicken wings, provided by Sickler at the criminal price of eight dollars a box, Raven and the di-rector studied a map of the area while Link fumed.

Mickey decided to start packing the gear in the truck.

"Where's the girl?" he asked Wahoo.

"Inside the shop."

"Go fetch her. We're outta here."

"Just a minute, dear." It was Raven, peering over the rims of her glasses. "You're not seriously quitting, are you?"

Mickey was taken by surprise. "I figured the job was over,

now that Mr. Beaver turned jackrabbit. But if you wanna pay me to hang around, ma'am, I'll gladly oblige."

Link spoke up. "Let'm go. We don't need him."

"I believe we do," said Raven. She tapped a finger on the map. "This place goes on forever. By now, Derek could be anywhere."

Wahoo and his father knew that wasn't true. Derek Badger wasn't some sly old swamp rat who could outwit his trackers. The man had no clue where he was going or what he was doing. Most likely he would steer Link's airboat wildly through the saw grass marsh until he beached it on dry land, plowed it into a stand of trees or simply ran out of gas.

"He won't starve," Mickey Cray said to Raven, "but there's other ways for a fool to die out here. I'll help you find him."

The director stared hopelessly at the green, featureless swath of map that represented the area where Derek had gone missing. There were no roads, no canals, no levees to follow. It was pure swamp.

Link said, "They's a gallon of water on my boat."

Raven was relieved. "That should keep him alive for a while." She stood up, all business, trying not to show her concern. "Let's get moving while the rain holds off."

Wahoo went looking for Tuna. He found her standing by the cash register in Sickler's tourist shop. "What'd you get?" he asked.

"Nuthin'." She handed him three one-dollar bills. He'd given her a five to purchase a snack.

"Well, you must've bought *something*," Wahoo said.

She seemed flustered. "Oh yeah. I forgot—I had a burrito. Hard as a rock."

Wahoo could tell that something was wrong. "What's up?"

"I'm fine," Tuna replied, but she definitely seemed different.

"Come on. You can tell me."

"It'll be fine." She slipped past him and headed for the screen door. "Which boat are we in, Lance? I want to ride in the same one as Link."

SEVENTEEN

Anyone taking the time to search Derek Badger's luxury motor coach would have found a clue to his strange and sudden departure.

Inside a silk pillowcase, tucked beneath his mattress, was a cherished collection of DVDs, volumes I through III of the Night Wing Trilogy. The movies were based on a series of popular novels featuring a handsome but sensitive high school baseball star named Dax Mangold and his girlfriend, Lupa Jean. In the first installment, *Cartwheel of Doom*, Lupa Jean turns into a vampire after being bitten by a bat during cheerleader practice. In the next volume, *Bark of the Dark Prince*, Lupa Jean bites Dax's dog—a dopey but adorable beagle named Bixby—and the dog becomes a vampire.

In the final saga, *Revenge of the Blood Moon*, Dax himself gets chomped by a bat, a flying squirrel, a crazed guinea pig, lovable Bixby and of course Lupa Jean (twice). Still, Dax manages to fight off the vampire curse and rescue both his beloved pet and girlfriend from the clutches of the undead. One reviewer, writing on Amazon, trashed the Night Wing Trilogy as "three of the most brainless books ever written in the English language, an insult to every unsuspecting reader who makes the tragic mistake of picking one up."

Derek Badger had never picked up any of the books

because he strenuously avoided reading. However, he loved movies, especially scary ones. Vampire flicks were his favorites—he couldn't get enough of them, going all the way back to *Dracula*, featuring the spooky Bela Lugosi. It was an addiction he kept secret, even from Raven Stark.

Not that Derek had been thinking about vampires when the mastiff bat bit him. He'd simply intended to gobble the stunned critter, one of his trademark TV moves. Loyal viewers of *Expedition Survival!* had come to expect at least one such disgusting scene in every episode.

Believing the animal to be disabled, Derek had been flabbergasted when it clamped onto his tongue. The pain was so piercing that he forgot about the lights and cameras and how ridiculous he must look on videotape with a flapping varmint attached to his face. Immediately he grew weak and woozy, slipping into a dream haze. The last thing he remembered was the redneck wrangler, Mickey Cray, bending down and tweaking the feisty bat with a twig.

Hours later, when Derek awoke inside his tent, he was drenched with sweat and twitching with fever. His tongue had swollen to the size of a knockwurst sausage, making it impossible for him to speak—or, at least, be understood. It didn't really matter, for he had nothing he wished to say.

A bat's teeth aren't particularly sanitary, and the mastiff had given Derek an exotic infection that fogged his thinking and set off deep, disturbing fears. All he wanted to do was run and hide.

The camp was pitch-black and silent when he tottered

from the tent. He picked up a flashlight and the expensive high-tech Helmet Cam, which he sometimes wore to film himself on the show and further mislead TV viewers into thinking he was alone on his expeditions.

Weaving through the dense hammock, Derek had no master plan. It was only later, when he was perched high atop a strangler fig tree, that his skittering thoughts returned to the creature that had chomped him. Could it have been a vampire bat? Could he himself be morphing into one of the sinister, night-roaming fiends?

Had he not been so ill, Derek would have scoffed at such an absurd idea. But once the notion took hold, his fever-racked imagination was unstoppable.

He decided to do what Dax Mangold did when he was attacked by a bat (and all those other critters) in the final Night Wing episode. Feeling the evil blood chill his veins, Dax Mangold fled deep into the woods to battle the terrible forces of the spirit underworld and to save his own soul.

The director and crew of *Expedition Survival!* were worried that Derek Badger had been stricken with rabies, but Derek himself was worried about something even worse. He spent the remainder of the night clinging to the branches, wondering if by morning he'd be hanging upside down by his feet, sporting bat wings and fuzzy crinkled ears.

Shortly after dawn, he heard an airboat arrive at the campsite. Soon Raven and some of the crew started shouting his name and launched a noisy search. When they passed beneath the old fig tree, none of them glanced up in the high boughs where Derek was hiding. Soon afterward, he scrambled to the ground and made his way to the moat, where Link's airboat was moored.

Unlike real survivalists, Derek had no natural sense of direction. He steered the flat-bottomed vessel across the liquid prairie in a snaking, aimless path that ended with him smacking into the embankment of another tree island. The airboat was traveling exactly twenty-nine miles per hour when it pancaked to a halt, ejecting Derek head over heels.

He landed on his Helmet Cam, bounced twice and then rolled into a bitter-smelling thicket of poison ivy. There he lay, scratching frantically, until a spear of sunshine lanced through the leafy canopy and caught him squarely in the eyes.

Derek recalled with alarm that daylight caused vampires to either melt or catch fire, possibly both. In a panic he crawled back to the mired boat and scrunched beneath its broad bow, where he cowered like an overgrown mole, shielding his face with the freshly dented Helmet Cam.

He braced against the dreaded first symptoms of vampirehood by reciting a chant of resistance that Dax Mangold kept repeating in *Revenge of the Blood Moon:*

"*Eee-ka-laro! Eee-ka-laro! Gumbo mucho eee-ka-laro!*"

The English translation was not known to Derek, but the word *eee-ka-laro* made him think of éclairs, his favorite dessert. Chocolate éclairs filled with French vanilla custard!

Soon Derek's stomach began snarling with hunger, a beast more bold and ferocious than any mere vampire.

*   *   *

Sickler wasn't losing any sleep over the missing survivalist. The longer Derek Badger stayed lost, the better it would be for Sickler's business.

Before setting off on the search, the airboat drivers and TV crew had loaded up on bottled water, sodas, coffee, snacks and sunscreen at Sickler's souvenir shop. Raven Stark had warned Sickler not to tell a soul that Derek was missing because it might leak to the media and then snoopy reporters would show up. Sickler had sort of agreed to keep his mouth shut. It would be good publicity for the shop if he got his face on the evening news, but for now he was willing to wait.

He was sitting alone, devouring a box of powdered donuts behind the counter, when a burly, unshaven man opened the screen door. The man was too tan to be a tourist. He wore a faded Buffalo Bills jersey, baggy gray gym shorts and soiled sneakers with no laces. His hair was matted, and his eyes were red-rimmed and oozy.

"Can I help you?" Sickler asked.

"I believe so."

"You look thirsty, sport. Want a soda?"

"Beer," the man said.

"Sure."

"In a bottle, if you got one."

"Absolutely."

"Is that real or fake?" The man pointed at the bleached

177

skull of a fox that was displayed on a pine shelf above the microwave.

"Course it's real." Sickler managed to sound indignant. "Shot it myself," he said, which was a lie. "It's yours for forty bucks."

"No thanks."

"How about thirty?"

"How 'bout lettin' me enjoy my brew?" The man swigged down half the bottle before he spoke again. "I'm tryin' to find somebody."

Sickler thought instantly of Derek Badger, but it didn't add up. The stranger didn't look like a TV reporter.

"Who're you lookin' for? What's his name?"

"Not he," the man said. "It's a she."

Sickler smiled and licked the sugary dust from another donut. "We don't get lots of women coming through here, sport. I'm pretty sure I'd remember."

The man slapped a wallet-sized photograph on the countertop. "She's not a woman," he said gruffly. "She's my daughter."

It was a school picture of the scrawny girl who'd been hanging around with Derek Badger's television crew. She looked exactly the same, except that in the photo she didn't have a black eye.

"She's real sick," the man said. "She run off without her medicine."

"What's the matter with her?" Sickler asked.

"It's called Floyd's disease. She could die from it."

"Never heard of that one. Floyd's disease?"

"It's rare," the man said. "Only one out of twenty-two million kids get it is what the doctors told us."

Sickler had seen enough trouble over the years that he wasn't looking for more. Maybe the stranger was telling the truth, and maybe he wasn't. In any case, Sickler had no desire to get in the middle of a family hassle.

He pushed the girl's photograph away. "Sorry. She don't look familiar."

"Oh, is that right?" The man lunged across the counter and hissed, "She called me from *here*, Slim!"

Sickler shoved him back. He was larger than the stranger—at nearly three hundred pounds, he was larger than almost everybody—but he was hopelessly out of shape. That's why he kept a claw hammer behind the counter.

He took it out and said, "Settle down, sport."

The man raised his hands apologetically. "Sorry, buddy. I just gotta find her, that's all, before she goes into a coma or somethin'. You can put that hammer away; I won't make no trouble."

Sickler didn't put it away. He said, "We get lots of tourists come in off the highway to borrow the phone when their cell batteries go dead. I don't pay attention to what they look like, or their kids."

"She's not a tourist."

The shop owner didn't like that the man had grabbed at him, or the meanness in the man's eyes. The "Slim" wisecrack was out of line, too.

"I told you—the girl don't look familiar. Now I got work to do, so be on your way."

"Hold on—"

"But first, pay for the beer." Sickler tapped the claw hammer on the countertop. "Four bucks even."

The stranger thumbed out the cash from a grimy wad. "Her name's Tuna."

"Tina?"

"No. Tuna."

"Like the fish?"

"She said on the phone she was in Aruba," the man said, "making lists of moths and butterflies. She told me not to worry, said she hitched a ride on a sailboat with some circus folks."

"Aruba?" Sickler laughed. "That's quite a story."

"Thing is, I got caller ID on my cell. That's how I know for a fact she was here."

Oh great, Sickler thought.

"The name of this place came up on my phone when she called," the man went on. "I looked up your address on the Internet, and here I am."

Sickler wasn't ever going to admit that he knew the girl, or that he'd charged her two bucks to use his office phone. "What time did she call you?"

"An hour ago," the stranger said. He checked his watch. "Make it one hour and eleven minutes."

"Whatever." Sickler shrugged. "I wasn't here; I was over

in Naples. But I'll ask the lady who watches the shop for me, see if she recalls seein' the girl. That's the best I can do."

"I'll leave her picture with you," the man said. "Hey, is that your motor coach parked outside? The big black number with tinted windows?"

"Sure is," Sickler lied again.

"Sweet. How much that bad boy set you back?"

"You don't wanna know."

"I got a Winnebago Chieftain that's seen better days. Lucky I don't have to drive it far."

Sickler said, "Hey, tell me somethin'."

"Sure."

"Why would this girl—"

"My daughter," the stranger interjected.

"Why would she call to say she's in Aruba if she ain't? Why the heck would she lie about somethin' like that to her own daddy?"

The man finished his beer with a burp and headed for the door. "Long story," he said.

I'll bet it is, thought Sickler.

EIGHTEEN

They searched all afternoon and couldn't find Derek Badger. The helicopter had to quit early because of mechanical trouble with something called a trim actuator. When the boats returned at sunset to Sickler's dock, the mood was grim.

Contrary to what TV viewers were led to believe, never in the history of *Expedition Survival!* had Derek actually been lost. He always stayed close to the snacks and beverages.

Raven had no confidence that the made-for-television survivalist would last very long alone in the Everglades, a fear shared by the show's director. Derek did not have a surplus of common sense, and it was only a matter of time before he accidentally ate a toxic berry or stepped on a deadly cottonmouth.

Assuming he wasn't already dying of rabies.

"You're Mr. Expert," Raven said sharply to Mickey Cray. "Any brilliant ideas?"

"Yeah. We try again tomorrow."

The director looked up from his iPhone. "Bummer. The forecast calls for more rain."

"So we get wet," said Mickey.

Raven threw up her hands. "That's your plan? Seriously? We get wet?"

"It's big country out there, lady. Plus, we're hunting for a knucklehead who doesn't want to be found."

"But that's ridiculous! Why would Derek be hiding?"

"Beats me. Critters I can figure out just fine. People like him? I got no clue what goes on in their itty-bitty brains."

Link, who'd hardly spoken a word all day, shocked the group by saying: "That man be wreckin' my airboat, I break him in two." He demonstrated by snapping a tree branch over one knee.

Raven immediately called for a private strategy session in Derek's motor coach. Mickey told Wahoo and Tuna to set up the tents while he was gone.

They selected an open area near some picnic tables at the edge of Sickler's property. The mosquitoes were thick and fearless, stinging any patch of bare flesh that wasn't coated with bug repellent—eyelids, earlobes, even armpits. Tuna and Wahoo swatted themselves constantly as they worked. Their cheeks, already windburned from the airboat ride, became pink and puffy from self-inflicted slaps.

Tuna paused to examine a mashed attacker in the palm of her hand.

"Okay, what's the verdict?" Wahoo said.

"I'm guessing *Aedes aegypti*." She flicked the dead insect away. "There are forty-three different species of mosquitoes in the Everglades, but only thirteen kinds like to bite humans. Isn't that weird?"

Wahoo smiled ruefully. "Where are the friendly ones?"

After the tents were in place, he and Tuna unrolled their sleeping bags. She wanted to build a campfire, but a big yellow sign warned against it. As darkness fell, they ate a tube of Pringles and washed it down with Gatorade. Wahoo was glad that Tuna seemed her usual perky self again.

"Who gave you the fish name?" she asked, out of the blue.

He told her about the agreement his parents had made soon after they were married. His mom would choose the name of the first baby—who turned out to be Julie, his older sister—and his father would get to name the next one.

"Too bad for you," said Tuna.

"When Pop was little, his favorite pro wrestler was a guy called Wahoo McDaniel. He was part Choctaw Indian, strong as a bear. He also played linebacker for the Dolphins."

"What's your mom think? Does she seriously call you Wahoo?"

"She's not thrilled about it, but she says a deal's a deal."

"You a wrestler, Lance?"

"Nope. I'm not on the football team, either."

"But don't you get picked on at school? Because of that goofy name?"

"I used to," Wahoo said, "until this happened." He wiggled the bony nub where his right thumb once had been. "Now the jocks leave me alone. Anybody who gets bitten by a gator and walks away, they think he must be super-tough. But that's got nothin' to do with it."

"I'm not so sure." Tuna opened her tote bag and saw, among her journals and nature books, the *Expedition Survival!* script. "I guess we can throw this thing away," she said.

"Wait, let's see how it was supposed to end." Wahoo took out the flashlight and sat on the sleeping bag beside her. They turned to the last page:

CLOSE-UP OF DEREK'S SWISS ARMY KNIFE, chipping away at the core of a log.

Only the log isn't just a log anymore. It's a dugout canoe, like the traditional craft once used by Seminoles to skim across the grassy shallows.

CUT TO MEDIUM SHOT of the finished canoe.

DEREK (exhausted): *Isn't she a beauty? I worked all night, and she's finally ready to float! I can't wait to get out of here, too.*

Crikey, I thought I was a goner after that monstrous gator ambushed me. One thing's for sure: I don't have the strength to fight off another one. It's time to go.

He straps on the HELMET CAM and grabs a tree limb for a paddle. Then he steps carefully into the canoe and pushes off.

CUT TO ANGLE FROM HELMET CAM, Derek's point of view, as he slowly makes his way across a lily-covered pond toward a sea of saw grass.

DEREK (breathing heavily as he paddles): *Everything looks the same in this part of the Everglades, no matter which bloody direction you go. By noon the sun will be so scorching hot that it could cause fatal heatstroke. My only hope is that somebody finds me way out here before it's too late. . . .*

ANGLE LOOKING UPWARD FROM HELMET CAM, buzzards circling. Derek keeps on paddling, the saw grass nicking his sunburned arms, until . . .

DEREK: *Maybe I'm hallucinating, but I swear I hear an airplane!*

CUT TO A SHOT FROM HELICOPTER CAMERA, looking down from high over the scene.

Derek's standing in the canoe and waving frantically. A small single-engine plane passes above.

DEREK (shouting desperately): *Hey, mates, down here! Come back!*

After several tense moments, the plane banks slowly and begins to turn around. Derek cheers and raises both fists in the air. The pilot dips a wing to signal that he sees the solitary traveler.

CUT TO HELMET CAM SHOT of the aircraft, now circling closer.

DEREK: *Yes! Yes! Yes! What a fantastic sight!*

CUT BACK TO HELICOPTER CAMERA, pulling away, higher and farther.

DEREK (now visible as just a dot on the immense Everglades prairie): *For a moment, as I battled for my life against that ferocious gator, I wasn't sure this expedition would turn out so happily. Now it looks like I'm actually getting out of this place alive!*

See you next week!

ROLL CREDITS.

Tuna tossed the script to the ground. "Nobody can chip out a whole canoe with a dinky pocketknife! Gimme a break."

"Welcome to the reality of reality TV." Wahoo switched off the flashlight, which was attracting a cloud of insects.

In the final layer of twilight, before the swamp darkness settled in, he heard Tuna say, "What if he croaks out there?"

"You mean Derek?"

"What if he's already dead?"

The same awful possibility had occurred to Wahoo. He reached for Tuna's hand and said, "The airboat probably ran out of gas is all."

Wahoo couldn't figure out why Derek had bolted from the base camp after the bat bite. Maybe he was just trying to stir up a little drama for the director and the crew. The man clearly enjoyed being the center of attention.

"Look, I know he's a total goober," Tuna said, "but I used to love, love, love his show. Every Thursday night, nine o'clock. Just about the time my dad would pass out."

Wahoo could picture the scene all too clearly, though he still couldn't put a human face on Tuna's father.

She went on: "The Walmart has a real good TV

department—that's where I go to watch *Expedition* and *Shrimp Wars* if Daddy's snoring too loud."

"Derek's not dead, Lucille. They'll find him."

"I sure hope so."

Wahoo hoped so, too. Of one thing he felt certain: whatever the so-called survivalist was doing at large in the Everglades, he wasn't carving a homemade canoe.

The snails tasted nasty, and Derek chewed up three of them in spite of his bloated tongue. They were small, and their thin, spiral shells crunched easily. He also captured a green tree frog, which he managed to gulp whole. It wriggled going down his throat and continued wriggling all the way to his stomach. He sucked on some leaves to get the slime out of his mouth.

This happened after the sun had gone down, when it was safe for vampires to roam.

Derek didn't yet feel like a vampire, though he was jittery with anticipation. Almost twenty-four hours had passed since the bat attack, and there was no sign of a transformation from mortal human to undead night stalker.

As thirsty as he was, Derek had no desire to drink blood from somebody's neck. A cold Diet Coke, however, would have been cause for rejoicing. Every so often he ran his fleshy fingertips along his capped teeth in expectation of fangs.

He was still sweaty and feverish, and now he noticed an annoying new symptom: dreadful, fiery itching all over his arms and legs. A knowledgeable person would have recognized the marks of poison ivy, but Derek was loopy from the infection. He wondered if the itch could be vampire-related, although he didn't recall Dax Mangold or any of the other Night Wing characters scratching so much.

He was still hungry after eating the frog and snails, which he had located using the small light mounted on the Helmet Cam. Despite being banged up in the crash, the device seemed to be working fine. Derek pawed through the items in the beached airboat until he came across Link's jug of water, which he guzzled heedlessly.

The night air thrummed and ticked with insects, and an occasional rustle came from deep in the brushy hammock. He stretched out on one of the airboat's bench seats and stared up at the sky, which was again filling with clouds. The unfriendly moon remained out of sight.

His stomach gurgled, and he desperately hoped it wasn't the frog, seeking escape. A fabulously clever idea entered his head: he would record a video of himself morphing into a vampire for *Expedition Survival!* The ratings for such a show would be sensational!

Derek activated the small camera connected to the Helmet Cam and propped it on the boat's driving platform. Illuminated only by the slender spray of light, he positioned himself in front of the dime-sized eye of the lens and began to relate his frightful story:

"Mmmphhrrrooofffttteeeeblahhhkkktunnnghhh . . ."

He was unable to speak regular words, of course, owing to

the swollen condition of his tongue. He tried several times, but all that tumbled out was gibberish. Eventually he turned off the Helmet Cam and lay back down to itch and brood.

Derek wasn't in a good place, either physically or emotionally. Although the bat that had chomped him wasn't carrying rabies, the germs from its saliva were toxic enough to blur his pampered sense of reality. In his overheated mind, the Night Wing vampire movies now loomed as true to life as a National Geographic nature documentary.

Another search of Link's airboat turned up a packet of leathery pork rinds that Derek struggled to swallow. His wounded tongue remained a major obstacle. A heron cawed in the distance, but to Derek it might as well have been a zombie calling.

He huddled in the boat and shut his eyes. Once more, his thoughts turned to food—specifically, the scrumptious dessert tray delivered nightly to his hotel suite at the Empresario. He could practically smell the spicy carrot cake and taste the silky crème brûlée. . . .

The dark side will never own me, Derek vowed to himself, repeating the mystic line from Dax Mangold. *Eee-ka-laro! Eee-ka-laro! Gumbo mucho eee-ka-laro!*

NINETEEN

Wahoo awoke before sunrise and chased off a family of raccoons that was snooping around the tents, scrounging for food. The low sky promised more rain, so he zipped on the fancy weather jacket given to him by Raven Stark.

Mickey Cray came out of the tent. He looked bleary and haggard.

"How many fingers, Pop?" Wahoo held up two.

"Aw, I'm just fine."

"No headache?"

"I slept poorly, that's all."

Wahoo knew why. His father was worried.

"How long do you think Derek can last out there?"

"Depends," Mickey said. "If he flipped that airboat, he's dead already. The prop would chop him into slaw."

"Say he didn't crash the boat. Say he just ran the gas tank dry."

Wahoo's father thought about it. "Well, the guy's got plenty of body fat. It'll take him a while to starve."

"A week?" Wahoo asked.

"At least. Unless he does somethin' stupid."

That's what everybody on the crew was afraid of, too. Wahoo asked his father if he thought Derek had gone crazy.

"Who could tell the difference?" Mickey said.

Tracking down a spacey TV star was not what he'd been hired to do. In fact, it was his first manhunt. That's why he'd tossed and turned all night. Although he had no respect for Derek Badger, Mickey was distressed by the thought of the man turning up dead—or not turning up at all.

Tuna emerged from her tent and declared she was ready for coffee and a microwaved burrito. On the walk to Sickler's shop they stopped at the dock, where the TV crew and the airboat drivers were getting a pre-search pep talk from Raven. Link was there, too, looking glum. Clearly the fate of his airboat was more important to him than the fate of Derek Badger. To Wahoo's surprise, Mickey was sympathetic.

"That boat's his whole life," he said in a low voice. "He probably built the darn thing himself."

"He tried to run you over, Pop."

Mickey smiled. "If that's what he meant to do, I'm pretty sure I wouldn't be standin' here right now."

Raven was perched on an equipment box, talking at the top of her voice. "Today's the day, okay? We're going to find Mr. Badger and bring him back safe and sound! Are we clear?"

There was a polite murmur of agreement, but Wahoo got the sense that nobody in the search party was bubbling with optimism. The weather looked ugly, and a distant quake of thunder caused one of the Miccosukee drivers to whistle unhappily. Anybody who knew the Everglades understood it was a bad place to be in an electrical storm. Tree islands were magnets for lightning bolts, and a metal airboat wasn't much safer.

"Everybody's got fresh batteries in their walkie-talkies?" Raven went on. "First-aid kits? Come on, people, look at your checklist."

Wahoo's father nudged him and said, "Let's go grab a snack. Where's your girlfriend?"

"She's *not* my girlfriend."

"Course she isn't."

Wahoo hadn't noticed Tuna slip away from the group. He peered around until he spotted her about fifty yards away, standing by a chain-link security fence that separated the parking lot from the rest of Sickler's property. Wahoo called out, but she acted as if she didn't hear him. Once more he called her name, louder, yet she still didn't turn around.

His father said, "Meet me at the shop. You want orange juice?"

"Sure."

"Pulp or no pulp?"

"Doesn't matter, Pop."

Wahoo was halfway to Tuna when she wheeled from the fence and started running toward him, running so hard that he knew it wasn't for fun. As she tore past, clutching her tote bag to her chest, her face was a gray mask of fear.

The souvenir shack was so busy selling junk food and stale protein bars to the search teams that at first Sickler didn't notice him standing in line.

"It's me again," the stranger said.

Sickler leveled a granite stare. "What's up?"

"Well, my daughter Tuna is what's up."

"I spoke to the help. Showed 'em her picture."

"Yeah?"

"They don't remember any kid like her askin' to use the phone."

Sickler hadn't run across the girl this morning, but he knew she was on the property somewhere. The last thing he needed was for her old man to see her and then the two of them get into it, scrapping like cats and dogs. Somebody might call the cops.

The man asked, "Can we talk private?"

"Now's not a good time, sport."

"Just take a minute. Then I'll be on my way."

"Sorry."

The stranger didn't move from his position in front of the cash register. "I believe you're lyin' to me, Slim. I believe my little girl's round here somewhere."

Sickler took out the claw hammer. "And I believe you've been drinkin'."

"What makes you say that?"

" 'Cause you stink of beer. Now git."

The drunk-smelling man shook his head. "Not till you show me where she's hidin'."

"I'll show you where," said a voice from behind.

Annoyed, Sickler looked past the drunk and saw the animal wrangler from Derek Badger's television show.

"In fact, I'll take you there right now," the wrangler said to the girl's father. "We'll go in my truck."

"Where's she at?" the stranger demanded, squinting bloodshot eyes. "Who're you?"

The wrangler held out his right hand. "Name's Mickey Cray. What's yours?"

"Gordon. Jared Gordon," the man said. His handshake was limp and insincere.

Sickler piped up. "Don't listen to him, Gordon. He don't know where your daughter's at, neither."

Mickey Cray tilted an eyebrow, hoping Sickler would get the message: *Butt out.*

"It's all right," Mickey assured Tuna's father. "She's expecting you."

Jared Gordon grinned. "How 'bout that?"

Sickler was glad the shop had cleared out. Now it was just the three of them. He was no saint himself, but he didn't like jerks who beat on their children.

"How'd she get that shiner?" he asked Jared Gordon.

"So you *did* see her after all!"

"What happened to her eye?"

"I tole you, she's got the Floyd's disease. That's one of the signs—black-and-blue marks on your face."

"You're so full of it," Sickler said.

Mickey cut in: "Come on, Jared. Let's you and me get in the truck. We got a long drive."

"Nooooooo thanks."

"You want to see your daughter, don't you?"

"I most surely do," said Tuna's father, "but I believe you're lyin' to me, mister, same as Slim. I believe she's still here, and I believe the both of you know 'zackly where she's at."

That's when Jared Gordon reached under his grungy Buffalo Bills jersey and whipped out the revolver. "And I do believe you're gonna lead me to her right this second," he said, "else somebody's gonna have a big-time hole in their head."

It was true that Link's homemade airboat was the center of his life. It was also true that his life wasn't very complicated. He lived by himself in a trailer near the tiny town of Copeland on Route 29. His interests were limited to fishing, hunting and tuning his boat's engine, an old 454 with compression issues.

Link's mind operated in a simple way, uncluttered by curiosity and ambition. He was mostly comfortable in the Everglades and enjoyed being alone, especially after experiencing such a rough childhood. He wasn't scared of bears, panthers or alligators, although snakes of all sizes made him skittish. Despite his thuggish appearance he was not a vicious person, but he wasn't afraid to use his fists. When he did, he usually won.

Few books or magazines could be found in Link's trailer, for he'd always struggled with reading. He watched plenty of television, although not the nature channels, so he had no appreciation for Derek Badger's fame. Link had accepted the *Expedition Survival!* job only because it paid two hundred bucks a day and he got to drive his airboat. So far he hadn't been impressed by what he'd seen, and he had no plans to start watching the program on Thursday nights. He would stick to cage fights on pay-per-view.

The manhunt for Badger wasn't Link's first. Usually the lost parties were amateur airboaters or backpacking tourists who were located within a day or two—sunburned, hungry and freckled with crimson bug bites. Link expected the searchers to find Badger in the same condition, miserable but unharmed. He couldn't recall the last time anybody had got eaten by a gator or died from a cottonmouth bite.

Of more concern was the fate of his precious airboat, which he'd put together by hand from a kit. He was the only one who'd ever driven the craft, until now. With a guy like Derek at the helm, anything could happen. Fearing that his creation might end up as a crumpled heap of aluminum, Link was a highly motivated searcher.

As the teams gathered at Sickler's dock to receive their final instructions from Raven Stark, Link fidgeted and paced. He couldn't wait to get out on the water. Raven had assigned him to ride with a young Miccosukee driver named Bradley Jumper, who was sitting beneath a nearby banyan tree and feasting on a glazed donut.

"Time to go," Link said.

"Dude, lemme finish my breakfast."

It seemed to Link that Bradley Jumper didn't appreciate what was at stake.

"Now!" Link said.

"Chill."

This wasn't the response Link had hoped for. Just as he was about to grab Bradley's long black ponytail and assist him to the dock, the girl named Tuna ran up.

"Help me," she gasped.

"Okay," said Link.

She hopped onto Bradley Jumper's airboat—a twenty-foot swamp-tour special with an eight-bladed turbo-prop. Link followed her aboard and quickly started the engine.

"Hey!" Bradley protested, spitting donut crumbs.

But Link was already untying the ropes from the pilings. Tuna was joined in the bow by the wrangler's son, who seemed to appear out of nowhere. Link didn't ask any questions because he could see that the girl was frightened to the bone. He remembered the feeling.

"Hurry!" she shouted over the rising whine of the engine.

On the edge of the dock stood Raven Stark, hands on her hips. "Where do you three think you're going?" she said. "The other teams aren't ready yet! Where's your radio?"

None of her yapping could be heard by Link, who'd pushed the boat clear and taken his seat in front of the big aviation propeller. As he revved the engine, something stung him sharply below his right shoulder blade. He grunted and turned to glimpse a stranger in a football jersey standing on the bank of the canal. With one arm the man was aiming a stubby black pistol. His other arm was locked around the neck of Cray, the animal wrangler.

Link was both puzzled and alarmed. He hit the gas and the airboat took off. Ten minutes and seven miles later, his brain finally made the unhappy connection between the worsening pain in his back and the stranger with the gun.

Maybe I been shot, he thought.

Everything in his vision—the clouds, the water, the tan waves of saw grass—began to turn fuzzy. The back of his T-shirt felt warm and sticky.

For sure I been shot, he thought.

Before collapsing, he managed to stop the boat. The kids apparently found the first-aid kit and started treating his bullet wound. Floating in and out of consciousness, Link picked up part of their conversation.

"Can't you stop the bleeding?" the girl was pleading.

"I'm trying," said the boy. "Did you see the gun? What was it?"

"A .38 revolver."

How'd she know that? Link wondered in a fog.

He lifted his head and cracked one eyelid. "You got a fix on who shot me?"

"Yeah," the girl replied. "My whacked-out dad."

"Ugh."

"A new low," she added, "even for him."

"Am I gone die?" Link asked.

"No way," the boy said.

"Good." Link closed his eye and took a nap.

Wahoo was experienced at first aid. Keeping a backyard full of animals, he and his father frequently got scratched, scraped or chomped. Pain-wise, monkey bites were the worst, with raccoon nips a close second. Such injuries weren't life-threatening, but they required speedy attention in order to prevent infections, which could be dangerous. From practice Wahoo had learned how to quickly stanch bleeding, clean a wound and apply antibiotics.

Tuna knelt beside him while he worked on Link. He began by using a screwdriver from the boat's toolbox to cut away Link's bloody shirt. Then he applied some hydrogen peroxide, followed by a dab of alcohol, which caused Link to groan from the sting.

After tweezing a crumb of broken lead from the pea-sized hole, Wahoo said, "The slug broke into pieces. It might've hit a bone."

Tuna took the jagged fragment and placed it in the palm of her hand. "Unbelievable," she said. "My father's officially out of his mind."

"How the heck did he find you?" Wahoo asked.

"I'm a total idiot, that's how. The battery in my cell was dead, so I borrowed the phone at the tourist shop. Sickler's name must have come up on Daddy's caller ID. Totally my fault—and now look what happened!"

She stared forlornly at Link unconscious on the deck of the airboat, where she and Wahoo had rolled him facedown after he'd tumbled from the driver's platform.

"This is horrible," she said.

Wahoo couldn't disagree. Despite what he'd told Link, he couldn't be certain that the injury wasn't fatal. Without X-rays and other hospital tests, there was no way to know how much internal damage the bullet had caused. It was overwhelming to think that Link might die, so Wahoo pushed the thought out of his mind. In that way he was able to remain steady-handed as he painted the gunshot wound with an antibiotic that looked like A1 steak sauce.

Tuna was explaining the frantic scene at Sickler's place: "When I spotted our dumpy old Winnebago in the parking lot, I almost had a stroke. . . . I couldn't believe he tracked me down. . . . The only thing to do was run."

"Why'd you call him in the first place?" Wahoo asked.

"I've got this pet hamster."

"So?"

"He needs to eat, Lance, just like your animals. I phoned Daddy to ask if he would please feed him," she said, "because he forgets when I'm not around. It's been four days."

Wahoo thought: *This whole mess broke loose because of a hungry hamster?*

"Don't be mad," Tuna said.

"I'm not mad. Slightly stressed is all."

The rain began to fall. Link stirred. His breathing sounded heavy, but at least he *was* breathing. Wahoo cross-taped a square of medical gauze over the bullet hole, which was no longer bleeding.

"What are we going to do? I can't go back while Daddy's there," Tuna said.

Wahoo didn't know where they were or how to find help. Most importantly, he didn't know how to run an airboat—and Link seemed in no shape to give lessons. The boats were fast and tricky to steer. Even experienced drivers flipped over on occasion.

He wondered what was happening back at Sickler's dock. Wahoo couldn't picture his father standing around doing nothing while some drunk with a pistol went nuts. It wasn't Mickey Cray's style to lay back. When trouble sprang up, he usually got involved in a major way. Wahoo thought of himself as more calm and cautious—but then again, he hadn't really been tested.

"Was your dad trying to shoot you?" he asked Tuna. The question came out halting and raspy. It didn't sound like his own voice.

Tuna blinked the raindrops from her eyelashes and thought about the answer. Finally she said, "I think he was aiming for the motor. That's what I choose to believe."

Wahoo nodded and took a deep breath. Then the wind shifted and they heard another airboat, coming full speed.

TWENTY

Derek Badger knew from the movies that it was dangerous for vampires to expose themselves to sunshine—but what about dark cloudy days, when the sun was blotted out?

He decided to take a chance. From his shelter, a damp hollow beneath the grounded airboat, he cautiously extended a bare hand into the morning air. He was relieved when his flesh didn't burst into flaming blisters, which sometimes happened to careless vampires in the Night Wing Trilogy.

As Derek squeezed from his hiding spot, a cool rain began to beat down. He felt a slight chill crawl down his spine, as if the fever were breaking. He remembered a scene from a program he'd done in a Costa Rican jungle—a nifty trick that one of the writers had thought up. He took off the Helmet Cam and turned it upside down so it functioned as a bucket. The rain wasn't as sweet as the bottled Italian springwater in the refrigerator of his motor coach, but Derek drank eagerly. It made him feel like a genuine survivalist.

Afterward, using the airboat's propeller blade as a mirror, he checked out his dental situation: still no fangs.

His bat-punctured tongue had shrunk to a size that almost fit inside his cheeks. In addition, the dreadful itching rash that had tormented him all night seemed to be ebbing. A normal person would have been pleased by these developments, but Derek was disappointed. He'd sort of been looking forward to becoming a vampire, defeating the evil curse and then triumphantly morphing back into human form—just like Dax Mangold did.

Sadly, there would be no special vampire edition of *Expedition Survival!* The Helmet Cam's video recorder wasn't working because of water damage to the wiring.

Drenched to the bone, Derek struggled to shove the airboat off the bank and get it floating. It wouldn't budge. Three inches of water puddled in the bottom didn't help.

As too often happened, his empty stomach took control of his brain. He was overpowered by a delicious vision of buttermilk pancakes flanked by strips of lean Canadian bacon, smoked Scottish salmon and luscious jade wedges of kiwifruit. Hot tears of desire welled up in his eyes.

Derek wasn't accustomed to the solitary life. The previous night, spent hunkered under Link's airboat, was the first time he'd ever slept truly alone in the wilderness, a fact that would have shocked millions of TV fans. Derek missed having the crew and the director to boss around. He missed Raven Stark hovering constantly, tending to his every whim.

Most of all he missed the nightly helicopter flights back to the swanky hotel, where he could get a massage and soak in the soothing Jacuzzi.

As he watched the airboat continue to fill with rain, Derek grew more apprehensive. If the hull wallowed and the engine became submerged, he'd be stranded in the middle of the bloody Everglades with no way to get out. Resorting again to the Helmet Cam, he hurriedly began scooping water from the boat and dumping it over the side.

In a downpour this was hard work, and Derek only lasted about fifteen minutes. Grumpy and exhausted, he took cover in a stand of trees—absolutely the dumbest place to hide when the clouds were full of thunder. From a wild coffee bush he plucked a handful of scarlet berries, which tasted exceptionally gross. He spat them out in a gummy clump, something he did only when cameras weren't rolling.

Disgusted, he sat down under a bay tree. The leaves were dripping and the ground was squishy, so he propped the Helmet Cam under his butt.

As the wind freshened and swirled, Derek tried in vain to think about anything other than food. When a lovely butterfly with wings like white parchment landed on a vine, he snatched the unsuspecting traveler and popped it into his mouth. The taste was only slightly less awful than that of the coffee berries. As soon as Derek swallowed, he knew he'd made a mistake.

He would have thrown up instantly if the lightning bolt hadn't struck first.

"Did you find him yet?" Gerry Germaine asked.

"There's been a setback," Raven Stark said. The satellite phone felt like a barbell in her hand. "Two of our search boats were . . ."

"What?"

"Hijacked," she said.

"By who? Pirates?" Gerry Germaine said sarcastically. "Are you in Florida, darling, or Somalia?"

"I didn't mean 'hijacked.' I meant waylaid." Raven was in no mood to quibble. This was already the worst day of her entire adult life. "Apparently it's a family dispute."

"Give me the short version, please." The executive producer of *Expedition Survival!* was sipping a grapefruit-and-tangerine smoothie on the pool deck of his house, which overlooked the Pacific Ocean. He was wearing sunglasses, a short linen robe and ridiculous slippers lined with weasel fur. His laptop sat open on the table.

"Here's what I know," said Raven. "The animal wrangler we're using has a son. The son has a girlfriend. The girlfriend's father has a drinking problem. This morning he showed up looking for his daughter. He also had a loaded gun—"

"This is the short version?"

"Nobody was killed—"

"You're ruining my sunrise," said Gerry Germaine.

"—at least, we don't *think* anybody was killed."

"Meaning you don't know for sure."

"He fired the gun once," Raven said, "at the airboat carrying his daughter. Though, as I said, we don't believe anyone was hit. Then he—"

"Stop right there. While all this domestic drama unfolds, is somebody out searching for the unreliable and grossly overpaid Mr. Badger? The star of my show? Yes or no?"

"Not at the moment." Raven was sitting alone in Derek's motor coach. Rain lashed at the windows. "We basically have monsoon conditions right now," she said. Her free hand stirred a mug of hot tea. "Also, the other airboat drivers are extremely upset about the shooting and so forth—"

"As they should be." The seriousness of the situation was clear to Gerry Germaine. "Is that thunder I hear on your end, Raven?"

"Yup."

With a full production crew on standby, weather delays were always expensive. So were lawsuits—and the set of a TV program was no place for a trigger-happy drunk. Gerry Germaine knew what had to be done. There was no choice.

"Is the redneck with the gun still on the loose?" he asked Raven.

"Yes, however—"

"Then you'd better call the cops."

"They're on the way. Unfortunately, they can't do much until the storms pass. It's too hairy out there."

Gerry Germaine sighed to himself. "Did you happen to tell the police about Derek running off?"

"I did." Raven wondered if she would be fired. In a way, it would be a relief. "Frankly, I felt things were getting out of hand down here."

"The understatement of the millennium."

"The police said anybody who calls himself a survivalist ought to be able to survive a rainstorm. They said they're in the business of hunting down criminals, not TV actors.

They won't even start looking for Derek until after they've caught the nut with the gun!"

"Hmmm," said Gerry Germaine. It wasn't the worst news he'd ever gotten.

In fact, he'd already made a phone call to a buff New Zealander who starred in a low-budget outdoor program on the Evergreen Network. Once the young fellow heard how much money was involved, he said he'd be honored to take over as host and star of *Expedition Survival!*, in the tragic event that Derek Badger was unable to go on.

From his Google search, Gerry Germaine had learned that a person infected with rabies might not show symptoms for weeks, months or even years. That presented an inconvenient roadblock to replacing Derek on the show, which was Gerry Germaine's secret plan. Therefore, the executive producer wasn't totally upset to learn that the police were more concerned with finding the disturbed gunman than tracking down a wayward celebrity.

In Gerry Germaine's view, the longer that Derek remained lost in the Everglades, the more likely that he'd be in no shape to continue doing the TV show after he was found. *If* he was found. Either way, Derek's absence would give Gerry Germaine an opening to fly in the New Zealander for a tryout.

Raven said, "There's another complication, Gerry. It involves the wrangler—he's been abducted."

"Not now. It's time for my swim."

Raven's loyalty to Derek had its limits. At this point she

was getting worried about saving her own job. "Look, I know this is costing a fortune," she said. "But even if Derek can't finish the show, it isn't a total loss."

"How so?"

"The scene with him riding the giant alligator is golden, trust me. Plus, he gets nipped on the nose by a turtle, bloodied by a water snake—and then there's the bat attack, which will be an instant classic on YouTube. All I'm saying, Gerry, is that we've got enough video to stitch together a pretty exciting Florida adventure."

"Except for the end," Gerry Germaine said. "We don't really have an ending, do we?"

"No," Raven replied glumly. "I guess we don't."

When Wahoo was six years old, he experienced a brush with death. At least that's how he remembered it.

His father was hunting for snakes near a railroad, Wahoo tagging along. His sister, Julie, was there, too, carrying the frayed old pillowcases that served as capture bags. Mickey ran off in pursuit of a speedy coachwhip snake, and Julie chased after him.

Wahoo wandered away, following the railroad bed. He became preoccupied with counting the wooden ties that were set in gravel beneath the rails—his dad had told him there were three thousand planks for every mile of track. Wahoo didn't believe it.

He walked slowly to make sure he counted each tie, and

he recited each number out loud. At 104, the rails began to hum. Wahoo turned.

Speeding toward him was a freight train pulled by a dirty blue locomotive.

In Hollywood movies, trains always blow a long whistle when something appears ahead on the tracks. That didn't happen. Wahoo wasn't very tall, so the engineer might not have seen him.

Time crawled. Wahoo should have been terrified, but he wasn't. He should have waved his arms, but he didn't; he just stood there feeling the rumble in the soles of his feet. The train wasn't slowing down, yet Wahoo's legs seemed in no hurry to move. Later his father would tell him the locomotive was going fifty-eight miles an hour. That Wahoo believed.

The tracks actually began to vibrate as the locomotive drew close. Its headlight was like a blazing white eyeball. With only seconds to spare, a life-or-death switch went off in Wahoo's mind. He snapped out of his odd trance and jumped from the rails.

What he remembered most clearly was the incredible whoosh of noise—coal cars, tankers, flatbeds, boxcars flying past in a blur—as he crouched only a few feet away. Covering his ears didn't help much. For days afterward he awoke to the fearsome sound of that train in his head.

The sensation rushed back to him now, the difference being that he could barely see his hand in front of his face. Tuna was huddled beside him and Link was sprawled at his feet. Through gusty winds and sopping rain, another airboat was definitely roaring in their direction.

Wahoo thought: *Whoever's driving that thing must be crazy.*

Their own airboat had drifted into a tall patch of saw grass, making it even more difficult for them to be seen. Wahoo feared they would accidentally be run over.

His options were limited. One was to stand on top of the propeller's safety cage and hope the other boaters would spot him in time—although that was risky, with so much lightning in the sky. The elevated metal cage was a magnet for electricity.

Still, Wahoo knew he had to flag down help. Link needed a doctor, and the approaching vessel might be the only one to pass so close for hours, or even days.

"Lie flat," he told Tuna, "in case they crash into us."

She got down next to Link. "What about you?" she called up to Wahoo.

"Just stay low," he said, and scrambled ape-style up on the safety cage.

There, gritting into the wind, he made himself as tall as possible. For balance he wedged the waterlogged toes of his sneakers into the wire mesh. He hoped that the *Expedition Survival!* jacket would make him stand out, a glossy blue beacon above the grassy brown horizon.

Although Wahoo still couldn't see the other airboat, he knew it had to be very near—the high buzz of the engine cut through the weather like a million angry wasps. As the noise grew louder, uncomfortably loud, he felt the same racing sense of anticipation as he did all those years ago on the train tracks. Only this time he wouldn't freeze.

A violet flash in the clouds was followed by a thunderclap that made him wobble.

"Get down, dummy!" Tuna shouted.

"No!" Wahoo fixed his concentration on the engine sound. He squinted fiercely into the rain and prepared to shout with all his might.

A sparkle-green airboat burst from the mist, a streaking silhouette that crossed perhaps forty yards behind the stern. The good news was that it wasn't going to hit him. The bad news was that the two men on board were looking the other way.

Wahoo began to wave and holler—then, suddenly, he stopped.

Tuna watched him leap down so fast that he left his shoes stuck in the safety cage. He lay with his cheek pressed to the deck and he didn't stir until the other boat was gone, a faint drone in the distance.

"What's wrong?" Tuna asked.

"We've gotta wake him up." Wahoo was shaking one of Link's shoulders. "I don't know how to drive this stupid thing. Help me wake him up."

"Take it easy, Lance. The dude's been shot, remember?"

"You don't understand." Wahoo's voice was taut. "Your dad was in that other airboat!"

Tuna looked puzzled. "Are you sure?"

"It was definitely him," Wahoo said.

"But Daddy doesn't know how to drive one of those things."

"No, *my* dad was the driver. Your dad was the one with the gun."

The color left Tuna's cheeks. "Did he see us?"

"I don't think so."

"Oh God. He must be out hunting for me."

"Well, now we're going hunting for *him*." Wahoo pinched one of Link's grimy fingertips. "Come on, man, wake up!"

TWENTY-ONE

Derek Badger probably would have died if he hadn't been sitting on the Helmet Cam.

The lightning bolt shot down the trunk of the bay tree and came out at the roots, striking the metal headpiece and launching Derek like a bomb.

He woke up later in a tingling daze, clueless about what had happened. For a while he failed to notice that the seat of his pants was smoldering, a wisp of smoke rising from the matted leaves where he sat. He picked up the Helmet Cam and stared curiously at the scorched, fist-sized hole. It was a mystery.

In fact, the whole morning was a blank. The lightning strike had wiped out all memory of the storm. Still, Derek felt different, changed in some important way. At first a ringing filled his eardrums like the bell of a fire truck, though gradually it faded to a dull hum. Then he noticed a fluttery tickle running in a weird current up and down his body. It made him want to flap his arms and try to fly, like a hummingbird.

Or maybe a bat.

Finally! Derek thought. *It's really happening.*

Oddly, he was no longer hungry. In fact, the thought of chocolate éclairs made him queasy. To Derek it was proof that his mutation from mortal to vampire was in progress, for the vampires in the Night Wing movies showed no interest in food. They hungered only for human blood.

Standing up, he felt a painful sensation on his butt. Reaching around, he discovered a hole in the backside of his khaki shorts, and inside that hole was a tender wound—a small burn caused by the lightning bolt punching through the Helmet Cam, which of course Derek didn't recall.

"It's a mark!" he exclaimed. "The mark of the undead!"

Actually it was the mark of the stupid, which is what you get for sitting under a tree during a thunderstorm. The jolt from the deflected lightning had frayed Derek's last fragile link to reality. Combined with the nagging effects of the bat infection, it had left him marooned in an imaginary underworld where evil night creepers roamed.

"I *must* resist," he whispered to himself.

Dizzily he made his way out of the trees to the place where he'd grounded the airboat. With dismay he saw it was now full of rainwater, way too heavy to move. A leopard frog swam happy circles between the seats. Derek felt no urge to snack on it. He shivered from the remains of his fever and returned to the shelter of the woods.

In *Revenge of the Blood Moon*, the last of the Night Wing series, Dax Mangold took refuge in Slackjaw Forest, where he constructed a sleeping platform in the boughs of a towering wing nut tree in order to be safe from prowling critters.

Derek had used a similar platform during an episode of *Expedition Survival!* in Sumatra. The structure had been built by local villagers and not by Derek himself, contrary to what he'd told his TV audience. Derek had been snoozing in an air-conditioned hotel suite two hundred miles away while the treetop hammock was being erected, so he had no idea how it should be done.

Now, out of options, he flopped down on the soggy ground. Gingerly he probed inside his mouth—still no bat fangs, although he was pleased to discover that his tongue was nearly back to its normal size. His limbs continued to tingle electrically even as he let himself drift toward sleep. He needed to be rested by nightfall and ready to roam.

Mickey Cray wasn't thrilled to have a gun pointing at him. It had happened before, late one night when he was getting money from an ATM outside a bank. A young man in a slime-green hoodie stuck a pistol in Mickey's ribs and demanded cash. Mickey gave him all he had—seventy-five dollars—and the robber hopped in a car and sped off.

He didn't know Mickey was following. He found out later when he awoke in his apartment with a strange hand around his throat. The muscles in Mickey's fingers were extremely strong from handling pythons and boa constrictors, and the robber was having an awful time trying to breathe.

"Give me back my money," Mickey advised.

The gasping kid pointed to a pair of jeans on the floor, in which Mickey found his seventy-five bucks.

"Now the gun," Mickey said to the robber, who coughed up the fact that the weapon was stashed beneath the bed.

Mickey confiscated the pistol, which he later tossed in a lake. "Where you from?" he asked the kid.

"West Virginia."

"Go back," Mickey said. "I mean first thing tomorrow."

"Seriously?"

"Unless you want me to come here with the cops. Also, I went through your wallet and found your mother's name."

"Leave her out of this!" the robber pleaded.

"Safe travels, then," said Mickey.

Now, steering the airboat through a driving rain, Mickey doubted that Tuna's father would be as sensible as the young robber. Jared Gordon had already fired his gun recklessly, once when he shot at the other airboat back at the dock and again at a floating gator that Mickey had recognized as Old Sleepy, Sickler's stuffed tourist decoy.

Mickey didn't doubt that Jared Gordon would use the pistol again if the urge came over him. That was a problem when dealing with drunks. They weren't rational.

Under different circumstances, Mickey would have put the airboat into a steep turn to throw the man overboard. However, Tuna's dad had used his belt to strap himself upright to the driver's platform, where he could keep the gun barrel pressed to Mickey's neck. He kept his finger on the trigger, too, which meant that Mickey had to be extra careful. The situation called for patience, which was not Mickey's strong suit.

The truth was he didn't like guns, period. He seldom carried one and, when he did, often didn't bother to load it. At the moment, his own pistol was under the front seat of his truck back at Sickler's place. For once, Mickey wished he'd brought it with him.

"Where are they? Where'd they go?" hollered Jared Gordon, spitting through the raindrops.

Mickey said, "It's a big swamp, brother."

He felt lucky his captor had been looking the wrong direction when they'd whisked past the other airboat, Wahoo waving at them. Jared Gordon hadn't seen a thing, so Mickey just kept driving. By now they must have traveled several miles, giving Link enough time to take the kids back to Sickler's dock. The police would be arriving soon, if they weren't already there.

"Okay, hotshot, slow down!" Tuna's dad commanded hoarsely.

Mickey stopped the boat. Jared Gordon unhitched himself from the driver's seat and threw up over the side, somehow keeping the handgun aimed at Mickey.

"Gimme a beer," he said, wiping his mouth on the sleeve of his Bills jersey.

"Sure," said Mickey.

Before hijacking one of the search boats and giving chase, Jared Gordon had dragged Mickey back to Sickler's store and swiped a cold twelve-pack. That's why Link and the kids had gotten such a good head start.

"Why's your daughter running from you?" Mickey asked, as if he didn't know.

" 'Cause she forgot who's the boss, that's why."

"She looked pretty scared to me."

"Ha!" Jared Gordon took a swig of beer. "It's called respect."

"What's your line of work?"

"Security. That's how I got a carry permit for this bad boy." He was referring to the revolver. "Right now I'm sorta between jobs. Hey, you hear somethin'?"

"Nope," said Mickey Cray, which was untrue. He heard the sound of another big engine. Maybe it was the police coming, or maybe it was . . . Link?

But that didn't make sense—chasing after a gunman who was chasing *you*. Not with two kids on board.

Link was no Einstein, Mickey thought, but he wasn't a total blockhead.

"It's just the weather you heard," Mickey said to Tuna's father.

"Naw, that wasn't no thunder."

Quickly Mickey started up the airboat in order to drown out any other sounds.

Tuna's father lobbed the empty beer can into the water. Mickey usually had harsh words for litterbugs, but this time he said nothing. The gun was definitely a game changer.

"It came from over there," Jared Gordon insisted. "Go thataway."

"You're the navigator," said Mickey.

His plan was to go the opposite direction of the second airboat, in case it was Link and the kids. He wanted to keep Tuna's father as far from them as possible, so he set off driving in an extravagant figure eight. Soon Jared Gordon got suspicious.

"No, I said, *that* way!" He twisted the gun barrel painfully into Mickey's flesh.

They were riding nearly blind through the rain, which was hairy but at the same time helpful to Mickey's strategy. In clear, calm conditions, the other boat would have been too easy to hear, and to follow. Tuna's dad would have figured out right away that Mickey was giving him the runaround.

"I can't see nuthin'!" Jared Gordon shouted.

"Join the club."

That's when they struck a cypress log and flew from the water, reminding Mickey of what crusty old Everglades poachers used to say about such mishaps:

Why do you think they call 'em airboats?

"How are you feeling?" Wahoo asked Link.

"I kin drive."

Tuna spoke up. "No, you can't. Not with a bullet hole in your back."

Wahoo agreed. Link was weak and shaky.

"Can you teach me how?" Wahoo asked.

"Not if you're as thick as your pappy."

"The guy who shot you just went by us in another boat, and he's got my dad as a hostage."

Wahoo knew Link wasn't fond of Mickey Cray, so he watched his reaction closely.

"The man that shot me? Where?" Link peered out across the wet savanna.

Tuna said grimly, "The one and only Jared Gordon. My pappy."

Link nodded. He didn't ask about Mickey.

"Git up there and drive," he told Wahoo. "Foot pedal is for gas. Stick is for steerin'."

"Where's the brakes?" asked Tuna.

"Ain't no brakes," Link said.

Until then, the fastest thing that Wahoo had ever driven was the creaky old golf cart that his father used for hauling supplies to the animal pens. An airboat was five times faster, louder and harder to handle. The rudder stick worked awkwardly compared to a steering wheel, and Wahoo struggled to master the feel. After several stalls and jerky starts, he finally got the boat planed off evenly.

"Which way dey go?" Link shouted.

Tuna pointed out the matted trail made by the other airboat. Wahoo headed in that direction, but he was careful to take it easy on the gas pedal. He had no idea what they'd do if they caught up to Jared Gordon. He hadn't thought that far ahead.

From the driver's platform, he could see better than Link and Tuna, and soon he forgot about being nervous. The sensation of gliding across wild water was thrilling, better than any theme-park ride. He didn't mind the sting of raindrops on his face or even the ear-pounding roar of the big engine. Whenever he needed to move the steering stick, the airboat turned as fluidly as a hawk in flight. Wahoo felt totally in control and totally focused.

They tracked the other boat's watery path until the saw grass gave way to a wide, lily-covered pond. With one arm Link made a stirring motion, so Wahoo began to steer in ever-widening circles, searching for signs of Jared Gordon.

Lightning crackled overhead, and Link turned toward the flash. "Bad" was all he said.

Wahoo read his lips and nodded. It was dangerous to stay exposed on the marsh prairie during a violent storm: in a split second they could all be fried.

The next lightning bolt produced a thunderclap that sounded like a bomb. Tuna let out a frightened cry, and Wahoo stomped on the accelerator.

"We're getting off the water!" he yelled.

They barely made it. The engine blew a piston and died just as they were closing in on an island. Under a pelting deluge, the airboat coasted sluggishly to the bank.

Within minutes the three of them were huddled under an oilskin tarp that Link found in a dry box bolted beneath the seats. By pure luck, they'd landed at the flat scrubby end of the tree island, a safe distance from the forty-foot cypresses that might attract lightning strikes.

Dejectedly, Wahoo said, "I can't believe I cooked the motor."

"Wasn't you," Link muttered. "That Bradley Jumper, he don't take good care of his 'quipment."

"Did you bring a phone?"

They were a long way from a cell tower, but Wahoo thought it was worth a try. Link dug into a pocket and retrieved a flip-top cellular that turned out to be waterlogged—and useless.

Tuna eyed it gloomily. "I hope you got insurance, dude."

Link was shivering. He had no shirt, and the rain had soaked through his trousers. Wahoo took off the slick *Expedition Survival!* jacket that Raven Stark had given him.

"Here, put this on," he said.

The jacket was way too tight and the sleeves were short, but Link was grateful. He reached back and fingered the gauze that Wahoo had taped over the bullet wound.

Then he turned slowly to Tuna. "Why'd your pappy try'n kill me?"

"It wasn't you, Link. He was just shootin' wild, like a whacked-out fool."

Then, in a rueful voice, she added: "He promised me on a stack of Bibles that he pawned that stupid gun. Obviously he lied."

Wahoo couldn't shake the image of Jared Gordon holding the revolver to his father's neck as their airboat sped by. The guy was definitely out of control.

And, thanks to the falling iguana, Mickey Cray wasn't his usual indestructible self. One of those crushing headaches could dull his reflexes—and his judgment. Worse, a spell of double vision might cause him to crash the boat.

Wahoo tried not to dwell on the dire possibilities. He knew the storm had reduced to almost zero the odds of catching up with his father before something serious happened.

Link said, "I cain't breathe so good."

Every time he inhaled, they heard a rasping in his chest. Wahoo wondered if a fragment of the bullet slug had punctured a lung. If so, there was only one thing to do: as soon as the weather cleared, they had to rush Link back to Sickler's place for medical help.

Leaving Mickey Cray alone to deal with Tuna's crazed father, somewhere out in the boggy wilderness.

"Lookie here," said Tuna, plucking a cocoa-striped snail from a bush. "This would be the lovely *Liguus fasciatus*."

In spite of everything, Wahoo had to smile. "You're too much, Lucille."

The wind yanked at the corners of the oilskin while the rain drummed down. Another boom of thunder made them all flinch at once.

"I'm gone pray," Link wheezed.

Tuna patted his arm. "Excellent plan," she said.

TWENTY-TWO

Raven Stark occasionally puzzled over her loyalty to Derek Badger, who was bossy and demanding, and who didn't appreciate all her hard work. But she was a team player, and she took personal pride in the success of *Expedition Survival!* As exasperating and childish as Derek could be, he was still the star—and her main responsibility.

"Never heard of him," said the police sergeant, whose name was Ramirez.

"Are you serious?" Raven asked.

"I don't watch kiddie TV."

"It's not 'kiddie' TV. Fifty-seven percent of our viewers are adults!"

They were sitting inside Derek's motor coach, sipping coffee, hoping for the weather to clear so that a proper search could begin. Every passing minute was frustrating for Raven, knowing Derek was alone somewhere in the wilderness. Given his lame sense of direction, he had virtually no chance of finding his own way back to civilization.

"I understand your concern," Sergeant Ramirez said, "but we've got a violent suspect out there who's holding at least one hostage. That's our first priority: catch the guy before somebody gets hurt."

In her heart, Raven knew the policeman was right.

Derek had run off on his own, but Mickey Cray had been kidnapped against his will. And those two kids—what if the gunman caught up with them?

It's a disaster, Raven thought.

The Everglades show was in chaos, completely out of control. *Real* reality had thwarted TV reality.

A local news crew had shown up at Sickler's place five minutes behind the police, and by tomorrow an army of media would be camped outside. The director and the cameramen were making morbid bets on how long it would take for Derek's body to be found. What else could go wrong?

Meanwhile, back in California, Raven's boss didn't seem to be losing much sleep over his star's disappearance. It was show business, after all. Anybody, no matter how famous, can be replaced. Raven knew the cold-blooded rules of the game.

Ever since signing on with *Expedition Survival!*, she'd hoped to someday become a big-time TV producer, like Gerry Germaine. Now that dream would likely never come true, thanks to Derek's latest fiasco. The script had said nothing about eating a bat!

Raven partly blamed herself. Who knew Derek better than she did? The man would do anything to shock his audience and to make himself appear fearless.

In truth, Raven wasn't totally crushed that she'd lost her opportunity to become a producer. Being stuck in a Hollywood office all day long—taking meetings, yakking on the telephone—it didn't sound like loads of fun.

Coddling an egomaniac like Derek was a chore, but Raven did enjoy traveling to exotic locations and working outdoors. Maybe another job like that would open up at a different network.

"This particular individual, Jared Gordon, we busted him a year ago for a DUI," the police sergeant was saying. "He tried to punch one of our officers and got himself Tased."

Raven said, "His daughter had a black eye when she got here. I think she's running from him." It was something the authorities should know.

"The witnesses said he stunk of beer," Sergeant Ramirez remarked. "He also stole a twelve-pack from Mr. Sickler's store. Alcohol and firearms—not a good combination."

The sergeant kept peering out a window to see if the rain was letting up. "Soon as we catch a break, we'll get the chopper airborne," he said. "Who knows—maybe they'll come across Mr. Beaver while they're looking for the others."

"It's *Badger*," Raven said.

"I never met a 'survivalist.' How do you get a job like that, anyway?"

She smiled wanly. "First you need a TV show."

The more she thought about it, the more ashamed she felt for suggesting to the police that finding Derek was more urgent than capturing the dangerous Jared Gordon.

"What do you know about the hostage?" Sergeant Ramirez asked.

"See for yourself," Raven said. She placed a disk into the

DVD machine and played the uncut footage of Derek being thrashed by Alice, the wrangler's giant alligator.

The sergeant was fascinated. "Who's the chubby dude with the orange hair?"

"That would be Mr. Badger."

"And the crazy guy who jumped in to save him?"

"That's Mr. Cray. The one who got kidnapped by the gunman."

Sergeant Ramirez cocked an eyebrow. "Could I see the video again?"

"Certainly."

They watched the gator scene two more times. Afterward, Sergeant Ramirez said, "Wow. That Cray dude has no fear."

"He's an unusual person," Raven agreed.

The sergeant put down his coffee cup. "I'm betting Jared Gordon's got his hands full right now. What do you think?"

After T-boning the cypress log, the airboat crashed upside down in the grassy flats. Mickey Cray landed on a natural cushion of cattails ten yards away. Surprisingly, his head didn't ache, and his vision was perfect.

When he saw the wrecked boat, he felt sure that Tuna's father was either dead or badly injured—but he was wrong. Jared Gordon clambered from beneath the overturned hull and trained his pistol on Mickey.

"Don't you move!"

"Anything you say, brother."

"Come grab the beer!"

Jared Gordon had chipped a front tooth but otherwise was unhurt. The leather belt with which he'd strapped himself to the driver's platform had held tight, saving him from being thrown under the weight of the boat. Mickey was amazed that the man had hung on to the gun.

"Let's go!" Jared Gordon snapped.

"Take it easy."

Together they set out through stinging rain in search of high ground. Mickey led the way, lugging the carton of beer. Overhead the sky continued to flash and quake.

The muck was so thick that it sucked the boots off their feet. Jared Gordon staggered and cussed, then staggered some more. Mickey kept watching for an opportunity to snatch the revolver, but not once did Jared Gordon fall. It was very discouraging.

After an hour, the lightning stopped and the downpour let up. They came upon an elevated ridge of hardwoods, and Tuna's father insisted on stopping for "an adult beverage."

Mickey handed him a beer, which he chugged down hastily. He signaled for another and asked, "Now what?"

"We wait."

"For what?"

"Help."

"I don't need help," Jared Gordon said. "I need to find my little girl."

"Can you walk on water?"

"What're you talkin' 'bout? Course I can't walk on water."

"Me neither," said Mickey, "which means we're stranded."

Tuna's father waggled the gun menacingly. "Oh no, we ain't."

"What—you expect me to carry you through the mud? Like a baby?"

"If that's what it takes."

"Not happening, amigo."

"Huh?" It dawned on Jared Gordon that his captive wasn't particularly afraid, despite the threat of a loaded weapon.

"Without me," Mickey said, "you'll never find your way out of here. You'll croak in this swamp—lost, drunk and all by your lonesome. That's a fact."

Even on a good day, Jared Gordon's brain didn't run like a smoothly oiled machine. And today wasn't a good day; it was a rotten day. He decided to show Mickey Cray that he meant business.

"Git down on your belly," he said.

"Why?"

"Just do it."

Mickey had been thinking hard about his situation and the smartest way to handle it. His main mission was to prevent Tuna's father from finding Tuna and Wahoo, wherever they might be. For that reason, Mickey couldn't afford to do something dumb and get himself shot. Until the police arrived, he was the only one standing between Jared Gordon and those two kids.

So, reluctantly, he did as he was told. In the wet grass he lay down, prepared to roll away violently if the man began firing at him.

However, Jared Gordon stepped off in another direction.

"Look here," he said, and leveled the pistol at a tall white heron in the reeds.

Mickey raised his head. "Hey, don't do that. I'll catch us some fish."

"Ha! This ain't about lunch."

It required every bit of Mickey's self-control for him to remain still while Jared Gordon took aim. Herons were wondrous birds, sly and elegant stalkers of minnows. A curious young male sometimes visited the pond of the Everglades set behind the Crays' house—Wahoo had named it Harry.

"What the bleep are you trying to prove?" Mickey said.

"Shut up." Tuna's father pulled the trigger and a single shot echoed.

The white heron flew away, squawking indignantly.

"Damn," Jared Gordon muttered, lowering the gun.

Mickey thought: *Good. Only three bullets left.*

The rain eased to a drizzle and the thunder faded. Wahoo and Tuna couldn't sit still anymore. They left Link resting under the tarp and ventured out to explore the island.

"Stay quiet," Wahoo whispered.

"Duh," said Tuna.

With caution they picked their way through underbrush.

Wahoo spotted a patch of poison ivy and detoured around it. The first major sign of life—and death—was a Burmese python coiled around a limp purple gallinule. The python was only a seven-footer, much smaller than Beulah, but still the bird had no chance.

Tuna stopped as if she'd walked into a brick wall. Never had she witnessed such a scene in person—only on TV nature programs. Unable to identify the reptile, she wanted to look it up in one of the field guides in her tote bag.

"No, let's keep going," Wahoo said.

"It won't come after us later?"

"Don't worry, Lucille. We're not on the menu."

He could see she was rattled. Memorizing the scientific names of wild species wasn't the same thing as entering their world. The bird had died so that the snake wouldn't starve.

"Pretty brutal," Tuna said.

"Humans can be worse. They do things out of pure meanness."

"Tell me about it."

Wahoo heard the pain in her words. "I didn't mean it that way," he said.

"No big deal. Daddy is what he is."

They circled the feeding python and moved on. Tuna's flip-flops kept sticking in the mud, so she kicked them off. Because of the heavy downpour, the borders of the tree island had shrunk with the rising water. Wahoo pointed out a drag mark where a hefty gator had crawled up on the bank to sleep.

"Where's he at now?" Tuna asked, looking around.

"Stop worrying."

"I am *not* worried."

Wahoo was the first to spy the empty airboat, its propeller blade showing through a gash in the cattails. He crouched low and pulled Tuna close.

"Is it them?" she whispered anxiously.

"I don't know. Stay here while I check it out."

"No way."

"I'm serious," Wahoo said.

"Me too, Lance. I go where you go."

They approached with cat-like caution. Tuna's legs were speckled with mosquitoes, but she didn't dare slap at them for fear of being heard. Wahoo listened intently for voices—especially his father's. The woods remained silent except for the murmur of raindrops on the leaves.

Wahoo halted a few feet behind the beached airboat. "Wrong color," he said.

The one that Tuna's father hijacked had a glam sparkle-green hull. This boat was hand-painted in dull camo colors.

"It's Link's!" Tuna said with relief. "The one Derek took."

From deep in the underbrush came a grunt, followed by an odd, quavering chant.

Wahoo edged closer. "Mr. Badger?"

"Go away, mate!" The bogus Steve Irwin accent was unmistakable. *Gah why, mite!*

"It's totally him," whispered Tuna.

The off-key chanting resumed: "*Eee-ka-laro! Eee-ka-laro! Gumbo mucho eee-ka-laro.*"

"Are you hurt?" Tuna called.

"Get lost!" Derek barked. "If you know what's bloody good for you!"

Tuna followed Wahoo toward the hoarse voice in the woods. They came upon the TV star scrambling awkwardly up a Brazilian peppertree. The punctured Helmet Cam sat crookedly on his head, and a burn hole was visible in his shorts. He looked haggard and wild-eyed.

"Come on down from there," Wahoo said.

"No! I've got the curse!"

"What curse?" Tuna asked.

"Run for your lives, both of you! Chop-chop!"

Wahoo said, "We need that airboat, Mr. Badger."

"Are you blind, boy? The bloody thing's full of water."

"You're going to help us bail it out."

"Just leave me alone!"

"Take it easy up there," Tuna advised. This was her second up close encounter with the legendary survivalist—the first being his botched attempt at bat eating—and so far she hadn't been dazzled. He certainly wasn't much of a climber.

"*Eee-ka-laro! Eee-ka-laro! Gumbo mucho eee-ka-laro!*" he yowled from the peppertree.

Wahoo threw up his hands. "Who has time for this?"

"It's the curse of the undead!" Derek decreed hoarsely.

More like the curse of the unglued, thought Wahoo.

They heard a sharp pop, like a car backfiring. Then a heron began to screech.

Tuna spun around. "Was that a—?"

"Gun. Yeah." Wahoo tensed. They were downwind from the shooter, although the distance was difficult to guess. One hundred yards? Two hundred?

Something tumbled through the branches and landed with a thud at Tuna's feet. It was the battered Helmet Cam.

"Help me!" cried Derek Badger, suddenly with no trace of Australia in his voice.

He was dangling upside down, arms flailing, one fleshy leg hooked over a bough that was plainly too thin to support his tubbiness.

"Are you shot?" Tuna yelled. "Hang on tight!"

"Somebody catch me!"

"Uh-oh," said Wahoo, tugging Tuna out of the way. "He's gonna fall."

And fall he did.

TWENTY-THREE

Mickey Cray's plan wasn't complicated: trick Jared Gordon into wasting his last three bullets, then jump him.

"Hear that?" Mickey asked with false excitement.

"I don't hear nuthin'," Jared Gordon grumped.

They were slopping across the flats, following a line of scrubby trees. Once the rain had slacked off, Jared Gordon had become restless and insisted they continue moving. Mickey had tried to stall, saying that the chances of finding Tuna were about a million to one since they no longer had an airboat to carry them across the marsh.

Jared Gordon refused to be persuaded, his logic having been hopelessly polluted by beer. He was on a mission to catch and punish his runaway daughter.

"Wait!" Mickey put a finger to his lips. "You hear it now?"

Jared Gordon shook his head.

"Sounds like a bear."

"Aw, no way," scoffed Jared Gordon.

"Seriously. Sickler said this place is crawlin' with 'em."

"Bears?"

Mickey dramatically dropped to one knee. "There! Over in those bay trees."

Jared Gordon craned his neck, but he couldn't see a bear or any other varmint. His mouth was as dry as sawdust.

"Is it a big one?" he asked Mickey.

"How good are you with that gun, brother?"

"Jest show me where he's at."

Mickey pointed. "See those branches moving?"

"Yeah!"

There were branches moving everywhere, of course. It was only the wind.

"Go ahead—take a shot!" Mickey urged. "Even if you don't hit him, you'll scare him off."

"You say so." Jared Gordon fired.

The slug pinged harmlessly through the trees.

"Aim six feet to the right," Mickey instructed.

"No sweat." Tuna's father pulled the trigger again.

"See that? You got him on the run!"

"Not for long!" Jared Gordon took his third and final shot.

As the echo of the gunfire died, Mickey rose up and said, "That's darn good shootin'."

"You sure he's gone? Better go have a look."

"Oh, he's gone. Don't worry." Mickey was already eyeing the pistol.

"I'll wait here," said Jared Gordon, stepping back.

Mickey played along. He entered the cluster of bay trees and pretended to scout for tracks. He didn't mind stringing out the act a little longer. His plan had worked perfectly—Tuna's father had emptied the gun at an imaginary beast. Finally it was safe for Mickey to take control and put an end to Jared Gordon's nonsense.

He returned to the clearing and said, "Nice job, brother. That poor critter's halfway to Shark River by now."

Tuna's father wore a smug grin that featured his jagged front tooth. "I told you I was good!"

"Well, you weren't lyin'," Mickey said, but the words trailed off in dejection.

He was staring at Jared Gordon's left hand. It held six shiny new bullets, which Jared Gordon loaded one by one into the cylinder of his revolver.

"I always keep a handful of spares," he said, "jest in case." He clicked the gun shut and raised the barrel. "Okay, Sparky, let's get movin' 'fore the rain kicks up again."

Mickey Cray nodded heavily. "Onward," he muttered.

For once in Derek Badger's show-business career, being chubby turned out to be a blessing. The flab cushioned his fall from the Brazilian peppertree.

"I'm alive!" he gasped, his accent still missing in action. He lay flat on a spongy bed of wet leaves and stared up at the two pesky kids, who stared back.

"You are definitely alive," Wahoo confirmed.

"Did I break my neck?"

"I think you'd notice," Tuna said.

Derek was a mess. Without his TV makeup and spray-on tan, he displayed all the vivid damage from the Everglades fiasco—the nicked nose from the snapping turtle; the tooth marks on his chin, arms and thumb from the water snake;

the scabbed lip and skinned knees from his wrestling match with Alice; the angry rash from the poison ivy; the punctured tongue from his bat encounter.

"Where's Raven? Oh, never mind." Derek sat up.

Wahoo said, "We need to go. Link's been shot and my dad's in trouble."

"No, *you* need to go," said Derek, "before the sun sets."

"What are you talking about?"

"Get out of here, both of you! I've got the dark curse, don't you see?" His gaze settled on Tuna's canvas tote. "Hey, you wouldn't happen to have a bottle of sparkling mineral water?"

"Why'd you run away from camp?" she asked.

Derek struggled to his feet. "Because I was savagely attacked by a vampire bat. You know what that means."

"What attack?" Wahoo said. "It bit you because you tried to eat it."

Tuna added, "It wasn't a vampire bat, Mr. Badger, it was a mastiff. The scientific classification is *Eumops glaucinus floridanus*."

"Which translates to what in the King's English—'hairy bloodsucking fiend'?"

"So what's this 'curse'?" Wahoo asked.

In an icy whisper, Derek replied, "The same one as Dax Mangold got. *That* curse."

Wahoo turned quizzically to Tuna, who said, "Oh-my-God."

"What?"

"The Night Wing Trilogy."

Derek nodded. "Exactly! You know what happens next!"

"Okay, I give up," Wahoo said impatiently. "What's the Night Wing Trilogy?"

Tuna's review was harsh: "I barely got through the first book. It was the stupidest thing I've ever read."

"The movie was a classic!" Derek protested.

"Wall-to-wall vampires," Tuna went on. "Vampire short-stops, vampire cheerleaders, even a vampire beagle. I'll spare you the plot."

"This isn't funny. We need to go, like *now*." Wahoo kept thinking about the lone gunshot they'd heard earlier. Had it been a signal? Or had Jared Gordon shot at Wahoo's dad?

Derek tilted his stubbled chin toward the clouds. "What time is it?"

"Time to get real. You're not a vampire." Wahoo reached for Derek's arm, but he ducked away.

"How long until dark?" he asked anxiously. "Will there be a moon?"

Tuna rolled her eyes.

"Mr. Badger, if you don't knock it off," she said, "I'm going on your Facebook page and rat you out big-time. I'll tell all your fans how you got lost in the Everglades and started whining like an epic crybaby. I'll tell about your bogus parachute jump and the bat on your tongue and the puny little water snake that almost gave you a heart at-tack and how you can't even climb a tree, you're such a pitiful phony. Is that something you want the whole world to know?"

Derek paled. "Hold on, sweetie, don't get your knickers in a knot. I'll help you with the boat."

The lightning zap had not scrambled Derek's senses so much that he couldn't recognize a serious threat to his stardom. Regardless of whether he was destined to become one of the undead, he wanted to keep his reputation—and his TV show. How else could he afford the payments on his magnificent *Sea Badger*, the yacht of his dreams? As spacey as he was at the moment, Derek still understood that he could never, ever go back to being Lee Bluepenny, unknown Irish folk dancer.

"Just start walking," said Wahoo. They'd wasted too much time already. His dad's life was in danger, and this nutcase was yammering about weird curses and vampires.

A close examination of Link's airboat proved disappointing. From bow to stern it brimmed with rainwater. Wahoo located a rusty drain plug in the transom, but the release lever broke off in his fingers. The hole in the Helmet Cam made it useless as a bucket, so they were forced to bail with their hands.

Derek proved worthless as a helper. He dribbled more than he scooped, complaining all the while. Ruefully Tuna thought of all the hours she'd spent glued to episodes of *Expedition Survival!*, even the Sunday repeats. She felt like a fool for ever thinking Derek's adventures—and his ruggedness—were real. He was no tough guy; he was just a Hollywood fake.

And obviously a whack job, if he really believed in vampires. Tuna no longer had any desire for an autograph.

Meanwhile, Wahoo bailed furiously. If they could lighten the weight in the hull, they might be able to slide it off the bank and into the shallows. An airboat like Link's could float in only three or four inches of water. The next challenge would be getting the engine started.

"Mates, I need a break," Derek said wearily.

Tuna snorted. "Oh please. You think Dax Mangold would take a break?"

Wahoo noticed that Derek didn't look too lively. His forehead was pink and beaded with sweat, as if from a fever. Although he'd received first aid at the base camp, it was possible that he'd still gotten an infection from the bat bite. That had happened a few times to Mickey Cray after being chomped by various critters.

"Take a rest," Wahoo said to Derek, who nodded gratefully and sprawled next to the boat.

"Here," he said, and handed one of his "survival" soda straws to Wahoo. It was imprinted with a tiny likeness of Derek's signature. "Use it as a siphon," he suggested.

Wahoo wasn't sarcastic by nature, but this straw was, literally, the last straw. "Gosh, I'll cherish it always," he said thinly, and flicked it away.

With her hands, Tuna ladled another cup-sized portion

of water over the side of the boat. "This is gonna take forever, Lance. You get that, right?"

Wahoo refused to become discouraged. The airboat was their only means of finding his father and Jared Gordon before something bad happened.

If it hadn't happened already.

And if Link's medical condition didn't take a turn for the worse—in which case, they'd need the boat to haul him straight to the mainland. Mickey Cray would be on his own.

Don't think that way, Wahoo told himself. *Stay positive.*

It wasn't easy. He was the one who'd talked his dad into taking the *Expedition Survival!* job, and he was the one who *had* talked him out of quitting when quitting would have been the smart thing to do.

Tuna lowered her voice so Derek wouldn't hear. "I'm really sorry for all this. You don't know how sorry."

"It's not your fault," Wahoo said.

"I'm the one who dragged you guys into this mess. I should never have run away. I should've stayed and hidden at the Walmart."

"What are you talking about?"

"The garden department is immense. It would take Daddy a week to find me in there."

"Okay, that's just crazy," Wahoo said.

Between the two of them, water was flying out of the boat in all directions.

Tuna clenched her jaw, fighting back tears. "I never thought he'd shoot a person. Not in a million years."

"Maybe it was an accident, like you said."

"No, he's totally gone off the deep end. What if he kills someone, Lance?"

Wahoo didn't look up. "My father can take care of himself."

"Well, my father . . ." Tuna laughed bitterly. "My father can't take care of breakfast—"

Three more shots rang out, one after the other. Wahoo and Tuna stopped bailing and turned to listen. Derek, who was dozing, didn't stir.

"How far?" Tuna whispered.

"Closer than before."

Most likely, the gunfire was coming from Jared Gordon. Maybe a bobcat or a python had crossed his path—or maybe Mickey Cray was trying to escape. The thought made Wahoo's stomach pitch.

A gust of wind brought a faint, swirling fragment of human conversation. They were male voices, two of them, which likely meant Mickey was still alive—at least that's what Wahoo elected to believe.

Had to believe.

"Sounds like they're heading this way," he said to Tuna.

Derek woke up and asked what was going on.

"We need to hide," Wahoo told him. "Let's move."

"Hide from what? Vampires?"

"Worse," said Tuna. "Lead the way, Lance."

TWENTY-FOUR

Once the weather began to improve, Sergeant Ramirez sent the searchers into action. Four airboats, each with a police officer aboard, departed at high speed from Sickler's dock. A sheriff's helicopter carrying infrared equipment was flying in from South Miami, and the Coast Guard was sending a chopper from Opa-locka.

Meanwhile, Raven Stark had locked herself in Derek Badger's motor coach in order to hide from a throng of news reporters who'd learned that the famed survivalist was missing in the Everglades. The reporters were trying to make a connection between Derek's disappearance and the "crazed gunman" who'd terrorized the crowd at Sickler's store, but a spokesperson for the police department said the two incidents were totally unrelated.

The media frenzy got even more stirred up by the director of *Expedition Survival!* He blabbed to a tabloid columnist about Derek's bloody encounter with the mastiff bat, sparking speculation that Derek had been stricken with rabies and was dying alone in the murky wetlands. Thousands of frantic fans posted messages on Derek's Facebook page and Tweeted anxiously among themselves.

Raven was miffed at the director, but, back at his office in California, Gerry Germaine remained unfazed. The executive producer believed that the publicity surrounding Derek's predicament—no matter what happened—would increase the TV audience for *Expedition Survival!* That would lead to higher advertising rates, which would lead to bigger profits for the Untamed Channel.

In the semi-tragic event that Derek indeed perished from rabies (or some other tropical disease), Gerry Germaine was preparing to broadcast a two-hour tribute, with highlight reels. The ratings would be epic from coast to coast.

"Let's release a statement to the media," said Raven, "saying we're confident that Derek, being such a skilled outdoorsman, is alive and well."

"Not so fast," Gerry Germaine cautioned. "It isn't such a terrible thing to have the whole world worrying about him. Remember those trapped miners down in Chile? When they got out, they were total rock stars."

The comparison was flimsy. The Chilean coal miners had been true survivalists, the real deal. Derek Badger wouldn't have lasted twenty-four hours in that cold black hole without losing his marbles, as both Raven and her boss knew.

"It'll be getting dark here soon," she said. "That will slow down the search."

"Hmmm." Gerry Germaine was cleaning his fingernails with a sterling silver letter opener. Engraved with his initials, it had been a gift from one of *Expedition Survival!*'s biggest sponsors, the company responsible for Pit Power, an underarm deodorant for "the raw adventurer in all of us." Derek Badger refused to endorse the product, saying it smelled like rotten mangoes.

"With a little luck, the cops will come across Derek before they track down this lunatic Gordon," Raven was saying. "If that happens, we're golden. Derek will be the top story on every newscast in America!"

Gerry Germaine agreed politely. "Raven, dear, have you ever seen this reality show from New Zealand called *Snake Diver*?"

"What does that even mean, 'snake diver'?"

"The star is a fellow named Brick Jeffers, and he's quite good on camera—witty, down-to-earth and seriously ripped. He does the blindfolded parachute entrance, like Derek, only for real. No stuntmen."

"What are you getting at, Gerry?"

"You know. Worst-case scenario?"

Raven was stunned. "You mean, if Derek doesn't make it out of the Everglades, this guy would replace him on *Expedition*? This Brick Jefferson snake-diving nobody?"

"The name is Jeffers. And we're flying him in from Auckland for an interview."

"I can't believe this!"

"Worst-case scenario, like I said. It makes sense to have a backup ready in case Derek can't do the show anymore."

"Like if he's dead, you mean."

"I'm just saying."

"Well, he's *not* dead," Raven asserted. "I just know it."

Gerry Germaine said, "Call me as soon as you hear something."

Then he hung up the phone and asked his secretary to make some calls. He wanted to know which restaurant in Beverly Hills served the tastiest New Zealand lamb chops.

Wahoo had more patience than his father did, but Derek Badger was pushing him to the limit.

"You call this a hiding place, mate?"

"Keep your voice down," Wahoo said.

They were hunkered in a thicket of sticky vines and coco plums. Derek wouldn't quit griping. He insisted his fever was worse. He prattled on about muscle cramps and strange tremors in his feet.

Tuna fished in her tote bag. "Here, try these." She handed him two of the same chalky pink tablets that she'd been giving to Wahoo's father.

"What's this?" Derek asked skeptically.

"Twenty milligrams of advanced formula Raguserup 2800."

"Ragu-what?" He made a face as he swallowed the tablets. Yet soon he stopped complaining about his aches and pains, and within an hour he was napping again.

Wahoo asked to see the bottle. "What kind of medicine is Raguserup? I definitely need to stock up on this for Pop."

Tuna laughed. "It's not medicine, Lance. It's just a sugar pill."

"What?"

"Seriously—I made up the name myself. It's *pure sugar*, spelled backward," she explained. "I even printed up a label for the bottle."

"I don't get it," Wahoo said.

"You ever heard of the placebo effect? That's when doctors test a new drug by giving it to half the sick patients, while the others get a placebo—a pill with no medicine, just sugar. Nobody knows who's on the real stuff and who's not, but here's the awesome part: some of the patients taking the bogus pills get better anyway. It never fails."

Tuna smiled and tapped a finger to her temple. "The mind's a powerful force for healing. If you believe something can cure you, it just might."

"But if the pills are only sugar, why do *you* need them?"

"Oh, I feed 'em to Daddy. Sometimes it quiets him down," Tuna said. "He gets lots of 'headaches,' too. And back pains, chest pains, neck pains, you name it. He thinks Raguserup is some sort of fantastic miracle drug. That, and the booze."

Wahoo was troubled to think his own father's symptoms were mostly mental and could be cured by fake medicine. "So, basically, both of our dads are whack jobs," he concluded glumly.

"Don't even go there," Tuna said sharply. "They couldn't be more different from each other."

She was right about that part. "I'd better go check on

Link," Wahoo said. "You okay staying here with Dracula Junior?"

"Aye, aye." She crossed her heart and gave a salute. "You go. We're good."

Quietly Wahoo slipped through the woods, pausing every few steps to listen. There had been no more random gunshots, no more voices on the breeze. Either the men they'd heard earlier had changed their course or the wind had switched directions, smothering the sounds of their conversation.

In his father's absence, Wahoo had come to feel responsible for the safety of everyone on the island—Derek, Link and especially Tuna. It was a new experience, being out of Mickey's shadow. Things looked different to Wahoo now that he was making the key decisions. Gut-check time, as his dad would say.

Link hadn't moved far from the glen where the kids had left him. He was sitting up, bare-chested, with Wahoo's *Expedition Survival!* jacket draped over his knees.

"I tried to walk," he said. "No gas in the tank."

He looked drained, and his breathing was still ragged. "Food?" he asked.

Wahoo was carrying half of a granola bar. He gave it to Link and said, "Good news. We found your airboat."

"Totaled?"

"Nope. Believe it or not, Derek didn't wreck it."

Link's expression was one of pure relief. "Miracle," he said.

Wahoo was glad the weather was breaking. Slices of clear sky were showing among the clouds.

"Did you hear those gunshots a while back?" he asked Link.

"Yep. Dey's a ways off."

"There were men talking, too."

Link shook his head. "All I heared was some owl."

Wahoo peeled back a corner of the bandage he had taped to Link's back. The bullet wound remained fairly clean, and there was no fresh blood.

"Still hurt when you take a breath?"

"Some," Link admitted.

"Worse than before?"

"Little."

Wahoo was practically certain that one of Link's lungs had been punctured. It was shocking that a little piece of lead could put down such an ox of a man.

"Hang in there," Wahoo told him. "We'll get you to a hospital."

"How far's my boat?"

"It's a hike. Just stay here and chill."

Link took a shallow gulp of air. "What 'bout the dude that shot me? The girl's old man."

"The police will catch him for sure. He'll be in jail soon."

"Jail?" Link grunted. "Das it?"

"Can I ask you something?" Wahoo said.

"Guess so."

"I know you don't like my dad, and that's okay. He can

be a pain. But the other day, when he was in the water and you were driving straight at him . . ."

Link hacked out a chuckle. "Heck, I only meant to scare the man is all. You think I's really gone run him over and put a big old dent in my airboat? No way."

"You sure fooled me and Tuna," Wahoo said.

"Not your pappy, though. He weren't one bit 'fraid."

Wahoo had to smile. "Don't go anywhere. I'll be back in a little while."

"You's just a kid. What you gone do?"

"Get us all out of here."

Link chuckled dryly again. "Here, take your jacket. It don't fit me anyhows."

"Listen!" Wahoo raised a finger in the air. "You hear *that*, right?"

"I do."

"Airboats! A bunch of 'em!"

A hopeful spark showed in Link's eyes.

"I was you," he said to Wahoo, "I'd start me a big ol' campfire."

The problem was—and Mickey Cray would be the first to admit it—he wasn't much of a "people" person. He preferred hanging out with animals (with the exception of his family, whom he adored unconditionally).

Because he spent so little time in social situations, Mickey wasn't good at behaving passively when the circumstance seemed to call for action. His experiences as an animal wrangler had taught him to respond on instinct—no fooling around. Psychology doesn't work when you're dealing with a stubborn six-hundred-pound gator or a cranky fourteen-foot python. The task calls for sure-footed commitment and quick reflexes, not mind games.

Mickey believed Jared Gordon's brain was less complicated than that of the average reptile. However, the average reptile didn't carry a loaded gun and guzzle beer.

"Gimme another one," Jared Gordon barked. "I'm a thirsty soul!"

He didn't seem to mind that the beer was as warm as spit. Most people would have been groggy after drinking so much, but he kept the pace, trudging along in Mickey's muddy footprints. Every time Mickey glanced over his shoulder, he saw the pistol pointed at his back.

"Don't try nuthin' funny," warned Tuna's father.

"Wouldn't dream of it."

They'd been hiking for a while, and soon the sun would be setting. Mickey hoped that by now Link had returned to Sickler's dock and that Wahoo and Tuna were safe.

A swarm of airboats could be heard in the distance— the search teams, fanning out across the marshes. It was a welcome sound, but Mickey wasn't ready to celebrate. Once darkness fell, the chances of being found would be slim. The Everglades by night was a tangled, boggy maze. Searchers would be relying on handheld spotlights and pure luck.

At the sound of the search boats, Tuna's father appeared to sober up. His shoulders pinched tensely and his steps got heavier.

"This ain't workin' out so good," he grumbled.

The plan to recapture his runaway daughter at gunpoint, which had seemed so brilliant in the early stages of Jared Gordon's beer binge, now looked like a big mistake.

"They'll catch up with us sooner or later," Mickey told him. "That's a fact."

"Why don't you shut up?"

Jared Gordon was no longer consumed with finding Tuna. He was focused on escape.

Sucking air through his teeth, he said, "Jest so you know—I ain't goin' to no prison."

"You are if they catch you with that .38."

"How far to the highway?"

"Too far," Mickey said. "Too far, too deep, too everything. We can't get there on foot."

Tuna's father jabbed him with the pistol barrel. "That's okay, Sparky. I always got a plan B."

"Does the B stand for 'brew'?"

"Ha! You're my ticket outta here and you don't even know it."

Mickey said, "There's no ticket out, brother. The cops know who you are."

"Don't matter. When they git here, I'm gonna make 'em a deal they can't refuse: your life for my freedom."

"You watch too many movies."

Jared Gordon was dead serious. "Like you say, they're bound to find us out here—if not tonight, then tomorrow for sure. And when they do, I'm gonna stick this gun to your fat head and tell 'em to give up one of their airboats or else. Which they will do, 'cause it'd make 'em look real bad if they just stood back and let me shoot you dead. Am I right?"

"Go on," said Mickey.

"Soon as we git a boat, you're gonna take me direct to the big road."

He was talking about U.S. Highway 41, the Tamiami Trail.

"Then what?"

"Then we say adios." Jared Gordon smirked at his own cleverness. "You drop me off on a nice, empty stretch, and I disappear like a ghost. Sneak away to the Bahamas, whatever. There's a place I saw on the Travel Channel called Harbour Island—you can ride horses on the beach. And the sand, they say it's the color of an Easter rose. I could seriously get used to that."

"What about your daughter?"

"Oh, I'll come back and deal with her later. She's the cause of all this trouble."

Mickey had no intention of letting Jared Gordon get away, but he played along.

He said, "We should stop and make a fire. They'll find us quicker that way."

"Fine by me, Sparky."

Not far ahead was a patch of hardwood trees that promised higher ground. When they got there, Mickey started searching for dry tinder. Most everything was still soggy from the long downpour, and the funky ground mulch had been disturbed by some type of animal activity. Mickey spied a single track in the dirt, and his heart began to thump against his ribs. It was a human footprint, belonging to a small person who wasn't wearing shoes. Mickey quickly smudged over the telltale mark with one of his boots.

To Tuna's father he said, "Too wet here. Let's look someplace else."

"It's wet *everywhere*. I'm sick of walkin'."

Mickey strained to hear the engines of the search boats. It was hard to tell if any of them had gotten closer.

Jared Gordon picked something off the ground and crowed, "Well, look here!"

He was waving a lime-colored flip-flop with rhinestones on the strap. Mickey didn't need to be told whose it was. He recognized it right away.

"What're the odds—like a million to one? Isn't that what you said?" Tuna's father was gloating. "But this here's her sandal, Sparky. That means she's around someplace, and I'm gonna git her. Million to one? Ha!"

The odds weren't really a million to one, as Mickey knew from studying Raven Stark's map. Within range of Sickler's dock were no more than a half-dozen tree islands, lush emerald groves rising from the pan-flat marsh. They were the most obvious places for a Glades traveler to seek cover, as well as solid ground.

But why did Link stop here? Mickey wondered. *Did his boat break down, or was there some sort of emergency?*

One chilling fact was clear: if Tuna was hiding on the island, so was Wahoo. He would have never left her alone. For Mickey, the stakes couldn't possibly get any higher. The kids were nearby. It was time to do something.

"Let's go find your girl," he said to Tuna's dad, and headed the opposite direction of where the small footprint had pointed.

Jared Gordon came up from behind and slapped the top of his head with Tuna's flip-flop. "Hey, you think I'm stupid or what? I got you figgered out."

Mickey balled his right fist. One solid punch to the jaw would knock the guy cold. He wouldn't have time to pull the trigger.

"I know what you're up to," Jared Gordon went on. "You wanna take me down, huh? You wanna be a hero."

Mickey shifted his balance. "I'm no hero. What're you talkin' about? Do I look like a hero?"

"Shut up and git your paws in the air."

"Why?"

"You got three seconds."

"That'll work," Mickey said.

He wheeled around, swinging hard, but the punch never got there.

TWENTY-FIVE

Wahoo smelled wood burning and wondered if Derek Badger had built a fire. Maybe even a lame TV survivalist could scrounge up some twigs for kindling.

But once he drew close enough to see the flames, Wahoo dropped flat and held motionless among the trees. Three figures were visible in the clearing, and Derek wasn't one of them. Tuna sat cross-legged on the ground, her curly-topped head bowed. Kneeling beside her was Mickey Cray, his brow bloodied and hands bound behind him with vines.

A stocky, stubble-cheeked man who Wahoo presumed was Tuna's father paced by the small campfire. In one hand was a revolver and in the other was a small green flip-flop, which he occasionally waggled over his head. Even from thirty yards, Wahoo could see well enough to put detailed features on the blank-faced attacker from his nightmare, the one who'd chased Tuna around the Walmart parking lot. In real life, Jared Gordon didn't look like a zombie monster; he looked like a loser with a mean streak.

The conversation rose and fell around the crackling flames. Wahoo could hear most of it. Jared Gordon's new plan was to escape with Tuna in Link's airboat, and he wanted Mickey to drive.

"We'll crash" was Mickey's raw response.

"And why's that?" Tuna's father demanded.

" 'Cause you brained me with your *pistole*, and now I'm seein' double."

"Ha! Nice try, Sparky."

Tuna looked up. "Mr. Cray's telling the truth, Daddy. He's had a concussion for months, and you just gave him another one."

Jared Gordon scowled. "He can still run the danged boat. Just go slow is all."

"Are you serious?" said Wahoo's father. "My head's about to split open."

"You want a bullet to finish the job?"

Mickey shrugged. "Couldn't feel any worse."

Again Tuna spoke up. "Daddy, just wait a little while for his vision to settle. Then he can take us to the highway."

Wahoo knew she was stalling for time, which was smart. Once darkness fell across the Glades, Mickey could steer the airboat in circles and Jared Gordon probably wouldn't know the difference.

"Hey, I got an idea." Jared Gordon kneed his daughter in the back. "Give 'im some of your magic pink pills."

Tuna didn't react. She made eye contact with Mickey, who said, "Sure, why not?"

There were four tablets left, and Wahoo's dad swallowed them dry. Jared Gordon tossed away the telltale flip-flop and plopped down to wait, as fidgety as a bug.

To Tuna he said, "I still can't believe you run off the way

you did. This is the thanks I get after all these years? You sneak off in the night?"

The girl's response was a whisper, but Wahoo clearly heard Mickey weigh in:

"Say, Gordon, you must be proud of that shiner you gave her. Tell me—what kind of sorry-ass excuse for a man would beat on a child?"

Wahoo lay there cringing. *Lay off, Pop, before he loses it.*

But all Jared Gordon said was: "Shut up, fool."

The flames were dying. Tuna found more dry sticks and peat, yet the freshened fire was still rather small—too small to be spotted by searchers, Wahoo feared. The buzzing of the other boats sounded as distant as ever.

Jared Gordon complained that the beer was all gone, but nobody had much else to say. The sun slipped below the western horizon and a buttery half-moon appeared in the east. It was the first cloudless sky in a week, and the stars began to sparkle as night deepened.

Still hunkered in the trees, Wahoo wondered what had happened to Derek. Had he done something to provoke Jared Gordon into clobbering him unconscious—or worse? Wahoo struggled to steady his nerves and think of a plan. One wrong move and his father might wind up dead.

Jared Gordon tossed a pocketknife to his daughter and told her to free Mickey's hands, which she did. Jared Gordon snatched the knife back and said, "Time to roll. Them pills got to be workin' by now."

"Not yet they aren't," Mickey said.

"Too bad for you, then. Suck it up."

Staying close to the ground, Wahoo frantically groped through the leafy mulch. He was hoping to locate a heavy stick or maybe a rock for a weapon.

He listened to his father saying: "Gordon, I'll take you to the highway but only on one condition: you let your daughter stay here and wait for help."

"No! I told you, she's real sick with the Floyd's disease. She needs a doctor, like, right away."

Tuna raised her voice. "Don't believe a word he says, Mr. Cray. I'm not sick—and Floyd happens to be the name of my hamster."

"Adorable," said Mickey.

"But I'll go with Daddy, if that's what he wants."

"No, you won't. Not as long as I'm drivin' the boat."

Wahoo gasped as he watched Jared Gordon step forward and level the gun at his father's heart.

"That girl's my flesh and blood, Sparky, and I ain't leavin' this swamp without her."

"Then you ain't leavin'," Mickey Cray said.

Wahoo was not prepared to watch his dad die right in front of him. Never in his life had he experienced such a powerful flood of emotions—fear, dread, desperation and rage. He wasn't as bold or impulsive as Mickey, but Wahoo's sense of devotion was equally fierce. He had to do something big, and he had to do it fast. In his own mind, it was never a matter of courage.

But courage it was.

Like his son, Mickey Cray didn't have a death wish.

Yet there was no way he could allow Tuna to go away with her father, not after what Jared Gordon had already done to the girl. If that meant Mickey had to take a bullet, so be it. At least the gunfire would alert Wahoo to the trouble.

Where is that kid, anyway? Mickey wondered.

Lying low, I hope. Playing it smarter than his old man.

The roundhouse punch that Wahoo's father had thrown at Jared Gordon never landed because Jared Gordon had seen it coming and clubbed Mickey with the pistol butt. Mickey had awakened with the second-worst headache of his life (the falling iguana was more painful) and with his wrists crudely knotted together with air potato vines.

He'd been lying to Tuna's father when he complained about seeing double. His vision was fine. He was merely scheming to get the man alone with him on the airboat, away from Tuna and Wahoo, wherever the heck Wahoo might be.

Although Jared Gordon's gun was now aimed squarely at Mickey's chest, he didn't panic. He was waiting for Jared Gordon to realize that, being unable to operate an airboat himself, he needed Mickey alive if he hoped to get out of the Glades.

The incredible stupidity of shooting his only driver would

have been obvious to a person of semi-average intelligence, but Tuna's father had so far failed to impress Mickey with his keen logic.

Mickey's other problem was his own anger and disgust for Jared Gordon, which he struggled to keep under control. Susan Cray sometimes joked that her husband needed a special filter implanted between his brain and his mouth to prevent him from blurting every single thought that entered his mind.

Such as when he called Tuna's father a "sorry-ass excuse for a man."

Probably not the smartest way to address a beer-soaked oaf with a loaded weapon.

Now the same oaf was holding his gun on Mickey and saying, "That girl's my flesh and blood, Sparky, and I ain't leavin' this swamp without her."

To which Mickey, who'd grown annoyed with the whole "Sparky" routine, replied: "Then you ain't leavin'."

An epic gamble, as the kids would say.

And possibly an epic fail—if Jared Gordon wasn't bright enough to see the foolishness of killing the one person who could guide his escape.

"Well," said Mickey, "what's it gonna be?"

Jared Gordon didn't answer. He was peering beyond Mickey, and his face was twisted like a dirty rag.

"Now what?" he growled.

"Wahoo!" Tuna cried.

Mickey felt a sickening chill and spun around. There was his son, jumping up and down at the edge of the trees. He looked like he was being attacked by bees.

"Wahoo, run!" Tuna shouted.

Jared Gordon said, " 'Wahoo'? What's that mean? Is it some kinda code?"

"No, Daddy, it's his name."

"Wahoo *who*?"

"He's just a boy from school," Tuna said.

"Sure he is. Doing jumpin' jacks in the middle of the boonies?" Jared Gordon distractedly let the revolver swing away from Mickey, who said nothing to give away his relationship with Wahoo. He understood what his son was trying to do. It was brave, but way too dangerous.

Wahoo was hoping to draw fire from Jared Gordon so that Mickey could jump the man.

"What's a matter with you?" Tuna's father called out.

Wahoo stopped hopping. "What's the matter with *you*?" he snapped back.

"Run away!" Tuna yelled.

"No, boy," said Jared Gordon, "you get your butt over here right now."

"Make me," Wahoo said.

"Make you?" Tuna's father cackled. "See this gun, boy?"

"See this phone, Mr. Gordon?" Wahoo held up Link's waterlogged cellular, which from a distance appeared undamaged. "I'm calling the cops and telling 'em exactly where you are!"

"No, you ain't! And how'd you know my name?"

"It's got a GPS, too!"

Jared Gordon purpled with rage. He shook the pistol at Wahoo, who retreated into the hardwoods, where he resumed bouncing like a cartoon kangaroo.

"Hold still, you!" Jared Gordon hissed.

"Daddy, leave him be," Tuna pleaded. "He's sort of sick in the head."

"Yeah, well, he's fixin' to be dead in the head."

Wahoo's father hastily stepped in front of the gun. "Don't waste a bullet on that crazy kid."

"You're right," said Jared Gordon, and shot Mickey Cray point-blank.

Wahoo came bolting in horror out of the trees. "Pop! No!"

"Did he say 'Pop'?" Jared Gordon grinned. "Now we're gettin' somewheres."

Derek Badger had gone off into the woods to relieve himself, and wasted no time getting lost. He was peering up at the half-moon, wondering if it meant he would turn into a half-vampire, when another gunshot split the air.

Hoping it was a signal from a search team, Derek aimed himself in the general direction of the sound. Thrashing clumsily through the underbrush, he began making up a script for the occasion of his rescue, which could be later reenacted to juice up the ending of the show:

"My harrowing Everglades adventure is finally drawing to an end, and not a moment too soon. I'm completely out of food, out of water and dangerously weak after being attacked by a rare but deadly vampire bat.

"Its savage bite left me dazed and delirious, racked with fever. Why, at times I even imagined myself morphing into a real-life vampire! Hopefully, the gunshot I just heard means that search crews are approaching, and my ordeal is almost over. . . ."

But it wasn't over.

A bulky shadow appeared in Derek's path, and he lurched to a halt. Cloaked by darkness, the creature was difficult to identify—a bear? a panther?—but it produced a series of volcanic snorts that were unmistakably hostile.

For protection, Derek whipped out his famed Swiss army knife, a cheap replica of which was sent to lucky viewers of *Expedition Survival!* who correctly answered a weekly trivia question. (Example: What does fried cobra meat taste like? Answer: Chicken.)

Derek tested the knife's blade, which was barely long enough to slice a kumquat.

"Scram!" he said to the mystery intruder.

Another surly snort was the only reply. The thing made no move to flee.

Derek was rethinking his decision to stage the Everglades episode without Mickey Cray's captive animals—to "put the 'real' back in 'reality' " by using only wild critters. The beast now blocking his escape probably never had laid eyes on a human, and it showed no fear.

Interestingly, Dax Mangold had faced a similar predicament in *Revenge of the Blood Moon*. A mutant possum the size of a Saint Bernard had cornered Dax deep in Slackjaw Forest, but the stouthearted young fighter had used his vampire superpowers to subdue the monstrous marsupial by wrestling it to the ground and gnawing through its jugular vein.

Derek wasn't sure that such a bold tactic would work for him, a doubt that was well founded.

Had he bothered to do any research about South Florida before his arrival, he would have known that the woods and marshlands had become plagued by wild pigs. These free-roaming marauders were descended from ordinary porkers that had escaped from farms, although the Everglades version was bigger, hairier and more foul-tempered. The boars were especially dangerous, growing long, curved tusks that were sharp enough to kill.

A funky heat radiated from the massive form confronting Derek Badger. In a way, the night shadow was a blessing, because Derek wasn't able to see the look in the creature's coal-black eyes. If he had, he might have fainted.

"Scram!" he said again, and the boar did exactly the opposite.

Derek tried to flee but, after years of French cheese and rich pastries, he wasn't exactly a speedster. The pig's tusks scooped the celebrity survivalist from behind and tossed him halfway up the trunk of a sabal palm, to which he clung like a terrified frog.

After circling a few times, the wild hog huffed loudly and trotted away. To better secure his elevated position, Derek attempted to spike his Swiss army knife into the bark of the palm. The blade promptly snapped off, and he hit the ground like a sack of beans.

That's it, he thought dismally, brushing himself off. *No more tree climbing for me.*

Mickey Cray looked up at his son and said, "Don't tell your mom."

"How bad does it hurt, Pop?"

"How bad does it look?"

"Pretty bad," Wahoo admitted.

Jared Gordon had put a bullet through Mickey's left foot.

"The same one Beulah tried to eat," he noted sullenly.

Tuna cried, "Daddy, what's wrong with you? Have you totally lost your mind?"

"The man wasn't takin' me serious. Now he will," said Jared Gordon.

Wahoo removed his father's bloody shoe and said, "Oh boy."

The bones in Mickey's foot were shattered, and his big toe had been shot clean off.

He winced at the sight. "Now we match," he said to Wahoo.

"Not quite, Pop."

"You're right. I'd rather lose a toe than a thumb."

"Be still." Wahoo pulled off his T-shirt and tore it into strips, which he wrapped tightly around his father's foot.

"Hope you're smarter than your old man," Jared Gordon grunted. "What're you doin' way out here, boy? Tell the truth."

"Working for a TV show." Wahoo didn't have to glance up to know that Tuna's dad was still brandishing the gun.

"What TV show is that?" Jared Gordon asked.

Tuna told him.

"The one with that Australian survivor dude?" Jared Gordon snickered. "No way! He's big-time."

"The Crays are professional animal wranglers, Daddy."

"You mean, like, they can teach a polar bear how to ride a bike? Stuff like that?"

Wahoo sighed and said, "Never mind."

Jared Gordon poked him. "Your daddy's good to go. Now let's git outta here."

"In case you didn't notice," Mickey said, "I can't walk."

"Yeah, but you can still drive a boat."

"It's not hard. I'll teach you how."

"No, Sparky," said Tuna's father. "You're gonna be my sho-fer!"

Wahoo knotted his *Expedition Survival!* jacket around the stump of a buttonwood branch and poked it in the embers of the fire to make a torch, which he handed to Tuna. Then he and Jared Gordon boosted Mickey upright, one on each side, acting as human crutches. Tuna led the way as they set off on the short trek to the water's edge.

With six hands scooping (Jared Gordon's being occupied by the revolver and now the torch), bailing the airboat took about an hour. After a forceful group shove, the craft was safely afloat.

Wahoo hopped up in the driver's seat and said, "I can do this."

His father frowned. "Since when?"

"I learned how this afternoon."

"Ha! No way," Jared Gordon said. "Git down from there, boy, and let your old man drive. Move it!"

Mickey rose to his knees. "Do what he says, son."

He was in major pain as Wahoo and Tuna helped him get positioned at the controls.

"Crank 'er up, Sparky," Jared Gordon commanded. "Take us to the big road."

"We'll see," Mickey said through gritted teeth.

The engine burped and stuttered, but it wouldn't start. He tried a half-dozen times, waited a few minutes, then tried again.

"Maybe some rain got in the bleeping gas tank," he said.

"Or maybe you're jest jerkin' my chain." Jared Gordon was glaring in the torchlight. "Maybe you don't really *want* to git 'er started."

Wahoo's father laughed emptily. "Yeah, that makes sense. I'd much rather stay out here and watch my leg rot off than get to a hospital." He gave Tuna a look of sympathy. "No offense, young lady, but your daddy's not the brightest bulb on the Christmas tree, is he?"

"Knock it off, Pop," Wahoo said.

Tuna cocked her head. "You hear that?"

Mickey raised his eyes to the sky. "Sounds like a chopper."

Now Jared Gordon was steaming. "Jest git the motor runnin'! Now!"

"Try again," Wahoo told his father.

This time the engine coughed to life, and the airboat's jumbo propeller began turning.

"Well, hooray," Tuna's dad muttered, though no one could hear him over the racket.

Then, just as suddenly: silence.

"No! No! No!" Jared Gordon was hopping with exasperation. "Are you kiddin' me? Did you flood this stupid thing?"

Mickey said, "Actually, I turned it off."

"What! You better have a damn good reason, Sparky."

"I believe the owner of this vessel wants a word with you."

"Uh?" Tuna's father swung the torch toward the shoreline, where a broad-shouldered stranger loomed.

"Git out my boat," he said. It was Link.

Jared Gordon sneered. "And who the heck're you?"

"The man what you shot in the back."

"Yeah? Well, I'll shoot you in the front, too, you don't *vamos* outta here."

Tuna shouted, "Daddy, that's enough!" She lunged to grab him, but he shoved her to the deck.

Wahoo helped her sit up. *Where is that chopper?* He scanned the sky anxiously.

"Gimme my airboat," Link said, and he began sloshing toward them.

Mickey Cray raised a hand. "Easy, brother. It ain't worth dyin' over."

"Says you." Link was wheezing.

"Stop!" Wahoo said. "You'll get your boat back, I promise."

But Link kept coming.

Jared Gordon steadied himself against the propeller cage. He raised the torch higher to better illuminate the intruder, and with his gun arm he took aim.

"I warned you, Tarzan," he said.

His mistake was taking his eyes off the wrangler's son. Wahoo nailed him broadside with a flying tackle that carried both of them overboard. The revolver in Jared Gordon's hand went off harmlessly, and the torch flew up on the muddy bank.

The option of doing nothing had never occurred to Wahoo, even for a split second. He was acting on gut reflex and pure adrenaline. There'd been no time to ponder the extreme danger of tangling with Tuna's whacked-out father. The man plainly intended to shoot Link—and not just in the foot, either. His pistol had been leveled at the center of Link's forehead when Wahoo had sprung at him.

Tuna jumped in to help while Mickey, cursing his crippled foot, watched from the driver's seat. The scene in the shallows was pure turmoil, a frantic thrash of arms and legs.

It reminded Mickey of bull gators fighting. Link was trying to gain control of the gun as the kids struggled to subdue Jared Gordon, who kicked and flailed like a madman.

Mickey couldn't stand being a bystander. He restarted the airboat and nosed it against the shore at an angle from which the propeller's gale-force backwash blew full blast into Jared Gordon's face.

Incredibly, the man didn't go down. Somehow he got his back turned and held his balance. Soon he shook free from his daughter, then from Wahoo.

Only Link kept his hold on Jared Gordon, though barely. The pain from the lung shot had sapped his strength. Mickey could see him begin to wobble and wheeze, while the revolver remained firmly in Jared Gordon's fist.

Meanwhile, Wahoo and Tuna were preparing to rush at her father again. Mickey shut off the boat engine and hollered for them to stay back. A rumble drew his gaze to the southern sky. It wasn't thunder; it was the helicopter, locked in a low hover no more than a mile away. Its violet search beam was sweeping back and forth across the black swamp below.

"Let's go, Sparky!" Jared Gordon rasped. His shirt was in tatters and his face was clawed. The airboat's slipstream had made a spiky nest of his hair.

Mickey saw Link keel and go down. The kids began hauling him toward dry land, trying to hold his head above the water.

Jared Gordon fired into the air. "I said let's go!"

Wahoo's father motioned him toward the boat. "Whenever you're ready."

The helicopter was moving closer. Jared Gordon glared up at it. "They spotted our fire," he mumbled sourly.

"Hop in," Mickey said. "I'll take you wherever you want."

Wahoo and Tuna had placed Link on the ground and were working to make him comfortable. Jared Gordon waded to shore and snatched his daughter by the jacket collar. Wahoo grabbed him around the knees but got booted in the jaw and fell back.

Furious, Mickey attempted to climb off the boat and help his son. His mangled foot was useless, and he tumbled in agony from the driver's platform.

"Git up, you! Git up and drive!" screamed Jared Gordon as he slogged with his daughter toward Mickey.

Wahoo rolled over and tried to call Tuna's name. She couldn't hear him over the din of the oncoming chopper. She fought to break away, but her father hooked a beefy arm around her neck. The gun he waved at Mickey Cray, still crumpled on the deck.

"I'm gonna count to three!"

"I can't move, brother."

"You *will* move, Sparky! Or you'll die!"

"But—"

"One! . . . Two! . . ."

The counting faded away. Wahoo rose to his knees and saw Jared Gordon hunched in a bright spear of bluish light,

Tuna writhing in his grasp. The police helicopter was no more than a hundred feet above them.

Under a halo of flitting insects, Jared Gordon appeared demented in the eerie cone of the search beam. Squinting like a shrew, he ranted and cussed up at the chopper, his drooling threats smothered by the heavy thump of its rotor blades.

Wahoo knew what would happen next, and he knew he couldn't possibly cover the distance between him and Tuna's father in time to stop it.

Jared Gordon aimed his revolver directly at the cockpit of the helicopter.

Sick with dread, Wahoo almost looked away. Had he done that, he would have missed a truly unforgettable sight, one he could never have foreseen.

Derek Badger exploded with a howl out of the woods. At a dead run he bounded from the bank of the island to the bow of Link's airboat, from which he vaulted himself at Tuna's father, who stood there gaping in disbelief.

The three of them toppled with a heavy splash—Derek, Jared Gordon and Tuna. By the time Wahoo reached them, Tuna was back on her feet and she was clutching the gun.

Jared Gordon had worse problems. Gagging on swamp muck, he found himself pinned underwater by a plump, wild-eyed stranger.

A stranger who, for some reason, was chomping him ferociously on the throat.

TWENTY-SIX

"It's not even a full moon," Tuna pointed out.

Derek Badger shrugged. "What can I say?"

He had no future as a vampire. Jared Gordon's blood had tasted awful.

Wahoo reached out and shook Derek's hand. "That was huge. Thanks."

"No worries." Derek didn't know what in the world had come over him. It wasn't in his nature to risk his life for others. Attacking the gunman seemed more like something Dax Mangold would have done, in the movies.

"Incredible," Tuna agreed. "We should get your saliva tested. Yours too, Lance."

They could hear the rescue boats racing through the saw grass prairie toward the island. Overhead the helicopter circled, the pilot expertly keeping the search beam trained on them to mark their location.

With Tuna standing guard, Wahoo had bound Jared Gordon's wrists and ankles with a nylon rope from the airboat. Link himself had helped secure the knots, which would later have to be cut with a fish knife.

The bite wounds on Jared Gordon's neck were painful but not life-threatening, due to Derek's lack of proper fangs.

Still, he'd clamped onto Tuna's father with enough force that it had required all of Wahoo's strength to pry him off.

One cheek in the dirt, Jared Gordon glowered up at the man who'd flattened him. "You sure don't look the same as on TV."

"Pipe down, mate," said Derek. "You got owned."

Wahoo's jaw was throbbing as if he'd been slugged by Mike Tyson. Before dousing the campfire, he relit the torch that he'd made from his *Expedition Survival!* jacket. Then he returned to the airboat and sat down beside his father, who was still lying on the deck.

"I'm proud of you," Mickey told him.

"I didn't do anything."

"Tell that to Link. You saved the man's life."

"I didn't save *you* from getting shot," Wahoo said.

"Hey, I asked for it." Mickey winked. "Alice got me, okay?"

"What?"

"Mom asks how come I'm limpin', it's 'cause Alice chomped me."

"Weak," Wahoo said.

"Yeah? Isn't that what happened to your thumb?"

"Okay, Pop. We'll give it a try."

Link was upright again, his breathing shallower than before. It hurt to talk, so he didn't. He was so elated to see his beloved airboat that he wasn't worrying about the bullet in his body.

Derek asked, "What are you people going to tell the police?"

"The truth," Wahoo replied.

"Everything?"

"He wants us to leave out the Night Wing stuff," Tuna said. "Right, Mr. Badger?"

He nodded uneasily. "Please."

"Okay—but only if you sign my coat." She fished through her bag and took out a black Sharpie.

Derek looked dubious. "You want my autograph?"

Tuna said, "You're the first real TV star I ever met. Plus, you did a seriously brave thing tonight. Twisted, but brave."

"Bull!" her father blurted. "That maniac tried to drown me!"

"Hush up, Daddy." She pulled off one of Jared Gordon's moldy wet socks and crammed it in his mouth.

Then she handed the Sharpie to Derek. "The name's Tuna," she said, "like the fish."

With a flourish, he wrote on her coat sleeve: *To my friend Tuna, a true survivor! Your fan, Derek Badger.*

She was still beaming when the first rescue boat arrived. With no small effort, the driver and the police officer lifted Link off the ground and laid him on one of the bench seats. Next they loaded Mickey Cray.

Wahoo gave the torch to Tuna and climbed in beside his father.

"These two need a doctor," said the driver, who wore a frogger's lamp on his head. "We gotta go."

Wahoo waved his thumbless hand. "Later, Lucille."

Tuna laughed and wiggled four fingers in return. After the boat sped away, she gave her father's pistol to the police officer, who'd stayed behind to read Jared Gordon his legal rights and officially place him under arrest.

Meanwhile, Derek Badger was basking in his heroic moment. "Say, mate, would you happen to know if that chopper's equipped with a video camera?"

The cop said he wasn't sure. "You're the Beaver guy from cable, right? My kids watch your show every week."

"It's Badger," Derek said tightly.

A second rescue boat pulled up carrying two more uniformed officers, who jumped out and yanked Tuna's father to a standing position.

He spit out the sock and said, "I want a lawyer."

"You got a name, mister?" asked one of the policemen.

"No comment."

"*Homo sapiens*," said Tuna, "but a really lame specimen."

She tossed the torch into the shallows, where it hissed and went cold.

EPILOGUE

Episode 103 of *Expedition Survival!* was broadcast nearly three months after the crew departed the Everglades. Derek Badger's final appearance drew 17.2 million viewers worldwide, a cable-television record for non-sports programming.

The director and editors did a clever job of splicing the video clips into a believable story, the climax being Derek's thirty-three-second struggle with Alice, who was of course portrayed as a random wild alligator instead of the old show-business pro that she was.

Derek's embarrassing encounters with the snapping turtle and the water snake were digitally "improved" to save him from looking like a total klutz. At the urging of the Untamed Channel's lawyers (who feared young viewers might try to imitate the stunt), Derek's ill-fated attempt to eat the mastiff bat was cut entirely from the program. However, the scene would turn up later on the director's private DVD of Derek's worst bloopers, another smash hit at the crew's end-of-the-year bash.

Jared Gordon watched the Everglades episode in the medical wing of the Miami-Dade County jail, where he was faking stomach cramps in order to receive favored treatment. Imprisonment had been depressing, especially when his defense attorney advised him to take a guilty plea rather than risk the wrath of a judge and jury. Tuna's father hadn't yet made up his mind what to do, but in any case the odds were slim that he'd be a free man before his ninety-ninth birthday.

Meanwhile, the person responsible for his bleak predicament was grinning down at him from a jailhouse television, flashing the same bleached teeth that had been embedded so ferociously in his throat, leaving a pattern of niblet-sized scars.

"Turn off that idiot!" Jared Gordon begged, but no one at the infirmary paid him any attention.

Raven Stark TiVo'd the Everglades broadcast in Derek's luxury motor coach, which she'd been driving all summer, ever since the night Derek was found safe on the tree island. The bus was a sweet ride, and Raven—sporting her sombrero-sized sun hat—had decided to take the slow, scenic route back to California. She'd already visited Disney World; her mother's house in Fairhope, Alabama; the French Market in New Orleans; the Great Smoky Mountains; and Graceland, the famed estate of Elvis Presley. Still ahead lay the Grand Canyon, Pikes Peak, the Custer battlefield and Glacier National Park, where she hoped to see a wild grizzly.

After everything that had happened, Raven felt she deserved a vacation.

It was she who'd composed the glowing press release about Derek's starring role in the capture of a dangerous gunman and the rescue of four innocent persons. She had kindly made no mention of his daffy vampire delusion or of his biting Jared Gordon's neck.

It was Raven who'd set up the secret doctor's visit so that Derek could be tested for rabies (negative) and pumped full of antibiotics to combat the lingering infection from the bat wounds. It was also she who had arranged for Derek to be interviewed by Matt Lauer, David Letterman, Jimmy Kimmel and even Dr. Oz.

And it was she who'd persuaded the governor of Florida to present Derek with the Sunshine State Medallion of Distinction, which was shaped like a navel orange and not usually awarded to TV celebrities.

The wave of media attention gave a major ratings boost to *Expedition Survival!* Consequently, no one (besides Derek himself) was more shocked than Raven when Derek's contract wasn't renewed. The show's executive producer, Gerry Germaine, went on *Entertainment Tonight* to say that, after the grueling Everglades ordeal, Mr. Badger would be taking some time off to "recharge his batteries" and "explore other career opportunities."

That was Hollywood code for getting fired.

It was Derek's own fault. Hoping to cash in on his new hero status, he'd demanded an even more outrageous raise for his new contract, which Gerry Germaine had been all too happy to reject. Brick Jeffers, the buff young outdoorsman from New Zealand, was grateful to work for half of Derek's salary.

Raven had been bitter about Derek's dismissal until Gerry Germaine called her on the road. She assumed he was going to yell at her for taking the motor coach, but instead he offered her a line producer's position on the new, revamped edition of *Expedition Survival!*

At first she had said no, but then she Skyped with Brick Jeffers for an hour. He turned out to be charming, extremely good-looking—and he was at least twenty-five IQ points smarter than Derek Badger.

So Raven had accepted the job, and now Derek wasn't returning her calls.

He was sulking on his yacht, the *Sea Badger*, moored off the Caribbean island of St. Barts. That's where he watched his final appearance on *Expedition Survival!*

He thought the program was suitably flattering, although his life-or-death fight with Jared Gordon would have made a more spectacular ending than his wrestling match with Mickey Cray's pet gator. Unfortunately, the police helicopter pilot had forgotten to turn on the video camera, so there was no tape of Derek's real-life act of valor on the swamp island.

Getting fired from the show had dented his oversized ego. He'd immediately filed a grievance with his TV union— Guild 154 of Mountaineers, Ice Truckers and Survivalists— but he'd received no response. A couple of other networks wanted him to star in new reality programs, and he'd been pondering his options.

He was leaning toward the Catastrophe Channel, which had offered him a sick pile of money to intentionally place himself in the path of oncoming hurricanes, typhoons, lava eruptions, wildfires, mud slides, avalanches and tidal waves. Best of all, the show—titled *Bring It On!*—would be shown during the same Thursday-night time slot as *Expedition Survival!*, giving Derek an opportunity to humiliate young Brick Jeffers in the ratings contest and make Gerry Germaine miserable.

There was only one catch: the producers of *Bring It On!* wanted Derek to perform his own stunts, including the opening parachute jump. Currently he wasn't in prime physical shape, having gained nineteen jiggly pounds during his sojourn in St. Barts, a cruel calorie trap for lovers of Brie cheese, soufflés and chocolate mousse.

Normally Derek would have relied on Raven Stark to endure his childish whining, but she'd deserted him. So he sat alone in the *Sea Badger*'s master cabin, engulfing his third cinnamon éclair of the evening and watching his own breathless finale on *Expedition Survival!* As soon as the show ended, he dialed up the menu of his private video library and ordered all three Night Wing movies, to be played one after another in high-def.

Through the port hatch, Derek spied a full moon, pale as the petals of a spider lily, in the tropical sky.

Life, he admitted to himself, *could be a whole lot worse.*

Back in Florida, surgeons had successfully removed a

bullet fragment from Link's right lung. Once he was out of the hospital, he bought another flip phone and called up Wahoo Cray, the kid who'd saved his life by tackling the shooter at the tree island.

"Thanks for what you done," Link said.

"Sure."

"You ever want 'nother airboat drivin' lesson, jest lemme know."

"It's a deal," said Wahoo.

After all the media coverage about the dramatic events in the swamp, Link found himself a minor celebrity among his fellow Gladesmen. That made him uncomfortable, since he wasn't a person who liked to socialize.

On the night of Derek Badger's last show, Link had reluctantly agreed to attend an *Expedition Survival!* screening party at Sickler's Jungle Outpost and Juice Bar. Sickler was in jolly spirits because the publicity about the lost survivalist and fugitive gunman had turned his cheesy roadside shop into a hot spot for curious tourists.

Scammer that he was, Sickler had acquired a large poster of Derek Badger, forged the star's autograph on the bottom and tacked it to the wall beside the cash register. He'd also strung the weather-beaten mount of Old Sleepy from the ceiling beams, telling customers that it was the very same alligator Derek had wrestled on the TV program and that it had drowned after he battled it to exhaustion.

Sickler's souvenir business was booming, with eager

suckers lining up to purchase overpriced coconut carvings, polyester rattlesnake skins and "authentic" Seminole bead shirts that were actually made in Vietnam.

The crowd at the store that night cheered throughout the broadcast of *Expedition Survival!*, the loudest applause erupting when Sickler's name appeared among the credits as a "location consultant," whatever that was. Link himself wasn't particularly enchanted by the television show and grew bored with the repeated slow-motion replays of Derek Badger being tossed like a rodeo cowboy by the gator.

Ten minutes before the big ending, Link snuck out Sickler's back door and went home to tinker with his airboat, which he'd recently named *Lucille* in honor of the kind-hearted girl with the mean, hard-drinking father, like his own. Eventually Link became a tour guide at the Miccosukee reservation, and he never took his boat on another TV job.

Wahoo Cray watched Derek's last episode at home. His mother had returned at long last from China (and, naturally, did not believe Mickey's version of how he'd lost his big toe). However, Susan Cray had been pleasantly surprised to learn that the house mortgage had been paid up, thanks to Mickey and Wahoo's earnings from *Expedition Survival!* She'd been even happier to see that her husband had completely recovered from his iguana concussion and was no longer suffering with headaches or double vision.

Despite his damaged foot, Mickey had resumed work soon after surgery, hobbling around the backyard pens and tending to his animals. Beulah the python had made the mistake of trying to chomp him again and gotten her teeth stuck in his cast.

The night that Derek Badger's Everglades adventure was broadcast, the Cray family sat down with a large bowl of buttered popcorn in front of the television. Wahoo thought the program turned out pretty tame, compared to what had really gone down in the swamp. Still, he was impressed by how the video editors had stitched the different scenes together in an entertaining way, including a shaky tree-climbing sequence they'd salvaged from Derek's broken Helmet Cam.

Mickey Cray didn't have much to say about the show, except that Alice had performed like a champ. Susan Cray thought the whole thing was overhyped and hokey.

The first phone call came from Julie, Wahoo's sister.

"Let's hear your review," he said.

"The show was okay. That Derek guy, though, he's still a tool."

"He's not so bad, Jule."

"I'm just glad you and Pop finally got your money."

"Thanks to you," Wahoo said.

Gerry Germaine at first had refused to give the Crays the agreed-upon wrangler fee, claiming their involvement with Tuna Gordon and her trigger-happy father had disrupted the show's production, endangered the crew and cost the company thousands of dollars.

The next day, Julie Cray had placed a phone call to Mr. Germaine, threatening to sue both him and the

Untamed Channel for gross negligence by failing to provide safe working conditions on the set of *Expedition Survival!* She'd noted that her father's traumatic foot injury had reduced his agility when handling large reptiles and other unpredictable creatures, which made his job more dangerous and even life-threatening. For extra ammunition, Julie Cray had also listed several obscure wildlife regulations that *Expedition Survival!* had ignored, information that she volunteered to share with the prosecutor's office in Miami.

Gerry Germaine backed down in a heartbeat. He told Julie Cray that he'd be happy to pay Wahoo and Mickey the full contract amount for their services, and also take care of Mickey's medical bills, which amounted to thirteen thousand dollars. It was Wahoo's belief that his sister had a bright future in the legal profession.

At the end of his conversation with Julie, Gerry Germaine had a brainstorm: Would Mickey consider a full-time role as Brick Jeffers's wrangler sidekick on the new, made-over version of *Expedition Survival!*?

Julie passed the offer along to her father, who responded with two words: "Bleep no!"

The next phone call after the show came from Tuna in Chicago, where she'd gone to join her mother.

"I saw my name in the credits!" she exclaimed. " 'Tuna J. Gordon—Taxonomist'!"

"You're a rock star," Wahoo said.

"How about you? 'Wahoo Cray—First Assistant Wildlife Wrangler'!"

"Okay, we're *both* rock stars."

Wahoo's parents had given him a cell phone as a birthday gift. He and Tuna had been texting regularly—he with one thumb—until Jocko, the bratty howler monkey, plucked the device from Wahoo's jeans and beat it to smithereens with a banyan branch.

Since then, Wahoo and Tuna had spoken only a few times, when she'd called him on the Crays' house phone.

"How's your grandmother?" he asked.

"She's hangin' in there, thanks to Mom. We're all hangin' in."

"And how's Floyd dealing with the move?"

"He's a hamster, dude. Every day's a good day."

Wahoo was curious to know if there was any wildlife to be classified in Chicago.

"Autumn is overrated," Tuna said. "It's already too cold for butterflies, though last month I logged a *Vanessa atalanta*."

"Which is . . . ?"

"A red admiral. He was just flyin' around Grant Park, having a big old time."

"Guess what I saw yesterday up in one of our palm trees."

"Not an iguana!"

"Oh yeah," Wahoo said. "A *serious* iguana."

Tuna chortled. "Did you show your dad?"

"Absolutely not."

"Smart call."

She told Wahoo about her grandmother's neighborhood

on the city's north side, which was overrun with obese and fearless raccoons. "They love chimneys," she said, "otherwise known as coon-dominiums."

Wahoo laughed, and he remembered how funny Tuna could be. He missed her, but he was glad she was safe, living in a place where she didn't have to hide in her room at night with the door locked.

"Daddy might plead guilty," she said.

"That's good news."

She and Wahoo had sometimes talked about hanging out together at the Miami courthouse while the case against her father was being heard. In truth, neither of them was looking forward to testifying while Jared Gordon sat only a few feet away, glaring murderously. It would be best if there was no need for a trial.

Selfishly, though, Wahoo felt disappointed that he might not get to see Tuna.

"So, you don't know when you'll be back in Florida?"

"At Christmas break, for sure," she said. "Mom promised."

"Really?"

"Maybe even sooner."

"Cool," he said. "We'll go catch some critters."

"I'd like that, Lance."

"Me too, Lucille."

CARL HIAASEN has been writing about Florida since his father gave him a typewriter at age six. Now Hiaasen writes a column for the *Miami Herald* and is the author of many bestselling novels, including *Skinny Dip* and *Star Island*.

Hoot, Hiaasen's first novel for young readers, was the recipient of numerous awards, including a prestigious Newbery Honor.

You can read more about Hiaasen's work at carlhiaasen.com.